1430 W. Susquehanna Ave
Philadelphia, PA 19121
215-236-1760 | treehousebooks.org

WILLIAM F. VAN WERT

MISSING IN ACTION

A COLLECTION OF SHORT STORIES

D1457199

YORK PRESS LTD.

Canadian Cataloguing in Publication Data
Van Wert, William F.
    Missing in action
    ISBN 0-919966-75-6
I. Title.
PS3572. A4228M57   1990   813'. 54   C90-097583-0

Copyright © 1990 by William F. Van Wert

Typesetting: YORKTYPE

===

YORK PRESS LTD.
P.O. Box 1172
Fredericton, N.B. E3B 5C8, Canada

To Daniel, my judge

Acknowledgments

The following stories have been published previously:
"Missing in Action" in THE MISCELLANY
"Varee" in QUARRY
"The Man With the Umbrella" in THE ANTIGONISH REVIEW
"Night Baseball" in NORTWEST REVIEW
"The Interpreter" in QUARTERLY WEST
"Johannesburg Diary" in ZONE
"Recycling Dante" in ZONE
"The Kleptomaniac" in THE LITERARY REVIEW
"Krishna's Flute" in MINNESOTA REVIEW

CONTENTS

Missing in Action

Livingstone walked into the 8th Aerial Port of Ton Son Nhut Air Base. The heat rose up like the sound of warm applause in his ears. He began to sweat. The monsoon season had just ended in Vietnam, but the air remained moist and the sun at four in the afternoon had the same intensity as it did at noon in the United States. Livingstone was indifferent to the weather. If this were Anchorage, Alaska, he would still be sweating. But except for the sweating, he felt no outward signs of life. There were none of the usual quick heartbeats, jumps in the throat, or stomach cramps that accompanied him each time he walked into a terminal. There was only the sweat.

His feet still worked. Nothing else seemed important. He had learned to use his feet two years ago in basic training. Since that time he had become quite adept at walking, whether it was an oblique right, an about-face or merely standing in place at attention. Next to his rifle, the can of Desenex in his duffle bag was the most important piece of equipment that he owned. He had turned in the rifle, because he was going home. But he still had the Desenex. He stepped forward without really looking. He heard the crunch and squash of something like egg shells cracking under his right foot. He stepped back. It was a cockroach. He had been careless. Three days ago it might have been a mine.

"Would you say it again, Sarge?"

Livingstone was not thinking in the present. His feet had gotten him to the ATCO counter where he would get his boarding pass, but his mind was still with the cockroach.

"I said, 'what's your name?' "
"Livingstone."
"You on WOT5Y?"
"What?"
"I said, 'you on Whirly Ogre Tango Fiver Yankee?'"
"Yes. That's it. What do I need, Sarge?"
"Copy of travel orders, valid shot record, MTA, bags on the scale."

Livingstone thought that the Sarge must have had to say that same thing in precisely the same order a thousand times a day. There were wrinkle lines around the Sarge's mouth and his belly flipped slightly on the counter edge every time he moved, like a seal flips on pavement. He had a "Flying Tiger" patch on his short sleeve. He had been here a long time. He wasn't flying any more, but still he was here, getting others off the ground. At least he didn't have to use his feet.

"These two are mine. That one is Carter's."
"Oh. You the one they called about. You be coming back to us, eh?"

Livingstone didn't smile. He may have cut down on his lip a little, but he wasn't sure. The Sarge was a lifer. What had happened to Livingstone and

5

Carter, the Sarge had lived through many times before. He could afford to make a joke.

"Sorry, buddy. No offense meant. What you guys went through was hell. I heard about it at the barracks. Heard you might even get a medal. Seems a crying shame, though. Eleven guys to save two. No offense, you understand. I know you guys was doing your loyal best. But it was sure one hell of a thing. You got to give them guys in the Jolly Greens one hell of a lot of fucking credit. When they rescue, they go the whole nine yards. The only 'missing in action' for them is a dead one. Know what I mean? Course you do. You was there."

"Sarge, that all?"
"Huh? Oh yeah, the boarding pass. Here it is. Boarding time is eighteen hundred. Seat number five. Gate number one."

Livingstone began to walk toward the seats, conscious only of his sweating and the movement of his feet.

"Say, Livingstone."
"Sarge?"
"Your buddy. Fucking shame."

Livingstone didn't answer. He just turned his back and began walking again. The Sarge had been through it all before. He couldn't really be sorry or he wouldn't still be here. He had to be hard to it all by now. Yet Livingstone felt what he thought to be shame beginning to color and surface on his own face. Maybe that was why he didn't answer. He had to turn quickly and walk away. He kicked a dixie cup he hadn't seen there before. Was it the same old carelessness this time or was it disgust? He knew he would have diarrhea soon if he kept on trying to think in this heat. So he tried not to think.

He stepped up on an elevated platform of green hard-backed chairs, almost all of them filled with bodies in varying degrees of sitting or sleeping. Bare light bulbs extended over steel girders above them. Livingstone could see dust moving in the air near the light. The light was an off-yellow, and those who sat directly under a row of bulbs looked like they were jaundiced or already enbalmed. He dodged around knees that jutted out, looking for a place. A few looked up at him without moving as he passed. Their eyes told him nothing, even though they squinted. They all had the look of insomniacs. Were they perturbed at him because he had moved the stale air, stirred it up and caused them to sweat a little more? Or was it because he alone was still walking? It shouldn't have made any difference to Livingstone. These were complete strangers. Yet for some reason he felt like their servant, their house-boy. He didn't want to offend even one of them.

He found a place two seats away from the fan. At first he wondered why there was still an empty place so near the fan in all this heat. As he sat down, he knew why. Every thirty seconds the fan would blow full force in his face and dry the sweat. It would shake his hair as wind shakes a wheat field and make it stand up. As the fan passed on and blew on others farther down the row more softly, his hair would collapse on his face. The sweat would reappear, as if it had only been in hiding, as if it had sprung from a source deep in his cheeks. The sweat would make his hair stick to his forehead. Every thirty seconds he would raise his hand and brush the hair back. He thought it must have looked to others like he was saluting. He wanted to move, but he sat rigidly still in his seat. The only way to move was in front of the others again, and he didn't want to bother them any more than he already had. Besides, he couldn't move. It was the only empty seat.

The man in the first seat nearest the fan was smoking a cigar. By his markings he was a captain, but it was difficult to tell, since he wore camouflage. Even Captains had to be in a Class A uniform to get on the Freedom Bird, the plane to the States. Livingstone knew that. Obviously, the captain was not leaving. He seemed to anticipate Livingstone's stare.

"Just saw my best friend off. On leave to Bangkok, lucky bastard. He was sitting right there where you're sitting now. Just a minute ago. In a couple hours he'll be there in Bangkok and off to one of those Turkish baths."

The captain smiled as he talked. His eyes were staring at the wall, but still he was smiling. Obviously, he wasn't even seeing the wall.

"Yeah, he got off all right. Amazing how many flights get off like clockwork from this place. Thinking of him in Bangkok, then thinking of going back to the BOQ, well, I just had to sit here a minute and prolong the agony. You know what I mean?"

Livingstone nodded, but he didn't know what the captain meant. Livingstone had never been able to prolong agony. How could he know what the captain meant? When his father died, he would have liked to prolong the agony, like the captain said, because it was graduation week from high school for him. When the draft notice came, there again he would have liked to prolong the agony. But he didn't see how he could, so he just shut his mind the best he could and walked right into it. And when he left home, there was no agony. His mother was making wedding announcements. The captain was still laughing.

"You know what that bastard is going to say when he gets back? He's going to say he spent the whole week working on the railroad. And to give him the last line, I'm going to have to say, 'what do you mean?' And he's going to tell me that he was laying Thai's. The bastard. I know he's going to pull it on me."

Livingstone wanted to move again. But there was no place to go. Two helicopters had to spot-land in a clearing twenty miles from Da Nang on a routine search-and-rescue mission. Only it wasn't routine. It didn't go like clockwork. He and Carter had held hands. He couldn't remember for sure, but he thought it was the only time in his life he'd ever held hands with another man. Eleven for two minus one. The captain was like all others. Livingstone didn't want to offend him.

"You going back to the world?"
"I'm sorry, sir. I didn't hear you."
"I said, 'you going back to the world?' "
"Yes, sir. Emergency leave."

"When you coming back?"

"Two weeks, sir."

"By that time I'll be really short myself. So I'm not going to say I wish I was in your place. You want to know how short I am?"

"Yes, sir."

"Hell, I'm so short I don't have time to smoke a king-size cigarette."

Livingstone didn't laugh. He tried, but it wouldn't come. All he got out was a turning at the corners of his mouth. He watched the captain stamp out his cigar and get up to go. The fan blew the captain's last puff in Livingstone's face.

"Well, gotta be off. Take care and a good flight to you. Don't do anything I wouldn't do."

Livingstone nodded as the captain walked by him. The captain didn't even look as he walked by the others. Livingstone wondered if not having to look at others was a sign of rank. Livingstone cleared his throat. He felt some phlegm at the back of his mouth, but he couldn't spit here, so he swallowed. The captain had probably never been on a Jolly Green. Watching the captain walk by the others, Livingstone knew why they had given him such sullen looks when he had walked by. It was because they were down and he was up. They were forced to look at his pockets, and he wasn't a captain. He hadn't felt that way when he was down, looking up at two green whirling blades in the air. Eleven for two. He knew why he didn't like the fan. Livingstone barely had time to close his eyes when an airman came up to the empty seat next to him.

"Hey man, this one taken?"

"No. Go right ahead."

"Say man, where you goin'? Home?"

"Yes. Emergency leave."

"How long?"

"Two weeks."

"Fourteen big ones! Don't make no difference. You still some kind a fucking lucky."

The fan didn't seem to bother the airman. He was running a big black comb very carefully through his hair.

"Where's at, your home?"

"Detroit."

"Detroit City, huh? Your folks know you're comin'?"

"No. No, they don't."

"Don't matter. They gonna get down on their knees when you walk in. I can see it now. What a scene. My shit's turnin' green already. Detroit, huh?"

"Yes."

"Got some crazy little women there."

"I, I guess so."

"Straight A, man. You can bet you gonna think about it some on the big bird. You gonna forget all these gook chicks in no time. Take you maybe eighteen hours to get there. You got time to turn it around. You gonna live this day twice, man. You cross that date line, you're home free. It'll all be a bad dream then. Wish I was in your shoes, no shit. I think about it plenty. Going, I mean.

8

Going and never coming back. I even thought about going AWOL some. It don't work out, though. They just sit back and wait till the chow runs out. Or the bread. And when you come strollin' back, you know they gonna be waitin' on you, all set to sock the chains on you. Shoot, the only way, man, it's gotta be missing in action. They just write the letter then and cross you off. Zero. Like the dateline. You gotta be home free then. Hey man, you listenin'?"

"Sorry. I guess I was thinking about something else."

"Sure, man. You got to have plenty on your mind now. Man, if I was you, I know what I'd be doing."

"That so?"

"Straight A. As soon as the old water-hopper touched down, I'd tear ass for the head, get outa these digs, see, get myself a good shave in some indoor crappers, man, indoors. No flies and sweet-smellin' cakes in the stalls. Decent! I'd have me a long bath, leisure-like, you know. The whole nine yards. Then I'd be in the phone book. Call me up a round-eye chick. A real fine one, one you'd even let your old lady see, understand? I'd fight down the old juices at first, you know, force myself to be gentle-like. Not too eager. Like to want to scare em off, some a these dudes, putting the moves on em as soon as they hawk em. Man, I'd treat her right, see? A fine meal. Detroit, you say? Gotta be some real nice places to take her there. Four-course, bills on the table, that's what I'd hit her with. Little California red and some candles, you know? Then when we was all full and warmed up, real cozy, I'd give her the strong rap, right out front. Been to the action, honey, kinda scared to be back, don't know if I'm still a man, been so long since someone really understood me like you. Even got hit once, honey. Leg still works okay, though. They got me out just in time. Then . . ."

"Shut up! Shut up please. I don't want to hear any more."

"What's the matter, man? You queer or something'?"

"No, I'm just tired. I'm sorry. Really. I didn't mean to say that to you. Please, go on. I want to know what you'd do then."

"Some dude! Knows he's going back to the world. It's real to him! And he won't even let somebody who's not going do a little fantasizing. You don't have to fly it in my face, you know. Isn't anybody forcing you to go, is there? Talk about back home and he goes ape-shit. Hell, I'm goin' up-country. But you don't see me wipin' the floor."

"I said I was sorry. Please go on with your story."

"Isn't any more story. If it was me, I wouldn't be caught dead in Detroit City. Anyway, I hear it stinks there, real dirty air. More war there than here. Just isn't any more story."

"I'm sorry if I spoiled it for you."

"Sure, man, sure."

Livingstone leaned back and down in his chair. It was impossible to sleep in that position. He wondered why he saw so many in the row like that. Now he knew. It was so they wouldn't have to talk to anybody. It was a warning signal that said that they didn't want to be bothered.

Livingstone could still see the airman out of the corner of his eye. He was taking a comic book out of his duffle bag. It was better this way. He could have tried to explain to the airman, but the airman wouldn't have understood anyway. How could anybody feel the way he did to be going home, to be leaving Vietnam, to be still alive . . .

9

They were still alive. The plane was grizzled and smoking. Pieces of metal were burning everywhere. Pieces were scattered all over the clearing. They were all burning like little Indian fires in the movies. The captain was dead. So was the co-pilot. They couldn't see the navigator. He was either dead or he was hurt in the bushes somewhere. Carter needed to be carried into the bushes. Livingstone still had his feet. That's all anyone ever had when a plane went down. Carter had a radio, but no feet. He was unconscious. Livingstone knew how to work the radio. He didn't even have to think. All he had to do was clear his throat and the Jolly Greens picked it up. They weren't the only ones who had radios. Don't call us, we'll find you. Rule one. Get into the bushes. Rule two. He'd already done it. Carter was regaining consciousness. He would soon feel the full pain in his legs, what were once his legs. He held Carter's hand and squeezed it tightly while they waited. Carter was mumbling that he would take care of Livingstone, and that Livingstone was not to die, no matter what else he did. They waited to go home.

Waiting to go home was the most difficult thing Livingstone had ever done. It was because others were waiting too. He didn't want to offend them. He wasn't sure whether or not he ever wanted to see Detroit again. So much had happened since Detroit. He felt like this was the only home left now. A plot of scorched dirt on enemy maps. 'Bags on the scale.' He knew why some of them stayed. Two green birds up high in the sky fanned themselves so peacefully with their blades. Mayday. Mayday.

May was waiting for him at the Happy Bar on Tudo Street. He didn't want to go. It was the only place he went to before going to the terminal. He had promised Carter that he would tell May. She could see it in his feet, the way he walked into the bar. He was glad he wouldn't have to explain. May said she was pregnant. She didn't know how long she could keep working in the bar. She looked older. He knew it would be a boy. A little gook boy with Carter's freckles and red hair. He bought some tea for her. They had very little to say to each other.

The loudspeaker had just finished announcing the flight. It brought Livingstone back to his senses. The airman had gotten up quickly and quietly. He had walked toward Gate One. The loudspeaker had announced the immediate loading and departure of the C130 for Da Nang.

Livingstone knew he had hurt the airman. He had hurt May too. He spoke to her of Carter. He told her that he loved Carter. Carter had been to him what no other man or woman had ever been. He saw that it was hurting her to listen to him. He didn't care. They had only this to share and no other time to share it. No other time.

WORLD AIRWAYS ANNOUNCES THE IMMEDIATE LOADING AND DEPARTURE OF MAC CONTRACT FLIGHT WOT5Y. ALL THOSE HOLDING CONFIRMED RESERVATIONS ON THIS FLIGHT PLEASE ASSEMBLE AT GATE NUMBER ONE WITH BOARDING PASSES IN HAND.

Livingstone retied his shoes laces and got up. It was time to go. He looked at the others. No one noticed him get up. For some strange reason, he had the strongest urge to choke one of them, to tell one of them that he was leaving now, that he wouldn't be bothering any of them any more, but that one of them had to look him straight in the eye before he would leave. The Sarge was weighing bags on the scale beyond the platform. A Vietnamese woman spit some beetle nut juice and then swept it along with the dixie cups and cigarette butts. A Red Cross girl was buying what looked like tomato juice in the snack bar. He knew he would not remember any of them.

The sun was setting as he walked through the gate. To the right and to the left of him the whole horizon was swollen with redness from the setting sun. The visibility would be good for the flight.

The plane was white. There was a red streak painted around the windows and where the windows ended, red letters announced 'World Airways.' The little windows of the plane seemed to him like mail boxes. He would be put in one, Seat Five. He would be sealed and delivered. It was all so ridiculously simple. It was hard to think that he was really leaving when it was that simple.

Livingstone knew that nothing was ever that simple. Something was missing. He wondered whether or not he was going in the right direction to find out what it was. Perhaps he would never find out. Surely there must be some answers that are withheld from a man. He had already fastened his seat belt. The plane had taxied to the runway and was waiting for clearance. When it shot forward, Livingstone's head went with it. Then back it snapped against the seat. He couldn't hear the engines any longer. Ton Son Nhut was only a miniature walled city that Livingstone had bought when he was a child and put together in three days. Saigon was made of balsa wood and airplane glue. The plane gave no more visible signs of motion. Suddenly Livingstone realized for the first time that the plane was going back.

II

I am out of breath. I am just in time. I can almost see the plane now. Wish you could see it too, Livvie. The visibility is not very good. I cannot see the yellow markers on the runway, but I think I smell fuel. The smell is strong. It makes me slightly dizzy. What'd I tell you, Livvie? That I'd take care of you. All you had to do was sit tight and not die.

Someone is hacking my brain with a crowbar. My mind has a heart of its own. My cheeks are pulling apart from my face. I am thinking of Queen Anne's Lace. My face must be red, but I cannot tell for sure. If it is, it's because I'm unable to sweat. Livvie could sweat, not me. I think he could end the war all by himself. The gooks fear the monsoons. I can see Livvie now, strapped to the bottom of an F4, flying over Hanoi. The pilot pushes a button and Livvie goes into his act. Hanoi is completely under water inside of a week. all his salt eats away at the crops. They surrender and we all go home. Livvie and I are going home anyway.

I am all alone. There is talking in my ears. Subways talk like that. Maybe there's a crowd forming. My elbows move. I have not told them to move. My shirt clings to me in back, but I have it all unbuttoned in the front. Elbows are like feet. What happens if I let them fall to my sides?

"Doc, what do you think?"
"He'll pull out in a minute, poor bastard. It's the fever. It's rising. Someone get the window."

I must have fainted. So there is a crowd. I can hear them talking. I know that I am not able to sweat, but I should not have fainted. I have called attention to myself again. I should play dumb. I should let them put their clammy hands on my forehead, let them probe my pulse. I must win them over. Until I am safely on the plane, I must make them think that they are helping me.

A girl in a Red Cross uniform stands in front of me. I am already seated. I think that we are in the terminal cafeteria. I can smell food, and the girl is nervous. She is not standing still. She fidgets and wavers in front of my eyes. I am thinking of a willow tree. Her hair is fastened up in back. Under her hat I can see a hair net. I wonder if she knows how to fish. Her face is turned toward me, but I have not said anything at all to her. Her eyes are down. I cannot see them. Her fists clench and unclench. They are close to my eyes, and I can see them very well. She may be a friend of the pilot. She may be getting a free ride with him. Perhaps she is nervous because she is afraid of getting caught. She doesn't have to worry. I won't tell on her. She is motioning to my mouth.

"No, man. I'm not too hungry."

The loudspeaker gives the ball scores. Detroit lost to Cleveland. Too bad, Livvie. It doesn't really matter. The scores are always different, but still they never change. Did Detroit lose to Cleveland when Roosevelt was President? I'm sure the loudspeaker said so if they did.

She is staring at me now. I cannot let her know that I'm uncomfortable. I must say something.

"Mind if we talk, mam?"
"Oh no. Please. You don't even have to talk if you don't want to."
"No. I want to talk."

The loudspeaker interrupts my thoughts again. Did it say the plane would be delayed? I should listen more carefully.

"Mam, are we ever going to get on that plane?"
"What plane?"

Foot in it again. She's not even going on the plane. What is she doing here then? And where is the pilot who is a friend of hers?

"You aren't married, are you, mam?"
"Yes, I am. Why?"
"Oh nothing. I just saw all the rings and wondered. Usually it's a sure give-away. Where's your husband?"
"Da Nang."

I think that she moved when she said it. Or maybe it was me. I have heard of women working in Vietnam just to be near their husbands, but she is the first one I have ever talked to. I must put her at ease.

"I was there once. It isn't so bad. Your husband's okay. The rockets are like a fourth of July. Really. I never went into the bunkers. I just stayed out and watched them. They never hit anything. Charley just sets them during the day by alarm clocks, but they're cheap clocks that have been stolen from the BX. They don't always work. At night when they go off, he isn't even there. Besides, you can always tell when they're going to hit. Saturday nights like clockwork. Sorry, mam. I didn't mean to make a joke. But you know the maids, we call them mamasans, they don't show up for work when there's going to be a hit. It's a sure giveaway. So your husband's okay."

I think her eyes are black. It must be a lie. Red Cross girls always have blue eyes. They wouldn't be picked, if they didn't. I am sorry that I told her what I did. Now she suspects me. She knows that I've been there. I am a traveling salesman. I am a banker from Hong Kong, just passing through. I have never been to Da Nang. It always comes to me too late. I must make her do the talking. She can't see me if she is doing all the talking.

"When will he get out?"
"Eleven months."
"Then what?"
"We'll re-enlist, I guess. Frank likes the Air Force. It's what he wants. He says it's the only place where he can fly those fast planes. He was commercial before he went in. But he didn't like it. Too many schedules. Now I worry about him, but I know that he's happy. We're both working, we're both doing our part. In five years we'll be out. We're going to buy a home in Texas. Near San Antonio, I think. Frank likes the rodeo. Maybe we can even get a ranch."
"Livvie always talked about going South. Fort Lauderdale mostly. Maybe he meant Texas too."
"Who's Livvie?"
"My friend, mam. We're going back to the world soon."
"Where is he now, your friend?"
"Already out there, I guess. He'll be getting a real good stink on pretty soon. Livvie always did sweat a lot."
"Oh. You don't say."

Yes, I do say. Why am I talking so much? I must kill time, stall her with talk, kill her, stall time with talk. I must make that plane. But it's no good. She suspects me. She will make me talk somehow. I must leave.

"Excuse me, mam, I have to go."
"But you can't go anywhere now. We're having a nice chat, aren't we?"
"Oh no. It isn't that. I do have to run, though. See about Livvie."
"But you said he was already out there."
"He is. But . . . well . . . you don't understand, mam. He's my responsibility. He didn't have anybody else. I told him I'd take care of him. There was only me."
"But I'm sure that he can take care of himself."

The pushiness comes out. Behind the red cross is another, only real, just waiting to be martyred. We are not in Africa. She is not a missionary. Why does she want to keep me here? Does she want to catch me in a lie so that she can make me stay? Eleven months until she gets out. Eleven. They're coming, Livvie. I can hear them coming.

"Excuse me, mam. I don't mean to be unfriendly. But I'm a little tired. I have been through this all before. I don't need your help."
"But I . . ."
"I know what you were trying to do."
"But I . . . what are you doing? Oh God, is that blood?"
"No, mam. It's . . . it's puke. It's the heat. Tomato juice."
"I'll go get something. Wait just a minute."

I must get away before she gets back. Yet I am waiting, rooted to my spot. My elbows are circling, but my feet have deserted me. I am a plane. If they find out that I did this, they won't let me get on the plane. I am face-down in a sampan. The Mekong is dirty. I can smell the dead fish. Livvie clears his throat too much. Charley knows the difference between that and a frog. Sit tight, Livvie. We're going to take the Freedom Bird.

Mayday. What did you say? Six-thousand piaster? About twenty-five in U. S. ? May, your hair is beautiful. You soak it in eggs? No, I not married. No, I not butterfly. I don't talk to many girls. Can I touch your hair? No, not the hair? It's sacred. Where's Buddha? May, you are not making sense. Hair's hair. When you go bald, does Buddha go away? The feet, then, let me touch something. No, I not butterfly. I need to touch something. I want it to last all night. I'm not usually that quick, honest. Yes, I come already, honey. I can start again, though. Please, May, your tea can wait. In a minute. I know it hurt you. What are you doing? What are you taking out of your squat? A guitar pick! God, May, I'm not some typhus. May, you don't keep babies away that way. Please don't say that! No, you don't want my baby. It would be a bad baby. It would run away. I think I'm going to be sick.

I am walking through the terminal now, but I cannot hear my steps nor can I see my feet. The dusty concrete floor does not give me back my echo. It soaks up footsteps. There is no one in the terminal. I must be the last one to board. I hope that I am still on time. I am out of breath.

A fan palm tree sways in the muggy breeze outside the gate. There are yellow arrows leading to the plane. It isn't necessary. I already know the way. My shirt and trousers stick to me in the back, but I know that it's not from sweat, because I am unable to sweat. My shirt is half-unbuttoned in the back. I think I will suffocate, but I must button up. They will not let me on the plane if I don't. The wind must be blowing from the back, because I sense a hollow space between my shirt and my chest.

I can see the plane now. The windows are all in rows. I know that they cannot open the windows in flight, so I will not ask them. Still I wish that they could. I cannot breathe very well.

I strap myself in automatically. I cannot feel the belt, but I have pushed my stomach in, so I know that I'm securely in place. There's a woman on my left. I think it might be the Red Cross girl, but I know this cannot be. She wasn't going on the plane. Why would she lie to me? Besides, she doesn't even recognize me. There's a fat man on my right. He is pulling at his collar.

I feel very uncomfortable. It is hard for me to think. I keep feeling a crowbar in my head, but the chips are softer now. Mushier. I may need to ask the stewardess for some aspirin. My fists are clenching and unclenching.

What is she doing? My arm feels pinched and stung. She's flicked her cigarette ash, and my fist is covering the ash tray. She's not even looking. I can't see her eyes.

"Lady, please."

I think she's going to cry. I just asked her please. I didn't even scold her. I mustn't talk anymore. I'll only be blamed. We don't even have to talk. I just want to touch your hair. Livvie, just sit tight. You know I'm responsible for you now. She's looking at the fat man. Asking him with her eyes if she's done anything wrong. She'll need a kleenex soon.

"My son . . ."

It's the fat man. He's butting in now. I must let him think he's won. Whatever he says. Why don't they sit together if they know each other? Why do they crowd me like this? I think they must know each other. On the same plane. It hurts my head to have to think of them. Mrs. Livingstone? Some reason why they have to sit apart. I knew your son. Something wrong, something illegal. The feet, then, let me touch the feet. Foot in it again.

"Lady, would you like to trade places with me?"
"Oh God, I can't take it."

She's too high-strung to be flying on this plane. The plane is shaking. We must be airborne. I didn't even notice. My knees must be shaking. There is something wet on my face. It cannot be sweat, because I am unable to sweat.

"My son . . . please . . ."

They can talk all they want now. I refuse to listen. They would only blame me anyway. I'm responsible now. His voice seems far away already. Yet I think I am being pushed from both sides. Why aren't the seat-belt signs on? There's no time to think about it. I am going to sleep. When I awaken, I will be in California. I must have insulted the Red Cross girl when I closed my eyes and didn't say anything, because she has slapped my face. It doesn't matter. I am going to ignore it completely. Let bygones be bygones. I am easing up now. I am getting loose. My elbows are no longer hard. I am not going to remember anything soon. I am no longer at attention.

Varee

It was my last day in Bangkok. I arrived at Dom Muang Airport at eight-fifteen, the same time I had arrived every Saturday morning for the past two months. During the week I taught courses in World Literature to American soldiers at Utapao Air Base, which was forty minutes by plane to the South. On weekends I escaped from the tribal camaraderie of the modern military into Bangkok with its air-conditioned hotels, its streets of silk and jewelry shops, its gilded temples and Turkish baths. I went to Bangkok every weekend for hot running water, although it was rust-colored, for real orange juice and French bread in the mornings, for the smell of cheese and vinegar in the streets to replace the previous week's storage of smoke and beer and fuel smells. I went to Bangkok to indulge myself: to sip cognac on the verandah of the Oriental Hotel in the afternoons, watching the paddle boats go by in the river as Tennessee Williams and Somerset Maugham must have done before me. At Utapao I had no other choice but to be alone at night. In Bangkok I would sometimes spend a whole afternoon deciding whether or not I would buy a woman for the night. More often than not, I spent the night alone, but the choice was still mine. The option to have a woman with me was often satisfaction in itself. It made being alone almost a delicacy.

At the Air Base I remained alone from Monday through Friday. I was not really alone, but I was not a part of anyone else's life either. Still there was something like the feeling of a nudist colony on the base. There was no privacy. I was constantly being exposed, from taking my pee with others in the outdoor toilets to eating the same meatloaf with others in the chow hall to sleeping in the barracks together where I was forced to share their snoring, forced to smell their breath of stale beer in the morning.

So I chose to be a hermit. I had no friends, because there were none to have. Everyone else worked during the day when I was free, and I taught at night when everyone else was free. My only verbal human contact was with my students, but that contact was parasitic, not symbiotic. It was based, not upon mutual dependence, but rather upon random collision. I would come in like Halley's Comet, deliver my lecture and vanish before they could probe my brain with picks and shovels. I would physically exhaust myself with each lecture to the point where any further actions for the rest of the evening were pantomime. The exhaustion was intentional, not because I was dedicated to the students, but because I wanted to be able to fall asleep immediately when I returned to the Barracks.

I was never quite successful. The bedsheets were always humid from the heat. They clung to my naked body as a rubber wet suit clings to the scuba diver. I slapped at imaginary mosquitoes that turned out to be sweat drops or strands of hair fallen out from too much itching and scratching. The B52's flew their bombing missions every hour on the hour after midnight, and their flight

16

path was directly over my bed. Each half hour a different crew would return. But coming or going, with or without bombs, the noise level was the same and the amount that they shook the bed was the same. When I was able to abstract it all, it struck me as syncopated tympany. Sometimes I would masturbate to help myself to sleep, imagining myself with a voluptuous drummer in an airport. In the intervals of pause I often stared at the baby lizard crawling on the window screen. I marvelled that such a small body could produce such a loud screech. I also marvelled at its patience, its all-night vigil, its tireless search for bugs. When sleep came, it came upon me as the lizard upon its victim -- without a sound.

When Saturday came, I was up to meet it. I rolled out of my week's cocoon and ran barefoot to the showers. I was going to Bangkok; I would soon be a butterfly again. I shaved in cold water or in no water at all, whichever was the case. I dressed in darkness and snoring, then walked to the terminal in darkness with the sound of cicadas singing on both sides of me to tell me where the road was. At the terminal I checked in and waited the customary several hours that the military calls "showtime" and finally boarded the C130 at seven-thirty. By eight-fifteen I would be at Dom Muang and boarding a bus on my way into Bangkok. By the time I reached Bangkok the sun was always up.

So were the farmers and the water buffalo. There were twenty miles of countryside between the airport and the city. The buffalo pulled ploughs and the men followed, the ropes of the ploughs around their necks. They could have been Ethiopians: they were invariably sunburnt beyond recognition. All were stripped to the waist where ox-hide hung draped like a towel. All seemed to be suffering from malnutrition or overwork. Their chests were caved in from all the pulling and bending. Their ribs looked purple to me -- a combination, I suppose, of the redness of the sun at that hour and the blue-tinted window glass of the air-conditioned bus in which I was riding. Every fifty yards or so, the field became a rice paddy. Here the women worked, knee-deep in the mud, their conical straw hats shining in the sun and protecting them from it. The houses in the distance were elevated by wooden slats at the four corners. This gave ventilation to the houses, kept the mosquitoes away and protected the houses from the erosive dampness of the soil. Suddenly there were billboard signs in the fields. I saw a Coca Cola sign which must have said "Things go better with Coke" in the cursive Thai language of curly-cue's and question marks. With more signs came more houses in the distance. Then suddenly the fields disappeared altogether. Fruit stalls and motorcycle shops replaced them. The bus slowed down. We were in Bangkok. It was almost nine o'clock and Bangkok was already one massive traffic jam.

I usually took a nap when I got to the hotel, but this time was different. This was to be my last day in Bangkok, and I wanted to live it to the fullest. I also wanted to exhaust myself, so that I would sleep on the plane that night. After the usual quibbling over what reductions in rate I was entitled to at the hotel, I went to breakfast. This was the only meal that I ever ate American-style in Bangkok. If it hadn't been for the orange juice, French bread and free newspaper, I wouldn't have eaten breakfast at all. There is a curious thing about the military when they aren't in uniform: they tend to wear the brightest colors at the most inopportune times. There were several men in purple velveteen pants suits and burgundy corduroy suits with wide orange ties at the next table. They must have gotten a discount on the material. Even in suits, they looked like they were in uniform. Imitation blue chandeliers hung from the ceiling. The table cloths were gold and seats were high-arched `a la Louis Quatorze. The official title for this dining facility was "Officers' Open Mess.' On the table was a placard which read: "Where the Elite Meet to Eat." I was glad that my courses in World Literature dealt only with fiction and not with poetry.

I read the Bangkok Post avidly, even though I was fighting off my usual morning yawning fits, because it was the last time I would ever read it.

Field Marshal Kittikachorn was quoted as having vowed to crack down on the corruption of the government's provincial chiefs. Anyone caught with his fingers in the till would be shot without trial. He said he would close down all the sidewalk markets, since they were only a front for drugs. He said there would be a midnight curfew imposed on all night clubs to eliminate the rapes, muggings and murders of tourists. And effective immediately, he would close down all the Turkish baths, since they were allegedly guilty of sexual improprieties. I laughed. How could a bath give you improprieties? Of course, I knew what he meant, though. I would miss the baths. Fortunately, I would be gone before they closed.

A man named Prasit Tanaveruseran had stolen two elephants from a farmer in Chiengmai and had arranged a ransom for them with the farmer. When they met in an open field for the exchange, the police were hiding behind the bushes and they promptly riddled poor Prasit with bullets. Where did he hide those two stolen elephants?

Colonel Likkit Suvannathat had been acquitted at a trial of his peers at Nakhon Phanom for allegedly having paid $200,000 five years ago for the post of Thai Base Commander there and then extracting bribe money from all the Thai military and civilians there.

I put the paper down. I needed to stretch my legs and give my eyes a rest. Reluctantly, I paid the bill and walked through the lobby to the elevators. It was almost noon.

When I awoke it was two o'clock. I didn't mean to sleep that long. I quickly went downstairs. As I passed the bar to the right of the front desk, I could see that it was already half-filled and quite lively. A heavy-set forty-ish blonde was standing on the stage, going through her numbers for the evening show. Her hair was rolled up into a bun in back. Her big breasts vibrated on the high notes like bobbers do when the fish are biting. She was singing "The Impossible Dream" with an Australian accent. At the end of each line, she dug into the stage with her spiked heels. She reminded me of a horse with her digging. The Thai piano player looked bored. I walked on.

In the barber shop there were three male barbers and a female manicurist. She rarely gave a manicure, though, for she was the mamasan. I nodded to her and she slid one of the wall mirrors to one side, revealing a row of seven closed stalls. This was the Turkish bath. I walked into the second stall, aware that what would follow would be the first dialogue I had had in a week.

"Hello, Somboon. Khun sawatdee krap?"
"Oh, khun Bob. Sawatdee ka."

For the past seven weeks Somboon had given me my bath. When I first got to Bangkok, I had tried out the bigger, more commercial baths like Chuvallo's where they had 700 stalls and where I had to choose one girl among fifty or more behind the blue tint when they couldn't see me. I preferred the company of the smaller Turkish bath, the familiarity with Somboon, even the familiarity by now of the language barrier. I knew the greetings and good-byes in Thai. For the rest I used my hands.

Somboon knew how to use her hands. After seven weeks I was still embarrassed to undress before her and get into the bath. But with her child-like innocence, or maybe it was just indifference, she always came forward and unbuttoned my shirt for me. It was always easier after that. I know there was no pleasure in the work for her, and yet I wanted to ask her each time I came why she worked there, as if she had any choice in the matter. When she washed my back, it was as if I were washing it. But when she passed over my genitals with the washcloth, I was always acutely aware that she was someone else, that she was another.

She lit a cigarette and waited for me to dry myself off. She motioned toward the cot, which was very much like those in a doctor's office. It was long and hard with a white paper covering on top. I lay face down, while she applied some talcum powder to my body. Then she mounted me and straddled my sides to massage my neck and shoulders. She did not know how to give a good massage, yet this was always the most interesting time of the whole bath. It was at this moment that the soldiers, Thai and American alike, propositioned the girls. For us it was at this moment that Somboon did most of the talking. Sometimes she sang old Thai folk songs and I would fall asleep. But more often she talked. She never failed to ask me if I had a "teelock," which was the slang word for mistress. I always told her no, but still she asked me every time. It must have puzzled her, I thought. If I didn't have one, then why hadn't I asked her by now? Why did I always go back to Utapao on Monday? A person didn't come all the way to Bangkok every weekend just for a Turkish bath, did he?

She was particularly insistent this time when she asked. She must have read the papers about the closing down of all Turkish baths. She would have to become someone's "teelock" very soon. I almost felt apologetic for taking up her time. I must have sounded more evasive than usual in my answer, because she pinched my shoulders very hard and my neck cracked as it snapped back from the pinch. Actually I was being evasive for another reason. I was not going back to Utapao on Monday. I would not be coming back to Bangkok for any more Turkish baths. I would not tell Somboon that I was leaving. For some reason I had accepted this course of action from the very beginning. It was just better this way. It was not the trauma of good-bye that bothered me, for I hardly knew her, but the need to explain a good-bye that seemed so impossible, so illogical, so unnecessary. Americans fly in and out of Bangkok every day. I was no different from the rest in that respect. And suddenly, abruptly, even sense-

19

lessly, I was going home, and there would be no more ritual, no more unbuttoned shirt, no more rubbing of hands.

"You bullshit me, khun Bob!"

She still thought I had a regular mistress hidden away somewhere. It always amazed me that she knew so many GI slang and swear words when she knew so little English. She pronounced these words so casually that it was as if I had heard them for the first time. Her voice was deadpan, as if she were giving a weather report. Mother, I would like you to meet Somboon. You bullshit me, khun Bob Mother. No, I could not imagine that happening. Somboon and I would never sit in pajamas at the breakfast table together. There was only the rubbing of hands.

"You want special massage, khun Bob?"
"How much does it cost?"
"You know how much it cost."

Even this was ritual. The special massage consisted of Brylcream or Vaseline, and the cost was five dollars. The idea of paying for something I could do better by myself was somehow repellent to me. The most bizarre perversion in all the Far East must be free sex. She always asked and I never accepted. It was part of the script. She always pretended that she was mad because I was so cheap, which was ridiculous, since I usually gave her a five dollar tip anyway. Perhaps I never paid so that I could keep coming back. This too was ridiculous, since I would not be back. It was time to go.

"Krap khun krap, Somboon. I have to go now. There are probably others waiting."
"No be others."
"What?"
"No be others. We close, no more bath. All close."
"Yes, I read about it. I'm sorry, Somboon. What will you do now?"
"I go Indian movie. You wait Somboon. You go movie too."

She went to change into her street clothes, while I waited outside in the barber shop. The wall mirror slid back behind me and I was left with my own reflections. I didn't quite know why I was waiting. I couldn't communicate with her in Thai, let alone munch popcorn at an Indian movie where the subtitles would mean as little as the original. I think that I waited because it was my last day in Bangkok to wait. The whole day was a kind of waiting. I was like an expectant father. My mood was always different when I knew that I was leaving a place and would never be back. It struck me for the first time, for example, that I had been a regular customer and that I had also been the very last customer. I felt obliged to wait.

While I waited, Varee emerged from behind the mirror. I did not know her name then. I only knew that she was the most beautiful girl that I had ever seen. Her thick lips parted and she smiled a smile as wide as her face. Her teeth sparkled in contrast to her dark, brooding eyes and olive cheeks. There was a space between her front teeth. I remembered what Chaucer had said

20

about gap-toothed women. I was so disarmed by her that I think I asked her what she was instead of who she was.

She laughed and announced herself as the first stall. For seven straight weekends I had gone into the second stall. Somehow I had never thought of the other stalls as even being occupied. She laughed again. She pinched my arm as if to say that I had lots of muscle. She said I had made Somboon very happy, because I was going to the Indian movie. Suddenly I knew that I would not be going to the movie with Somboon. I knew I would be gone before Somboon came out.

"Please . . . what is your name?"
"Sopa."
"Please, Sopa, tell Somboon that I sorry. I no can go to movie."

It always infuriated me that I slipped into their pigeon English in order to get myself understood without having to repeat myself. I left her before she could answer. I felt that she must be still smiling, even though she must also be bewildered. All I could picture was that smile as I walked past the bar and up to the elevator. I was confused. It is difficult to think clearly after a Turkish bath. But I was leaving that night, so I had to think both clearly and quickly. I turned around and walked back into the bar. I sat down just inside the door where I could see anyone coming out of the barber shop. I ordered a beer which I had no intention of drinking.

Somboon walked out. I was glad that her back was all I could see. Her little squat-walk carried her to the door. She would forgive me in time. What would she forgive me? There was nothing to forgive. There had never been anything, because I had never paid. Only payment could demand repayment: forgiveness. I was getting giddy.

Then the girl who called herself Sopa walked out and I was beside her.

"Please, Sopa. I know you no know me. But I want to buy you coffee."
"But . . . Somboon?"

She pointed helplessly toward the door through which Somboon had already vanished into the traffic. The Turkish bath had closed for Sopa too. A customer where there were no more customers must have been the last thing on her mind. I was asking her to be an accomplice.

"I know. Somboon. I know. Somboon . . . She just bath to me. You understand me? Khun siap mai? But you . . . I want talk to you. Just talk, no more. Please."

She frowned, and I could not tell whether it was a moral judgment or merely a misunderstanding of language. It should have discouraged me, but it didn't. She was even more striking when she frowned. I could never hope to know her any better than I had known Somboon after seven weeks, but I had to try. She consented finally, after making me promise that we would go somewhere no one would see us. We went to the bar of the Florida Hotel across the street, which was always empty during the day. There was no Turkish bath there.

Somehow I knew that she had not eaten all day. Now that she was no longer smiling as freely as before, I could see it in her face. I urged her to eat something, but she refused. Finally she compromised herself enough to accept a cup of coffee at my expense.

"Sopa, you look very sad."
"My name not Sopa."
"What is your name, then?"
"Varee. I use 'Sopa' only work. That work."

She was pointing again. She was pointing directionally toward the hotel we'd just come from. But she was also pointing to signify that she knew the work wasn't respectable.

"I know your name."
"You do?"
"Yes. Khun Bop."

I had to laugh. Varee was pronounced 'Walee,' something Americans would never understand. And Bob was pronounced 'Bop' for her, and she would not hear the difference if I corrected her. So I just laughed. She was laughing too, without knowing why.

"Why you laugh, khun Bop?"
"To make you laugh. You very beautiful when you laugh."

I didn't think she understood me, because she was frowning again. So I translated as best I could into Thai.

"Khun suey mak."

Her expression only deepened. She had understood the first time. And because she had understood, she had frowned. I was ashamed. I realized that I had treated all Thai girls as if they were little wooden wind-up dolls. They had acted like dolls in the bath. That she could be more complex than simply being beautiful, that she could have feelings deeper than I could get to both awed me and made me ashamed.

"Why you speak Thai to me, khun Bop?'
"I don't know."
"Please speak English. I no like you speak Thai. If you know Thai, that mean you know many 'pooying,' and I no 'pooying' girl like them."

Of course she was right. If I spoke Thai fluently, then I had to have learned it in school. But if I only spoke in snatches, I had to have learned it from bar girls and girls in the bath. My Thai had the same effect on her as Somboon's English had had on me. Mama, Pom cha'bai America with Khun Bop. No, it would never happen. Now I was frowning. Varee was laughing. It was a softer laugh than she had given me in the barber shop. There was still the sensual space between her teeth, and the slight lisp, she would say wisp, in her voice that it caused. But her quiet little whispered laugh had broken the language barrier between us. And perhaps other barriers too. We were no longer speaking in tongues. I looked at my watch. It was four-thirty.

"Varee, what does it mean? Your name, what does it mean?"
"It mean 'water' like in 'klong'."

The klongs were the canals of Bangkok. The guidebooks called Bangkok the "Venice of the Far East." But most of the klongs had dried up or had been replaced with streets. Those that remained reeked with the stench of human waste that poured into them daily. They were the sewage system. It was hard to imagine the Indian Gods of the *Ramayana* flowing all the way to Bangkok via the klongs, as the myth purported, to become the Gods of the *Ramakien*, the Thai national epic. But it was easy to imagine Varee meaning water. Perhaps it was because of the bath.

"What will you do now, Varee, now there no more bath?"
"I no know. I work."

She meant the future tense. Future uncertain tense. She was rubbing her fingers together. The massage was still going on in her fingers.

"I'm sorry. I didn't mean to make you sad."
"I know."
"I only want to make you happy. I must leave Bangkok, must leave Thailand tonight. So I do not want to make you sad. Before I go I only want to make you smile."
"You tell Somboon?"
"No."
"You make Somboon sad when you no go Indian movie."
"I know. But I told you, Somboon and me, it was only for the bath. Nothing else."
"You sure, khun Bop?"
"Sure I sure. Why?"
"Somboon work hard. She have many money. She give massage, but she give more too. She no only one. Other girl they give more. Give bath bad name. I give massage. Just massage. I no have money like Somboon. Now bath close."

And she closed her eyes momentarily. Her fingers were balling up into fists. Perhaps she had come with me because I had not gone with Somboon, and not in spite of it. But I had not seen through Somboon. I had only seen beyond her. I had never paid.

"Varee, if you need some money, perhaps . . ."
"No, khun Bop. I no take money. I work. There money. If I no work, there no money. I no take money."
"Are you hungry? Can I buy you something to eat?"
"No, I no hungry. I no eat much."

I thought of Colonel Likkit Suvannathat being acquitted. I thought of two elephants being stolen. Thailand was Siam. Like twins. It was a country of opposites.

"Varee, did your family know you worked in bath?"
"No, I never tell them. My father think I work in jewelry shop."
"Are you ashamed of what you do?"
"What you mean, khun Bop?"
"I mean, do you think it wrong?"
"It wrong. For Somboon maybe it no wrong. For me it wrong."
"Varee, can I ask you something? Are you a Buddhist?"
"Yes, I Buddha."
"Then you think Buddha angry that you work in Turkish bath?"
"He angry. But if I no work, there no money."
"Maybe Buddha will forgive you, because you had to work?"
"What mean, 'forgive'?"
"I mean, maybe Buddha wouldn't be angry. Maybe he would say it's okay."
"Buddha, he say it wrong. I not good. I no can say I sorry."
"What do you mean?"
"American, he can say he sorry. But I no can say I sorry. Buddha know I no can say. American say, it make all good. I no can say. I know before. I no can say after Buddha no forgive."
"Then you can't pray, can you? I mean, it wouldn't do any good?"
"Sure I pray. I pray all time."
"I don't understand."
"If I pray, maybe I die."
"Varee, don't say that!"
"No, it good. If I die, maybe I come back somebody better."

Even the religion was Siamese. There was no forgiveness for her. But then there was no final death for her either, so perhaps it didn't matter. It mattered only to me. I looked at my watch. It was six o'clock.

"Please let me buy you something to eat."
"No, khun Bop. I no take money."
"But it's not money. It's food."
"No."
"A steak, a sandwich, some fried rice."
"No."
"Some chicken, or fish, or maybe some soup."
"No. Okay. Maybe some soup."

Varee explained our order to the girl in Thai. The girl answered. Varee was explaining again. It took her a long time to order two bowls of soup.

"Varee, what did you tell the girl?"
"What you mean, khun Bop?"
"You know what I mean. What did you say to her after you told her the soup?"

She was blushing.

"Khun Bop, you know Thai very good."

"Come on, what did you say to her?"

"I tell her that I sick. That you find me when I sick. You buy me soup. If I eat steak or rice, she think I bad. If I no tell her I sick, she think I your teelock."

"Oh."

"You mad?"

"No, I'm not mad. just confused, that's all. You're something else."

"Jim, he always say I something else."

"Who's Jim?"

My voice seemed to go up an octave with the question. I certainly hadn't asked it very casually. I was jealous.

"Jim, he my husband before."

"What do you mean by before?"

"He not now. He go away. I think America, but I no know."

"But why?"

"I no want tell you. You laugh at Varee."

"I promise I won't laugh. Please tell me."

"Jim marry me, I know nothing. What Somboon do, I no know what is. Jim, he know. He do. He teach me."

"Was he a good teacher?"

"What you mean?"

"Nothing. Please go on."

"One day I feel sick. I no know why. Jim, he make me feel sick too. He smoke cigarette, my stomach come up. No good. One day I lock door. He come, I tell him go away. He come again, I tell him go away. I think maybe I no love him. One day he come, he tell me open door or he go away America, never come back. I let him go."

"That's very sad, Varee. But why?"

"He go away long time. One day his friend come to my house. I no let him see me. He go away. Then one day my baby come."

"That's incredible. You didn't know?"

"I know nothing before."

"Did you ever write to tell him?"

"No, I no know where he go. I no can say I sorry. It better. I love my baby. His name Jim. I work, someday buy my house. I work, my baby never know."

"You must love your baby very much."

"Buddha love him too."

The soup was cold. I hadn't even touched it. I had the feeling that I was fasting, that my senses were more acute than they had been the whole time I was in Thailand.

"Varee, did you ever find anyone else? I mean. the baby must need a father."

"My father his father. I no need love. I work."

"But you're still very young, very beautiful."

"I not beautiful. I bad."

"No, honest. You're beautiful. Surely there are other men."

"Only one. But he before too."

"Who was that?"

"His name Tom."

"And what happened to him?"

"Tom fight Vietnam. He come see me two time. First time he come to bath. He sad because I work in bath. He say it bad. He go back Vietnam, but he send money for my baby. He send money, say I should stay home with baby. I write him, say I quit work in bath, but I lie. I tell him so he be happy. But I need work in bath. I no can take money if I no work. He come back. He say we buy house when he get out. We go hotel, but he no touch me, we just sleep. He very good to me. He go back to Vietnam, say he come again, but he never do."

"What happened?"

"Maybe he die. I think maybe he die. One day I know he think of me. I know he like my hair. He always say my hair beautiful. One day I cut hair, put hair in klong. I pray Buddha he send hair for khun Tom. I think maybe he do."

"God, how sad!"

"I not sad. No sad now, khun Bop. You make Varee happy."

I took her hand and put it in my own. I wanted to unbutton my shirt and put it inside, but I didn't dare. She didn't squeeze my hand, but neither did she refuse my squeeze. We just looked at each other. There was a kiss a million miles away between our lips. Suddenly it was ten o'clock and the spell was breaking. It was time for me to go.

"Varee, I have to go."

She never blinked her eyes. She just kept staring at me, as if the language barrier had suddenly returned. Slowly her eyes were swelling up with tears. But none would ever leave her eyes. I was sure of that. I knew her that well.

"Khun Bop, why you no go Indian movie with Somboon? Why you talk to Varee? Sure I sad. You say you want to make me happy. You make happy. Now you go, you make me very sad."

"Please Varee, please don't talk like that. I only meant to make you happy, that's all. Maybe someday I can come back. But if I don't, I know you'll be happy. I want you to know it too."

"I know nothing."

We were crossing the street already. In ten minutes I would be checked out and into a taxi on my way back to the airport. I felt like I had just arrived. How could I be leaving? She didn't want to come up to the room with me. She said that she would wait for me outside.

As I passed the bar, the Australian singer was taking her bows. The men were whistling and clapping and calling for more. For me there wasn't any more. When I got to my room, I found that the bed had been remade. Varee would never see it. Even the hotel seemed to anticipate my leaving. They couldn't even wait for me to leave before making up the bed. I had a bitter taste in my mouth. I shut the door behind me.

26

The noise had not decreased at all in the bar. Maybe these were the flight crews of the B52's. If so, they were used to such noise. I wondered if anyone were sitting just inside the door where I had sat. If so, could he see me as I passed? He would be glad to see only the back of me. I was crying.

I was no longer crying when I got to where Varee was standing. A young Thai man shouted something to her from the other side of the street. Then he whistled. Varee jutted her chin out and said something very quickly to the man. Then she lowered her head and looked down at my feet.

"Varee, what did he say to you?"
"He say I very pretty girl."
"What else?"
"He say I need good man like him, not dirty American like you."
"And what did you say back to him?"
"I no can tell you, khun Bop. It bad."
"Yes, you can. Now tell me. What did you say?"
"I say . . . 'fuck you!'"
"Varee, where did you learn that?"
"Somboon. She teach me."

She was laughing, but it was the hollow laughter of the barber shop again. My taxi was there already. It was time to go.

"We have to say good-bye here. Here's another taxi for you. It's better this way. I don't want you to see me at the plane."

She was all pantomime now. There was much she could have told me that I would never hear. I was home.

"You know, I don't even know where you live."
"On road to airport."

I could only guess at Varee's Siamese self. This American hotel, the Turkish bath, the Thai cotton dress, the lipstick, the streets of Bangkok -- none of this was really her. This was Sopa. Varee was out there where her father followed the plough and the water buffalo, where her mother was knee-deep in mud with a cone-shaped straw hat on, where her baby waited inside the house on stilts.

I kissed her once, very hard, and she did not refuse. Most of me wanted to take just one taxi. Most of me wanted to take her back to the States with me. But it was not the other me, I who would step off the plane. It was just the me who would board the plane. I had spent too many nights alone.

I put her in the second taxi.

"Pom lak khun, khun Bop."

She didn't need to translate. I was fluent by now. She squeezed my shoulder as the hypnotist does to put his patient to sleep. I put fifty dollars in her hand as it drew back inside the car, and she did not refuse. I couldn't see her face. Her taxi had already gone. I had finally paid. And I would go on paying.

The Amateur Sword-Swallower

Cooper was one of those lanky, latter-day Southern gentlemen who find their way into the military for mysterious reasons, who never make sergeant, who never save any money but always seem to have money to spend, who fall asleep on the job, but who know every woman on and off the base by their first names, whose best approximation of standing at attention is an oblique slouch. To hear his drawl, you would never suspect that he was in Intelligence (and precisely because of his ability with languages). I was not the only one who thought that his drawl was less than entirely authentic. But he could put you to sleep with it, humming to you with those lazy, half-closed eyes and pouting lower lip, as if he were talking to himself. He called it his hangdog look, but I never saw any other, except perhaps once. Everything about Coop (everyone called him that) was deceiving. To look at him, you would swear that he was one of the Army's legion of select rejects, one of McNamara's hundred-thousand, a kind of American foreign legion in permanent exile. But if his body seemed one-hundred-percent drone, his mind housed the rest of the humming bee-hive. He filtered all of his intelligence through the smoke-screen of a razor-sharp wit that always left you wondering whether he really knew what he was saying, whether he could be that naive, that sincere, that self-effacing, that stupid, that ingenious.

If one could believe him, he came to the military quite naturally, in the only way that could be sanely called "naturally": through heredity. He swore that his ancestors had all worn uniforms, dating back to the only one of them who had ever fought for a losing cause: a Marcus D. Cooper, who was supposed to have been with Lee when the South surrendered. Yet Coop had to be drafted in order to sustain his allegiance to tradition. Coop's one obsession in life -- his love of swords -- apparently stemmed from the legacy of the aforementioned Marcus D.

I could never tell what kept Coop in the military, long after his time was legally up, or, for that matter, why the military bothered to keep him, since he was definitely more trouble to them in uniform than he possibly ever could have been out. It was one of those love-hate relationships that has nothing to do with time or place, that persists through habit and circumstance. If I quizzed Coop on the subject, he would just look at me patiently, benevolently, with that hangdog look of his that said: "You're the teacher, not me. You're supposed to know and I'm not going to tell you." And from those limpid, candid eyes and that orphan's smile, the smile of children caught in their mischief, echoed through the cavernous mouth, would come that inimitable "rivvet" sound, a cross between a frog's mating call and a primeval burp, which was the cue for a change of subject.

Coop was an encyclopedia of contradictions. Nobody really knew him, yet everyone (of equivalent rank or lower, that is) liked him, respected him, followed his lead. These were others who talked like generals, there were even generals who talked like generals, but Coop was the real general of the base. As soon as an order was given, everyone, including the officer who had given the order, would turn to Coop, would turn to see if he was in the mood to follow that particular order. You couldn't really say that Coop was lazy or even insubordinate; it's just that he lived life in slow motion. Thus, it was difficult to separate the real Coop from the Coop of legend. His presence, while taken for granted, was always considerable. His absences, which were frequent, were always explained by rumors that he was in bed with so-and-so's wife, so-and-so's mistress, so-and-so's prostitute. I had difficulty believing the rumors myself, since Coop had absolutely nothing to prove. He was already a "general".

I must confess that at first I disliked him intensely. I could never figure out why he enrolled in my course, except perhaps out of boredom or mischief, since he knew the material as well, if not better, than I did. The very first time I walked into the base classroom, I noticed him immediately. He stood out from all the others. His eyes were closed, his chin was tucked into his chest, and he looked as if he would break into a snore at any minute. Then, just as suddenly, his eyes opened, as cats' eyes open from an apparent sleep. They were clear and vigilant. The corners of his mouth turned up slightly, almost imperceptibly, as though to say that he was mildly amused with me, and that he was waiting to be entertained.

That first night was the only time that he was physically present when the class actually started. From that night on, he seemed to time his entry for precisely the moment when I had just finished filling out the required attendance sheets. Invariably, I would already have marked him as absent. I spoke to him after class. He nodded his head, smiled, and, when he had heard enough, he "rivvet"-ed the subject to its conclusion and left. He persisted in his tardiness. I threatened to make him stay those ten minutes after all the others had left. I threatened to lock the door, so that no one could enter after the class had started. I threatened to leave the absent mark on the sheet if he did not come on time. I threatened to lower his final grade. I even reprimanded him in front of the others. I cajoled and pleaded. I threatened him with everything I could think of, but it was all to no avail. I surrendered. Coop was the general.

A teacher depends to a great extent on eye contact with his students. This was another source of irritation between me and Coop. He would never look at me when I lectured. It became a challenge for me. I used to stay awake at night, planning exciting lectures, rehearsing my delivery. If I were good enough, he would have to look up, take notice, show the others that I commanded respect. But he never looked up. Instead, I found that the only way I could cope with the situation was to look down, myself, to tuck my chin into my chest, to lecture my ricochet. Coop was the general.

I have always been a conscientious teacher, both in the planning of my lectures and in my delivery of them. I would always know before the class how much time, for example, I wanted to spend covering this point or that. Again, I was in for a surprise. My tempo was not synchronized with Coop's. When he concluded that I had spent enough time on a certain point, he would go "rivvet" with that low throaty frog-grunt. If I persisted beyond this warning, I no longer had anyone's attention in the class. You see, I had no need of eye contact after all, no need ever to look up. Coop would tell me when it was time to move on to something different or when it was time to stop completely. His throat was my stop-watch. I found myself under-preparing for my lectures. I would unconsciously race through my notes, anticipating Coop's signals. A lecture that would have taken me the full hour to give in any other class took me thirty minutes in that class. It is always embarrassing for a teacher to finish ahead of time, to have to let the students go early, because there is no more to say. But Coop was the general.

As long as I resisted, I was at odds with the whole class. It was as if they had come out of spite -- to watch me squirm. I saw all kinds of barriers between us that were never really there. As soon as I adjusted to my proper place, that is, as soon as I stopped acting like the head of a class whose body was decapitated from me, as soon as I allowed the class to be of one body and mind, I began to like Coop as I have never liked another human being.

Admittedly, his actions must seem very infantile to anyone who wasn't there. But Coop never interrupted me indiscriminately. His sense of the class's heartbeat was much more accurate, I must say, than my own. And he was always entertaining. A visitor to the classroom would have concluded that there was a poltergeist or at least a professional ventriloquist loose in the class, for Coop performed with his mouth closed. He gave all the cues without taking any of the bows. And for some inexplicable reason, he put up with all my paranoia, with all my pedantry. I think he actually liked me.

He must have liked me, for I began to be accepted as an equal by the others. I began to be invited to their quarters before and after class. Class became an artificial landscape, a necessary formality between real get-togethers. Gradually, I knew that I had been really accepted, that I was really there, because everyone acted as though I weren't there at all, at least not as their teacher. They ran around naked in my presence; they gambled and swore; they took drugs and showed me their Polaroid snapshots of the women back home. It took me a long time to forget that we weren't in the classroom. I would begin preaching and Coop would go "rivvet". Everyone would laugh, and I would be accepted again.

The very best times were the drunkest times, the times of complete and sodden abandon. These were the nights of far-away shells, of planes with no more noise than a common fly's buzz. These were the nights when you could look up and see your own eye-lashes and imagine them as combs, quietly stroking your field of vision. But, above all else, these were the nights when Coop swallowed swords.

He had made it a habit to collect a sword from every place he visited. He had swords from Hong Kong and Tokyo, from Mexico and Thailand, from the Civil War and the time of Napoleon. He had samurai swords, he had saracen blades, he had scimitars. I don't know how he got to keep them, since swords are supposed to be dangerous weapons, at least in some armies. The amazing thing about Coop was that he not only collected, he also swallowed what he collected.

He would tilt his head back so far that his chin formed one continuous vertical line with his neck. His Adam's apple would swell to three times its normal size. With his feet rooted solidly on the floor (which, for obvious reasons, had to be level), his knees slightly bent, his stomach pulled in, the rhythm of his breathing adjusted to a set pattern and his hair falling over his collar in back from so much straining, he would push out his lips and open them, until the corners almost touched his cheek bones. He would poise the tip of the sword between his fingers. He would, thus, balance the whole weight of the sword at its smallest point with those nimble fingers.

Then slowly, ever so slowly, Coop would ease the glistening edge down the long hollow of his mouth and throat, the two of them becoming one. He would continue to breathe through swift sniffs of his nostrils and quick, quiet gasps from the depths of his throat. For several agonizingly interminable minutes, it was as if Coop had no body at all, as if he were completely empty inside. We watched the blade disappear into his body, until finally the hilt of the sword touched the corners of his mouth. At this point, Coop would momentarily close those bulging eyes, which, during sword-swallowing, were as big as his mouth. The penetration was complete.

With a slight twitch in his bent elbows, so that his muscles would not lock on him, he would begin to remove the sword. When he had removed it, he would always collapse on a bed and breathe heavily for several minutes. During this time, we always checked to see if there were any blood, any saliva, any phlegm, anything to prove that the sword had actually disappeared in Coop's body. We never found any signs. Completely relaxed now, Coop would become unabashedly indifferent to the rest of us. Those who knew him best would begin to make jokes about his prowess, usually of a sexual nature. I could only feel pity and awe for Coop at such times.

What keeps men from losing their minds in the military is usually some form of perversion. There were, of course, the dangerous missions that men volunteered for out of boredom, knowing that they might be killed, knowing that they needn't go at all. There were sexual games among the men, seeing who could grow the hardest, seeing who could hold the longest, seeing who could shoot the most. There were games involving intentional overdoses of drugs, and there were games of Russian roulette with their weapons. And there was Coop's sword-swallowing, the best kept secret on the base.

The worst-kept secret was the coming of the USO tour. They came three weeks before the semester ended. With them, whether it was ever authorized or not, came Edna Wheeler, General Wheeler's wife. Twenty years younger than her husband, she was still ten years older than the rest of the women who came with the tour. They had come to "entertain the boys". They were much prettier than the Red Cross women and much less jaded-looking than the women who worked for A.I.D. in town. But they all looked the same to me. They all looked like a former Miss Idaho or Miss Nevada of four years ago, women who had lost the most important beauty contest of their lives, but who had gotten hooked on airplanes and photographers. These were women who had waited around Hollywood, working as part-time models or Kelly girls, as drive-in waitresses or prostitutes for the indoor swimming pool set, waiting to be "discovered". These were women whose voices were always two octaves higher then they should have been, women who could easily pretend that all men in uniform were medieval knights, women whose hair was the parched color of manila envelopes and whose lipstick glared in the dark like the beams atop radio and television towers, women who looked more like dimestore dolls than women, and whose skin, from too many chocolates and malted milkshakes, felt like popcorn to the touch.

There were two exceptions. Edna Wheeler was one of them. Although she could not have been over thirty-five, her hair was completely silver. She had an Irish temper in her eyes and a small gap between her two front teeth when she smiled. She looked like a cocktail waitress or a hostess at Howard Johnson's. There was the savvy of handling men in the way she walked, poised herself before doors to be opened, carried her breasts to their full advantage. There could be no mistake. Edna Wheeler was definitely among the generals. She could ask what time of day it was, and you felt as if someone had just gift-wrapped your soul to hell. Her voice rasped; it invited you closer at the same time that it scolded you to keep your distance. Edna Wheeler's whole body declared that she had absolutely no illusions left in life; that she would settle for the intensity of moments instead of the responsibility of goals; that the only enemy was age and that the only weapon against the enemy was an organized, efficient body hysteria. It was impossible to imagine a baby picture of Edna Wheeler. It was equally impossible to imagine her as decrepit in some rocking chair in a midwestern old folks' home. Edna Wheeler was one of those women who were at the age they had always been and always would be.

The other exception was Eileen Ritter. Her face flamed with acne in the afternoon sun, which was the first clue that she was not a former Miss Idaho. She was a gangling eel of a woman, tall because she was thin and thin because she was tall. She wore bifocals and she stuttered slightly when she spoke. Her job was that of secretary, business manager, chaperone, confidante, mother superior for all the wilting beauty queens. She too was efficient in her self-effacing nomadic way. You could look at Eileen Ritter for two hours, and , after an absence of five minutes, you would have forgotten completely what she looked like.

The men in the barracks looked at these women as a wolf looks at a wounded chicken, as a pauper looks at an expensive house, as a janitor looks at the company president's waste basket, that is, with a mixture of desire and despair. They had ravaged so many imaginary women in their open barracks beds, where the lack of privacy wore on you like a boil, where the smell of black polish on marching boots rose from the floor and infected the damp pillow case, where the men would bury their heads in those pillows, pretending that there were no others present, suffocating their sex and their shame, the other hand moving back and forth beneath the sheets with the mechanical precision of carnival machines. And in the dark the hurried breathing and muffled grunts would finally subside, grow oppressive by absence like the lack of fresh air on a humid, summer day, then return again rhythmically in the anguished open-mouthed snoring of self-induced sleep, like that of babies after crying fits. Only Coop, his lips like two drowned lovers who have washed ashore from the bottomless ocean, their bodies locked in a death-embrace, kept his secrets sealed

33

inside and slept without snoring. I too kept my secrets sealed, because I slept alone.

It was around this time that I began to sense that I was a stranger to myself. I began to lose control of the looks and gestures that define a teacher. I began to forget my notes, to daydream during my lectures, to become engrossed in the counting of the buttons on my shirt. Every teacher experiences this time of dry swallows and sinking stomachs about two-thirds of the way through any course. My colleagues call it the limbo of teaching. With an equal mixture of apprehension and enthusiasm, both decreasing with age and experience, the teacher sets sail with his course. Half-way through the course, no land is visible, either before him or behind. And when he reaches the two-thirds mark, dry sand springs up before him in the distance, springs up like a reverse mirage, springs up like the hollow crystal spray from a fountain. He realizes that he has no more to give of himself, that he is as formless as the fountain spray, maintaining the illusion of being a solid form long after he has melted. He realizes that the uncertain beginning has become the inevitable ending, and that his followers must lead him to shore, then leave him. He realizes that inevitably he will have no more control over them. Like Moses with his enigmatic and irrelevant tablets, he realizes that all this time he has been spreading lies and dissension.

Two weeks before the end, I met General (three stars) Adam Wheeler. Coop and I were eating fried chicken that had the texture of athletes' feet in the cafeteria. Coop was lamenting the total lack of fresh green vegetables in the military, meticulously explaining in that teeter-totter drawl of his all the calories and cholesterol my body was absorbing with each bite of the chicken, all the while maintaining the deadpan look of a county coroner delivering an autopsy report to the police and next-of-kin.

My back was to the general, and I swallowed whole a large piece of chicken breast when the general tapped me on the neck with the thump of three-star authority.

"Mister, do you know who I am?"

I did not at first understand that he was talking to me. His voice boomed through the whole club as though through a megaphone, a voice that spread outward as it went, directed at everyone in general and at no one in particular, except that he still had his hand on my neck.

"Answer when you're spoken to, boy. I asked you a question."

The words struck me full-force in the face like a giant wave of ocean froth which slaps the shore and then slinks away on tiptoe. Surprise attack, then quick retreat to prepare for the next onslaught. The smell of cigar smoke and suppressed whiskey burps came with his words.

"I'm General Wheeler, you frisky punk. I run this base, and this is my club. Do I make myself understood?"

34

His words continued to strike, but they still had not sunk beneath the skin. I was like someone who has taken a shower and without drying off has walked out into a pouring rain. Water can displace anything but water. Because of his hold on my neck, it hurt my head to gaze upward, from the cheap off-duty Hawaiian shirt he was wearing to the off-color pink of his inebriated eyes. I started to laugh, because he began to look like an albino baby dressed in a rainbow. As he inadvertently burped with the same emphasis of authority, I could see behind him in the distance, rising up in embarrassment from the sudden clamor, the silhouette of one of the serving girls in the privileged shadows surrounding the general's table. She was buttoning her blouse.

'The man can't very well answer you, sir, if you don't let go of his neck."

General Wheeler turned toward Coop with the look of instant court-martial in his eyes. Undaunted, Coop patiently explained that I was a teacher who merited the courtesies of the base, that I was a civilian who was not subject to military rules, that I was, nonetheless, someone who neither demanded the courtesies nor flaunted the rules, and, thus, that I was obviously innocent of any wrongdoing. With those exasperating pauses of his that stretched a simple sentence into compound-complex sentence and a minute into ten, with his syrupy sing-song intonation, as if he were offering candy to a deprived and irrational child, Coop concluded that there must have been some mistake on the general's part.

"There's been no damn mistake here, Corporal, as you'll soon discover after I'm done talking to your sergeant about your sassy sweet-mouth. This is MY club, and I won't have any hairy-ape liberals eating in here like this one."

". . this one . . ." was orchestrated with another thump on my neck, as if my neck were a mere mass of jelly-shaped dough for the general's kneading. I was speechless before my accuser, my long hair feeling even longer, stretching down my back like a horse's mane stretches and stands up in anticipation of its rider. I suddenly felt nauseous. The blurred and gaudy splotches of the general's shirt matched the feeling in my stomach. With no regard for his own anonymity (security), Coop continued to come to my defense.

"Sir, I think that if you will check the Code you will see that this man does not come under your jurisdiction."
"Don't 'code' me, you impertinent pup. And you . . .?"

He was pointing to the black-suited manager who had left his cash register to ease my departure by giving me the bill in person.

"You won't have a job here anymore if you let this shag-mop in here again."

The look on the manager's face was one of fright and pleading, entreating me with his eyes to have pity on him. I could envision an epileptic wife and seven screaming children somewhere in his eyes. I paid the bill right there at the table. By leaving without a word in my defense, I felt that I would be saving not only the manager but also Coop, whom I signalled with my eyes to stay behind. As I walked toward the door behind the general's table, I could hear Coop's last remark to the general, who was following the manager back to the cash register: "Sir, you are indeed a philistine and a sybarite." And then: "Rivvet."

My path crossed that of the silhouette of the woman I had seen at the general's table. To my surprise, it was not one of the serving girls. It was Eileen Ritter. She was going to sit down with Coop.

There is an avalanche effect to everything that happens on a military base, perhaps because it is a totally enclosed universe, perhaps because there is so much in-breeding. To read the military logs, nothing happens that is not either cause or effect. But surprises, when they come at all, come in swarms, as measles lead to mumps. I have no other explanation for the midnight visit of Edna Wheeler to my private quarters.

"Do you know who I am?"

The question must have been a family heirloom. She whispered it, but it had the same unmistakably imperious tone that only a general's wife could effect under such circumstances. The lights were out in the room, but I could see the silhouette of her breasts pressed like two coconuts against the screen door of my room in the midnight moonlight. I could no sooner answer her question than I could that of her husband. Involuntarily, I scratched my hair. She had caught me totally off my guard. I had just begun the hand's evening ritual of self-gratification and self-denial. I was unusually excited that particular night, because I had savored a fresh and palpable image of flesh to which my mind returned reflexively over and over in tempo with the movement of my hand. It was the image of Eileen Ritter: not the real Eileen Ritter in the bare bald sunshine, but she of the shadows, the specter of the woman getting up from the general's table and buttoning up her blouse. After leaving the club, I had wondered whether her breasts were soft and white to the touch or whether the acne explosion on her face spread even there, as if she were some Hiroshima victim suffering from fall-out. The wonder was bliss. I had not felt this happy since coming to the base. Even in my embarrassment at being caught naked in the dark by the wife of the general("he has neither demanded the courtesies nor flaunted the rules"), I had to smile. If my fantasy of Eileen Ritter depended somewhat on the fact that she had been compromised in an intimate situation with the general (who might even have ordered her rather than persuading her), then the reverse of that fantasy was equally vivid, for here was the general's wife in a compromising situation with me. Victory comes to those who only know to wait. There is a poetic justice to all surprises, I decided with one of my uncustomary snap judgments.

"Don't turn on the lights. We don't need them. And don't put any clothes on. You won't need them."

Her hand enclosed mine over the light switch. The order given, she continued to squeeze my hand in the darkness. We sat down on the bed and leaned our heads against the wall. She leaned her head toward mine to whisper in my ear.

"I don't want you to act surprised or innocent or naive or righteous with me. That's all I ask. Do you understand? Act as though this had happened every night of your life, as though this will continue to happen every night of your life. I don't want you to question me or my motives. I do what I do, that's all. As far as anyone else is concerned, I was never here tonight, understand? If you cross me, you'll never get over being sorry for it."

Her head remained on my shoulder, but her tone of voice made it clear that it was really my head that was on her shoulder. Edna Wheeler knew how not to beg to get what she wanted. Her lips remained against my ear. Her breath was so warm that it seemed wet in my ear, as if her whispered secrets were leaking drops of rain down an eaves-trough. I placed my legs together, and there was sweat to make them stick.

"I'm not going to be here long enough to go through all the usual formalities of getting to know you. It's going to have to be instant. Do you see what I mean? I've heard the whole story of what happened tonight. It excited me. I found out a lot about you before coming here . . . as much as I could find out without coming here myself. I know that you won't be here long enough to reconcile with my husband or to leave many ribald tales about me after I'm gone. We're two of a kind, teacher, if you see what I mean."

If she had been a cocktail waitress in her former life, she must have been a good one. I admired her strength and her self-control. She must have been able to push away even the most persistently tactile customers. And she must have been able to extract drinking tips even from the Mormons. Her breasts and her breath weighed on my body with equal pressure, the one solid, the other liquid, the two merging into a wonderfully pungent gas. There was the smell of sex all over her.

She began to humm a low lullaby like a chant in my ears. It instantly became my own brain talking to me. Her throaty voice both frightened and soothed me. It was the humm of lying near a four hour-old fire. it was the release of the mind to sleep and irrational dreams. It was the complete surrender of a sauna bath. I was happy that the lights were out. I felt flushed like a lobster all over my body. The sweat that sealed my legs had turned cold and solid. My body was covered with goose-flesh, and the floor felt like the ice tray in a refrigerator to my bare feet. Her sex was infectious: I began to smell the smell of old wine in dust-covered bottles when it's first uncorked. It was the smell of my own testicles.

"We don't have time for both, professor. Don't be afraid. Who knows? I might be able to teach the teacher a trick or two. Besides, your hair's just the right length for me tonight. Adam hates anyone who's not going bald like he is. He thinks you're throwing it in his face."

She laughed at what must have been a long-standing Achilles heel between them. It was the laugh of a child who knows better than to laugh for no reason. I realized at that moment that without her laughter I would never have understood the situation. In this half-second of private laughter shared, she became a woman for me. I wondered how many human relationships in the world had been solidified by such shared liquid crying or gaseous laughter. Something between my legs was hardening, forcing them apart. I still had not uttered a single word.

"I think that you'll find an hour or so with me will more than make up for any embarrassment my husband has caused you. As I said, we don't have time for both. When you take me, I ask only that you talk to me. Keep talking to me. I want your mouth to say what your body says. If you stop talking, you pull out or I get off, do you understand?"

If a teacher has any self-assurances, one is certainly his ability to move his tongue. I had only to whisper, and, as long as I didn't stop whispering, this anonymous moment of complete madness, this child's play of give-and-take, this teeter-totter of absolution would go on and on. Would never end. I nodded my head, as much to myself as to her. I was not talking for eye contact. Her head bobbed with my nod. She began humming again, like bees over flowers whose smells are the strongest, and I knew that this humming was foreplay, the drum roll for him who had not yet known her, was prayer and was ritual that, though this might be the one time and place without memories or projections, would go on repeating itself forever. It was my turn to share that private privileged laughter with her. I understood why I had thought that Edna Wheeler had never been a child, why she would never be any older than she was right then and there cradled in my arms. Then the humming stopped. Suddenly in, then just as quickly out, she stuck her tongue in my ear, short-circuiting my brain. I pushed her and grabbed her at the same time. As I pushed her prone onto the pillow, my hands grabbed her breasts, as if they had always been there in that one place, as if my hands had always known where to go in the midnight darkness, as if they were blind men grabbing, without any fumbling, the invisible but familiar door knob.

"Wait, professor. There's someone here who wasn't here before."

I became a statue in an instant, petrified by what I knew was never there, suspended midway between sitting and lying down, supported from falling by the hands which mashed down on her breasts. Her hands were even more clairvoyant than mine. Deprived of our sense of sight in the black pitch of sex, we are able to hear and smell and taste and touch as never before and never again. Everything but our eyes becomes an eye in sex. We have no need to keep our eyes open. The mind surely sees what the eye has never seen. Her hand enclosed my hardened penis as it had enclosed my hand over the light switch.

"See?"

She laughed her voiceless rippling peal of ocean foam. Before her chest and belly had stopped their happy heaving, I was upon her.

Edna Wheeler was right. There was another person in the room: there was one of her and two of me. The me that spoke to her in licks and tickles, bites and squeezes, the me that spoke in everything but words, was the me I remember most about that night. I was surprised by that self which had never before surfaced. For the first time, I worried neither about protection nor disease. Those were learned fears, I discovered, fears of the mind which tortured the body. This self was total body, animal instinct, instant wish, instant desire, complete flow, complete fulfillment. The body knew from birth what the mind would never understand in a lifetime. The darkness caressed us like a cozy blanket in winter, the silk spun by seductive spiders. I realized that false illusions are born in the mind which is blind and in the light which is lies, for both depend upon reflection for existence. Edna Wheeler's body was twenty to my touch. The moon behind the screen door only looked like a fixed and rigid piece of pie. Actually, it was an ever-moving, ever-changing pool of lemonade. I wanted to pee from excitement.

Edna Wheeler knew that deprived men have bigger eyes than stomachs, more desire than control. I was amazed at her patience, her own body throbbing with electricity, yet patient enough to control the throttle of my body. Several times, she would open her wise and glowing cats' eyes. Without blinking, as if enchanted, she would smile her quarter-moon smile and withdraw my penis to squeeze it ever so gently, ever so firmly, in order to prolong the talking and touching, Edna Wheeler was right. She had a lot to teach me.

The other me babbled and stuttered, swallowed and drooled, could not finish phrases, could not make connections. I talked of the weather. I talked of fried chicken. I talked of my teaching. I talked in my sleep. I realized that senators who could filibuster were senators who could win re-election until they died of laryngitis. I wanted to scream from so much whispering like so many sins in the confessional. I wanted to swallow and drown in my saliva, so my words could be bubbles, buoyant and formless, that would swim freely out of my mouth. I said nothing but I kept on saying it, repeating the saying, and I longed for the silence that would be pregnant with meaning. Each time I swallowed, I would panic. This was silence, primeval silence, before the word was made flesh. This silence was sleep, numbing the body as freezing persons experience the warmth of the snow. But this was also death, and so I would chatter to thaw myself out. This was the clicking of teeth benumbed by the frost, the moving of muscles, though they but run in place, to keep from succumbing to the sweet but lethal final abstraction.

And then I hit on the subject of Coop. The two selves merged again. I didn't have to think, I didn't have to swallow, I didn't have to hurry. Coop was a legend I knew from my heart. I hadn't realized how much there was to be said about him. I would never have guessed that the subject of Coop could be so in tune with the rest of my body. I surrendered my selves, gave myself up to the magic chant of the dance. Coop was his drawl (thrust), a crack in the world. Coop was his "rivvet" (thrust), the croaking of frogs. Coop was his throat (thrust), an envelope for swords. I weaved my tale of Coop in and out, a tale of madness, now sane, now insane, in and out, my tale of trivia, tale of truth, up-down in and out, a teeter-totter out on the ocean. The night became an Arabian night, and sex would not end, and death would not come, as long as I weaved. Lost in the weaving, I suddenly came. There was so much more to tell. I wondered how she had not felt it coming this time. The spell was broken, as movies end, not with the story but with the camera. And then I collapsed.

Edna Wheeler was dressed and in the doorway before I regained consciousness.

"One more thing, my sweet. I want to have him before I leave this place. I want you to set it up. Don't fail me."

The doorway was empty, the screen door still swinging senselessly like a hanged man's feet. The sound of Edna Wheeler's fading laughter clung to my tongue and made it stick to my teeth, as my penis had stuck to my legs. The feel was moss on enamel from eating lemons. How could I have mistaken this laughter for life? It was rather the sound of dry leaves rubbing against each other. How could I have been so badly mistaken ? The moon was a solid whose form never changed. For the moon to be seen, there had to be light. The moon was a solid, a reflection of light, a mirror of glaciers out on the ocean.

The last week passed, while time stood still. It was a week of illusions, of haunting sealed memories of Edna Wheeler on my pillow. It was also a week of ghosts. Until the night before the final exam, I had not seen Edna Wheeler again. Yet I could see her shadow everywhere spying on me, accusing me of not obeying her parting wish. I could not obey, for I had not seen Coop all week. He had simply vanished. He was not in the barracks, he was not at his job, he did not come to class. There was a third person who disappeared during that last week: Eileen Ritter.

The Talent Show took place in the club on the night before the final exam. It was the first time I had set foot in the club since my confrontation with General Wheeler. I sat with my students near one end of the stage, as far away from the general's table and the door as I could possibly get. I could see the smoke from his cigar emerge from the darkness and hang like disaster in the dimly-lit air. I knew he was there. I sensed also that Edna Wheeler was there in the shadows with him. When the show began, the only lights in the room were those on the stage, the footlights that gave the now fading beauty queens long and soft shadows under their chins that looked like Dutch beards. I had to look away to keep from laughing. At the other end of the stage, seated in the front row, were Coop and Eileen Ritter. All eyes but mine seemed rooted on the stage. For me, the drama was being played out in the darkness.

The queens performed their mawkish medlies of falsetto thirties' show tunes, of chorus-line dancing, their leotarded legs kicking out toward the void in unison, of stooped-forward charlestons, their hands going patty-cake across their knees, their plunging necklines being applauded by clapping and stomping, by whistles and cat-calls, that arose and hung like crows over garbage.

When they had finished, Eileen Ritter announced that the local talent would begin. Private Ramsay played the trumpet. Laughter and snorted tuba-like boos from the audience. Captain Morrissey tapdanced. It looked like marching to me. More laughter and boos, more subdued than before, in deference to his rank. Sergeant Sparks did his impressions of John Wayne and Jimmy Stewart, Jimmy Cagney and Cary Grant. Before he could do his swashbuckling Errol Flynn, General Wheeler was on the stage, thanking him and ushering him off.

"I know all you men out there want to thank the gracious ladies for entertaining us all week. (Applause) It's been almost like being home to have them on the base all week. (Cheers and clapping) Let's give them a nice hand, and maybe they'll come back some day. And I'm sure we want to thank our own men for sharing their talents with us. Now for the finale of our program, we have a surprise performer, someone most of you know. What you didn't know is that he's kept his wonderful talent a secret all this time. We've taken the liberty to go to his barracks and get the one prop he'll need for his act. He may be a little shy about coming up here, so I'm going to issue a direct order in front of all of you out there. Any refusal to obey that order will of course result in the usual penalties. So, ladies and gentlemen, would you please welcome Corporal Cooper, who's going to do some sword-swallowing for us?"

I could not believe that I had heard correctly. But when they brought out the sword that had once belonged to Marcus D., I knew that I was beginning to feel the consequences of disobeying a direct order. I kept my eye fixed on the still-empty stage, so that I would not have to look at my students next to me nor at Coop getting up nor into the shadows of the general's table. I could not hear the applause which forced Coop to the stage.

His face was pale, as if it were enbalmed of its blood. His walk was stiff and erect, a sign that he was nervous and not himself. If he could have spoken, I was sure that it would not have been in a drawl. He neither smiled nor frowned. He neither stalled for time nor started his act. He simply looked with those hangdog eyes of his on an otherwise poker-flat face at the table where Eileen Ritter sat. It was a look of accusation and disappointment. Only I and one other person in the hushed underarm of the room understood that look.

The room was tense with expectancy, with a sense of mystery surrounding those who had not known Coop's secret, with a sense of compassion surrounding those who had. Coop took the sword and held it upright, covering the middle of his face, like a samurai about to commit ritual harakari. He sighed almost imperceptibly, but it seemed to me that his whole body was deflated in that sigh.

A non-existent drum-roll pounded in my ears. Coop thrust his knees forward, his head upward and backward. His Adam's apple jutted out, protruded like a bruise. When his face had totally disappeared, he raised the tip of the sword above the invisible face whose gaping mouth must have been a crack in the world. His spider-like fingers began easing the descent of the sword. There was absolutely no movement, no coughing, no breathing in the whole room. The eerie footlights cast their shadows along Coop's elongated chin and throat. It was as if we were watching an x-ray of Coop's insides. It was as if the shadows were transparent. It seemed that we would finally have proof of the descent into Coop's body.

He worked slowly, deliberately, methodically, like a puppet of wood. There was no trace of the flamboyant self-confidence of his previous swallowings. It was as if he were stretching the moment of his death, prolonging the anguish by living that moment in slow-motion. I realized that violence, to be violent, must be seen slowly. The poised fingers kept inching their way toward the hilt of the sword. I held my throat with him, unable to swallow. It was also my throat the sword was descending. Because I was so close to the stage, I noticed a curious thing. Coop had a hard-on. I realized that we had never looked below his stomach for proof during all those swallowings in the barracks. I wondered if this were the first time or the hundredth time that this had happened to him.

I knew that every stomach in the room was tied in knots from the inexorable watching and waiting: the frenzy of sentries during cease-fires. After an eternity of minutes, the hilt finally reached the invisible mouth and hung there suspended like the shell of a bug that's been squashed. Coop let the hilt hang there of itself, while he stretched his arms outward toward the audience, the gesture of a virtuoso, the gesture of a penitent. And then it happened.

"Rivvet."

The entire room was an instant pendulum of sickness. The sounds of coughing, choking, spitting, gagging and heaving filled the room. People were vomiting and fainting all around me. Just the smell of the bile was sufficient to infect those who had held their stomachs in check. The manager and the help were running around opening bottles of ammonia, which revived those who had fainted, only to make them vomit. Everyone was throwing up. I wondered briefly what was happening at the table in the shadows at the back of the room, but I dared not look.

I would never know if this were Coop's first accident or if this were Coop's premeditated revenge on all of us. I am sure, however, that only my eyes saw him whisk the sword back out and let it fall, sticking in the wood of the stage as a reminder of where he had stood. In an instant Coop was gone, off the stage, out of the building, away from the base.

Those who could stand on their feet did so and left shortly thereafter. My students, because they could not possibly have understood that look between Coop and Eileen Ritter, alone understood the true betrayal of a precious secret. They got up and walked out without even looking at me. I had assassinated their general.

The lights were on, and I noticed that the general's table was empty, but that the floor beneath it was covered with an oozing mixture of liquids and solids. I could not feel my feet beneath me as I walked out. For the second time, my path crossed that of Eileen Ritter. She stood stiffly before me, and her face was horribly blemished in the light. She squinted from pursed and bloodshot eyes of pain. her face was so close to mine that I could smell the stale sickness on her breath.

"How could I have pitied you last week? You . . . you . . . He was the only one . . . goddamnyou . . . the only one who ever really looked . . . who ever saw me . . . who ever understood . . . the only one. How could you do this to him . . . to me? You deserve . . . everything!"

My chin was on my shirt. I had no need of eye contact. I couldn't see that she had walked around me. I stood transfixed, shuffling my feet around an imaginary grave.

I slept as late as I could the next morning, after not being able to fall asleep for most of the night. I was covered with bites from mosquitoes that I had neither the strength nor the courage to kill. I stayed in my room most of the day, packing my things, prolonging the mindlessness of packing by rearranging my suitcases, as many as I could without repetition. When the time came for me to go to class and administer the final exam, I finally threw up all over the pillow that still smelled of Edna Wheeler's silver hair. They were dry heaves, heaves of gas that left little trace of my sadness. I called in sick at the Education Center and asked that they send someone to give the test for me and deliver them to me afterwards.

I was mildly surprised to find out that everyone in the class was there for the final exam. Everyone except Coop. I had expected them all to stay away, but their presence had more to do with ritual than with any loyalty to me. The soldier who brought the exams said that Coop had volunteered for his first midnight mission the night before and that he had not returned with the morning crews. They were searching for him. He was listed as missing in action. As far as I know, he is still missing. I gave him an "incomplete" for the course. What else could I do?

The soldier waited until I had finished the grading. He drove me to the airport in his open jeep. The smell of night fires and the sound of crickets told me I was leaving, because it seemed that I had never smelled or heard them before that night. The soldier asked me whether I was happy or a little sorry to be leaving. I couldn't answer. You can get attached even to a hell-hole like this, he said. I couldn't answer. He concluded that I was a very lucky man to be going back to the "real world". His open-mouthed crackling of chewing gum drowned out the natural sounds of the crickets.

Before he left me, he gave me an envelope addressed to me in care of the Education Center. It took me ten minutes to read the note inside. It said:

"Hold your head up when you teach. I'm sorry. Coop."

As my plane sped upward in the midnight sky, it seemed that the halo around the moon grew more and more pinkish with a kind of orgasmic flush. I understood that illusion is not a question of mind or light but of distance. It seemed that the plane was going straight at the moon instead of levelling off and going home. When the plane finally did right itself, parallel with the pockmarked earth below, I understood that the moon was neither a liquid nor a solid. It was a mirrored gas of yellow bile.

The Man With the Umbrella

When I first walked by the house, white and weathered like a sailor's face, I almost didn't notice her. Nor, I believe, did she notice me, although I stood beneath her window for nearly an hour or more. Her window was on the second floor, the second one on my left. Had the woman been in the dark, I would never have noticed her, not even her silhouette, not even if she had called out to me, because I was too accustomed to the dark itself.

I always sleep in the morning. As seldom as necessary and only in the late afternoon, I go out to steal food. At night I walk the streets. Before the night I saw her light, I had always walked the streets for the pure peace of walking, the chance to suck in every foreign sound, the chance to hollow out in the head. I was not in search of anything or anyone. In fact, I rarely noticed anything on theses walks. I had become completely accustomed to the night, its smells of charcoal, garlic, gasoline. I knew its cloaked buildings, the faint tinny music, the blare of horns and sometimes gunfire.

My thoughts have a way of running on now, accumulating energy while losing meaning, because I am unaccustomed to any listeners. I talk to myself. I pose questions that are never answered. I begin arguments that I don't really believe in, just for the sake of argument. The tips of my combat boots are turned up from use, but the soles are still thick and cushion my steps.

When I first walked by her window, it was the rainy season here. The rain must have had something to do with my stopping. Ordinarily, I walk with my eyes wide open, so I notice nothing. But this particular night the rain fell in slanted sheets, so that I was forced to squint. Squinting, I began to notice things. For example, there were different shades of night, which had nothing to do with artificial lighting, since there were no street lights on this particular street. Two streets over, the curfew beacon bathed the rooftops. Where I stood with my umbrella, the wash from the light was purple.

I could see through the layers of night, as one might leaf through the pages of a book. There were light grays that, if one stared at them long enough, could pass for whites. There were middling grays like the street itself. There were darker grays like the tropical grass or the thatched rooftops. Then there were the blacks: the insides of porches, the gutter where it meets the street, the unlighted windows. Like being frightened by unexpected fireflies, I stopped more out of fear than curiosity when I saw her window.

I was attracted first by the light, not by the person in the light. I thought of bugs that flew to mate at night. They always get distracted by just such a light. It excites them. They crash their little bodies against the light source, because they believe it to be a smell, not a solid. I was surprised to see a solid human form occupying the light, taking it up and casting it off, as if the form were the source of the light. And then I discovered that it was a woman's form. I spread my arms as walkers sometimes do, as though to relax my feet.

She was preoccupied with something beneath the window sill. The window was open, and I could hear the sound of a machine. I couldn't tell what kind of machine it was. I couldn't even tell immediately whether the form was that of a man or woman. But then I noticed that there were two balls, one smaller and flatter in back of the first. Her shoulders were arched forward and downward. They moved in a circular pattern. The light was not very bright. Perhaps I was experiencing a kind of quasi-blindness from looking into the night so long. Yet I was able to distinguish two different tones to her form. The lighter tone shimmered undefined. The darker one was more circular, more clearly lined. The second must have been her body, the first a transparent nightgown.

The rain obscured other sounds around me. The machine obscured other sounds around her. But somewhere in between the two sounds, I could hear the woman humming to herself. She was also humming to me. I felt that she was calling me. If she had actually called out to me, I would have run away. But because she was humming, I was unable to move. The sound was low and deep. The sound was monotonous, but also very plaintive. The woman had strong feeling. I spread my legs, relaxed and attentive.

I don't know how long I stood there without moving, without blinking, without noticing what time it was. I don't wear a watch anymore. The woman finally moved forward and away from the window. I waited for her to sit back, but she did not. I finally decided that she had fallen asleep. The window was still half-open and the light was still on. I felt a sense of joy and power that I had not known for some time.

When I returned to my room, I discovered that I was drenched from the rain. Perhaps I was shivering; I cannot remember exactly. I remember that my knees were weak from the standing, my eyes were tired from the staring, and I sneezed several times before I reached my street.

I had caught a cold. I was in bed almost three full days, sneezing and unable to sleep. I could only sleep for ten to fifteen minutes at a time. My nose kept filling up and overflowing on the pillow. I kept waking up, feeling dizzy from the cold and drugged from the lack of sleep. I dreamed constantly. The dreams were short and usually disconnected. In each dream it was raining furiously. In each I tried to protect my face from the rain, but the wind kept pulling my umbrella up. Then I would tug with both hands and pull it down again. At this point different things happened in each dream. But in some of them, the wind would let go suddenly, and the umbrella would snap back upon me. When the umbrella came down, it went all the way to my toes with me still underneath. I was squashed into a little ball. Just as abruptly the umbrella turned upside down, swelling and flapping on the ocean with me in miniature clinging to the spokes. The big black leather handle stood straight in the sky. It was the mast and the spokes were the sails. Only there were no sails, because the cloth was missing. In short, I had no control. I clung to the spokes with all my might. My feet swung out from under me when the waves poured in. Only by clutching the spokes with both hands did I keep from going overboard. The silver-tipped rudder went scurrying through the water as though on skates. It righted me as it went. Then other waves, always bigger than previous ones, descended on the boat. With each swoop there was salt water in my mouth. I choked and coughed up the water, but the salt remained caked on my gums. I squeezed the spokes until they cut my hands. A giant wave with a grotesque, gurgling laughter descended on me and swallowed me in its belly. The whirling surge sucked me underneath. I was pulled in all directions. The covers were on the floor. I was sneezing and blowing my nose.

The dreams persisted. In my waking moments I thought only of the lighted window on the second floor and the woman within. I wanted so badly to be out there in the street. The smell of old garlic infected the room. Illness has a pungent smell which perpetuates itself. I kept my curtains closed, so that I wasn't sure whether it was day or night outside. For me it was always night.

Once I went into dreaming, and there was no rain. There was no storm, no umbrella, and no human presence. There was only the ocean and the long rows of white caps like piano keys, repeating themselves endlessly, the mindless practicing of a schoolboy. I must have been standing miles away from the scene, for the white caps looked as though they had been drawn with a pencil. Suddenly, they were as wide as the street. I must have come much closer. I could see the fin tips of two giant fish whose bodies curved into each other. Between them, bobbing at right angles to the water, was a black periscope. The engines were humming. Dive bombers hovered overhead, confused, like bats confused and going every which way. There were so many white caps.

I woke up and I knew that I was getting well. I had slept very soundly for a long time. My nose no longer ran. Now it was plugged and sore, as though someone had thrown an anchor inside and stretched all the blood vessels. My mouth was wide open. I stretched my legs, and they felt good to me. I got up and walked to the window. It was day, but the sky was light gray and overcast. It would be night soon. I decided to drink some hot tea, shave and wait the hours out. I wanted to go outside and see the stars here where there were always so many stars.

I walked at a quicker pace than my usual stroll. I could sense that I was nervous, but I wasn't sure why. Then I remembered the window, every detail about the window. I had only seen it once, and once was not enough to make it real. I have seen many things once that I have never seen again. So maybe I have never seen them after all. I saw the ocean once with my father, but that was very long ago. I tried to calm myself, to convince myself that the window would still be there, that the light would still be on, that the woman would still be waiting, sitting, rocking, but it was futile. I had never doubted anything so much in my life.

Even in my nervous state, I still maintained my habitual way of walking. I never walked on the sidewalk if I could help it, especially these prefab sidewalks that clashed with these crushed wooden houses. And I never turned a corner at a right angle. I always walked in the street, near the edge when there was too much traffic, and in the middle when there wasn't any at all. When I got to between twelve and thirty feet of the corner, I always had to make a quick decision. If I decided to continue in the same direction, there was no problem. But if I chose to turn right or left, then I had to walk over the running gutter, the thin brown grass and one prefab sidewalk, then over someone's scorched and cratered yard, then another sidewalk, more grass, another gutter and finally into the street again. I never turned a corner at a right angle. And I never broke stride. Sometimes I quickened my stride or slowed it down, but I never came to a complete stop. Unless I was staring at something.

The window was still half-opened. The woman was in the same position in which I had first seen her. Only the light had changed. It seemed stronger to me. I wasn't sure whether or not it was actually stronger. The rain was barely a drizzle, so perhaps I was just seeing the same light better than I had before. The cool night air rushed through my sinuses and lungs like a drug and made me dizzy. Perhaps the light was brighter because I had anticipated it this time, had wished for it, had prayed that it would still be there. Whatever the cause, it was still not bright enough to make out the features of the woman's face. Only the nose stuck out in profile. Perhaps the woman was Eurasian, but I could not say for sure. The light was just enough to let me see her, but not enough to let me look at her. For instance, I could not tell her age. I could only guess that she was no longer young. No woman here is as young as she looks. Add five years and two children: old rule of thumb. I knew from what I could see that she was not old either. She was probably middling gray.

Once she sat straight back in her chair and stretched her arms out from her sides in a yawn. Her right arm shot out the half-opened window and made a fist at me. I jumped back a step. Her back merged with the back of the chair, and for the first time, I could see the full profile of her front clearly. The neck curved delicately and then became a plunging line at a forty-five degree angle to her back. The window still sliced off my view where I imagined that the line curved in again and became her stomach. It distressed me, though, that I did not know for sure whether the line curved in or not. I imagined very intensely that it did. It was important to me. Because if it didn't, I didn't want to think about it. When her back separated with the chair, a very strange and beautiful thing happened. I could only think that it was a miracle. Her hair, which had been rolled up in back, came loose and descended like white caps, blackened by a sudden summer storm, onto her shoulder. It happened very abruptly, and she herself did not seem to take notice, but it was like ballet to me, although I have never seen ballet. I have seen postcards of ballet.

Where her hair had been rolled up before, I could now see a picture on the wall behind her. The picture was very small. I cannot be sure what was in it. I thought that it was a bowl of assorted fruits, gaudy on black velveteen, the kind of pictures they sell on street corners here. I waited until she disappeared from the window and the light remained constant. As usual, there were no other lights on in the house. When I walked back to my room, I was unaware of my feet or of the number of steps that they took. I was happier than I had ever been before.

That night I dreamed that I was in my room, looking at my table. I never put anything on my table. No flower vase, no drinking glass, no pencil even. Because they would disturb the feeling of flatness that I feel a table should always have. In my dream, however, there was a bowl in which assorted fruits clung to each other. Each had its usual color and all were lifesize. But in my dream the assorted fruits were not a still life. They floated just above the bowl. They became a face. Two apples were eyes, a slightly over-ripe banana was the nose, and shredded lemon pieces were the teeth. A strawberry attached itself to one cheek. The bottoms of the apples pointed toward me, so that the eyes looked sunken in from the rest of the face. They were also squinting. Suddenly the lemon pieces contracted and squirted me in the face. I became furious. I descended upon the face, plucked the left apple out and bit halfway up the body. As I spit out the pits, I woke up in darkness. I swallowed and went back to sleep.

The next night I descended into the street very deliberately. The first time I had seen the woman, I had not expected her. The second time, I had expected her too much, had prayed that she would still be there. This time I knew that she would be there. I knew that something extraordinary was going to happen.

It had rained during the day, because the grass was wet and thick and brown or green. The rain had stopped, but the night air was hot and humid. As I walked, I could feel the perspiration dripping down my sides beneath my shirt. I kept my umbrella closed and twirled it like a baton. Once or twice I lunged and thrust the silver tip into the shadows of trees. I was hot and deliriously happy. I think I had a fever.

Nothing was as I had left it. The window was opened all the way and the light seemed ever brighter than before. The woman, to my surprise, was only one tone. She cast no shadows in the night. She was naked. Her hair was rolled up in back. Her shoulders were bare. For the first time, I was aware of my own position in relation to her. If just once she happened to glance at the street where I stood, I would be totally vulnerable. I had no excuses to give, no reasons to propose, no means of escape. In exposing herself she had also exposed me. She was humming to herself. She was yellow. She was beautiful.

She made me feel immodest. Perhaps if she had known I was there, if she had removed her transparent nightgown for my benefit, it would have been better than this innocence she so casually kept to herself, this indifference she so coldly shared with me. I was already too involved to pretend that I had never seen her. I couldn't help myself. I walked backwards to the opposite sidewalk. Her body was less top-heavy, less angular from there. Everything was more level without being appreciably more visible. Nevertheless, I could see that the line from her delicate neck which descended outward did indeed return inward again. I was sure that I had a fever. I felt ashamed, and at the same time, I wanted more shame. My pants were moist.

Throughout the long watch, the curfew beacon passed over her roof every two minutes. I was aware of the futility of my position. Although she was naked, she still retained a crucial advantage over me: she didn't know that I existed. I had to equalize that advantage. With a mixed rush of fear and joy, I realized that I had to establish contact with her. Simply to call out from the street was out of the question. It was too crude. She would reject me. A passing patrol jeep might hear. To write a letter was impossible, since I did not know her name.

Anyway, the name was unimportant. To wait there might be awkward and risky. I thought of waiting all night until she emerged from the house in the morning. I preferred to meet her without her meeting me, if that was at all possible. I wanted to give her a sign, any sign, of my devotion and my fidelity. I didn't dare to think of love. Again she was at an advantage. My emotions were well in advance of her own. Consequently, I couldn't trust myself with a chance meeting. We had to meet without any risk. At once I decided, as though the thought had always been present.

I walked across the street. It would be more correct to say I tiptoed an imaginary line, a tightrope. At any moment I expected to be discovered. But the sound of the machine continued, reassuring me of my safety. My safety had to be guaranteed; otherwise, my plan was unworkable, even ridiculous.

I suddenly realized that I had never noticed the house before, except for the window. I was surprised to find a wrought-iron gate in front of me and a high open porch beyond that. To the left between the gate and the porch, there was a clothesline which held no clothes. I was in complete command of my senses. I carefully placed my red umbrella with the curved, black leather handle against the gate on the inside. I could barely contain myself as I walked home. I felt the same excitement the criminal feels when he gets away from the scene of the crime. My whole being trembled with the knowledge that my salvation depended upon that crime and its apprehension. It struck me as quite odd that I had spent less time watching the woman this time when she was nude than I had the other times when she wore the nightgown. It didn't matter. I had established contact.

That night I was unable to sleep. I was too accustomed to being out in the street at that hour. I had come back much earlier than usual. There was nothing to do but wait until sleep overwhelmed me. It finally came in the middle of the morning. I must have dreamed many dreams, because I was still exhausted when I woke up. I can only remember the last dream I had before waking.

The woman's face, hair, shoulders and breasts were invisible to me. I could only see the mound of her stomach and what the window sill had cut off heretofore. Her legs were spread for me, snapping open and shut like a pair of scissors. I was on my stomach, crawling up to enter her. But before I could, she straightened her right leg out and over my back, kicking my buttocks with her heel. Her left leg went out perpendicular to the rest of her body. Her legs had formed a right angle. Without breaking stride I decided to enter at a slant and come out her side. But before I could, she held up her right arm. In it was the umbrella. She pushed it toward me. It was raining. I took it and shoved it in her as far as it would go. Only the curved part of the black leather handle remained outside. She looked like a sea horse. She complained of the pain, so I withdrew the umbrella half-way where I fondled the button and finally pushed it. She complained again, but this time from the pleasure. The umbrella must have opened inside her, because her stomach ballooned in front of me. The mound was a mountain. Whenever I turned the handle slightly to one side or the other, her belly bulged on the opposite side. I set an alarm clock on top of her mountain. Both hands of the clock inhaled and exhaled when she did. When the alarm went off, her stomach exploded. It descended like a giant wave with its grotesque, gurgling laughter. White caps rushed out of her along the handle of the umbrella. I withdrew the umbrella and it was red. I woke up as the sun was setting.

I dressed quickly and went out in the street. As my walking had been, so now the woman had become habitual for me. I expected that she would always be there. It was difficult to confess to myself that I was not so much concerned with her now as I was with the umbrella. I was very nervous, just as I had been on my second vigil after my illness. But this time was different. This time I fully hoped to find that the umbrella had disappeared, that it had become only a shared figment of our imagination.

It had not disappeared. It was still there, tilted on its black leather handle against the broken gate. I didn't even want to look at it. It was inconceivable that the woman had not noticed it. She had to have gone out of the house at least once during the day. Perhaps she thought that it belonged to someone else within the house. That was certainly possible. But what if someone else within the house, although I had never seen anyone else, were to take the umbrella by mistake? What if the hordes of orphan children, common these days, took it? I didn't want just any human contact. It had to be hers. I had trouble thinking, because it was raining. I couldn't use the umbrella to protect myself, because it no longer belonged to me. I decided to hang the umbrella by its handle on the clothesline beneath her window. She would have to notice it then. I did so and left without even looking at the woman that night.

I returned the next night a little earlier than usual. I was taking a chance, because it was not completely dark yet. I risked being seen, but I no longer cared. I had to establish a bridge between us.

The umbrella had not moved. It still hung upside down from the clothesline. The only difference was that the edges sagged downward with the rain water that it had accumulated in my absence.

I began to sense that something was incredibly wrong. I had never stopped to wonder before why the woman was there in the window, so faithfully, so predictably. Perhaps she never left her room. Perhaps there was a reason why she never saw the umbrella. Could it be that she was blind, that she would never see the umbrella, even if I hung it from her window sill? If so, then contact between us would be impossible. The thought depressed me, and I dismissed it immediately.

The window was still half-open and the light had not changed. But the woman seemed changed somehow. It took me almost an hour to figure out why she seemed changed. First, it was the neck. She was wearing a necklace. I couldn't say for sure, but it looked like a pearl necklace. Little silver circular tips all around her neck. Beneath the necklace she was wearing clothes, at least as far down as I could see. She wore what looked like a black silken dress, common in this region but uncommon for this weather. The rain descended upon me mercilessly.

In an hour or so more of looking at the woman, I noticed that her manner was different too. She was no longer as composed as before, no longer as

51

rhythmic in her motions upon the machine, whatever it was. Her shoulders jerked back and forth in the chair. She was obviously nervous. Had she seen my red umbrella? Was that what made her nervous? Was she deciding whether or not she should take it, and in taking it, accept my invitation? She gave no signs of being curious, just nervous. Not once did she ever look out the window. I thought it odd for someone who kept it always half-open.

She looked as though she were in a hurry, although she never left the chair. Then something happened which baffled me. First, she lifted both hands up to the light, and there was no more sound from the machine. In her hands was a piece of cloth. What it was I couldn't tell. She put it to her chest and lowered her chin upon it. She began rocking her body, as if she were holding a baby. I loved her for that rocking. Then she turned her head completely around, showing the full of her back to me. She seemed to be looking at the picture. She turned back again and put her head in her hands. She was crying. There was nothing I could do.

I moved cautiously across the street. Then very slowly I opened the gate. It creaked as it went. I froze, merged with the gate. She hadn't heard me. I went to the clothesline. When I took my red umbrella from the line, it snapped back and was taut again. I emptied the water very carefully. Then I tiptoed up onto the porch. From the street the porch was black, but when I looked out from the porch, everything was illuminated. The night was really white, if one looked long enough and from the right vantage point. I was surprised by my own boldness. I placed the red umbrella right next to the door. She would leave her room, descend one flight of stairs, walk through the hallway and out the door. At the precise moment that she closed the door, she would know me. I couldn't wait. One moment I was on the porch, the next I was home again. There were no transitions any more. Contact was immediate.

I still worried about the other people. But since I had never seen any other light, I hoped that all the other rooms were vacant. If that were the case, my happiness would be complete. After the umbrella had disappeared from the porch, I would go to the house and see if there were any rooms to rent. It was time for me to move. I had remained burrowed in my own unlighted room too long already. It was time to keep my window half-open.

I dreamed that I was in an open field with one tree in the center and bushes all around me. Buzzing in my ears. An army of bees or a man with a saw. My eyes close on the tree. A violent wind bends the tree. Rain splatters diagonally through the branches. A hurricane perhaps. Something is tearing on the branch. Tenacious fibre-like folds rip, surrender. Filmy spider webs dissolve. A cocoon hatches and destroys itself. A little needle body appears. Slowly unfolds its wings from around the back. Stretches them out like a giant Japanese fan. Red and black wings. A very rare butterfly. It prods itself, gathers up its confidence, paws the bark for its footing. Suddenly it lifts off the branch where it was conceived. Glides. Sideways and circular. Returns to the branch. Becomes immobile. Rigid. No more flapping of wings. It becomes a cocoon. Out springs an umbrella. Red and black. Hanging upside down. The curved handle moves. A caterpillar.

I woke to find my head at the foot of the bed. I went to the window and opened the curtains. It was still day. The alarm clock perched atop the giant turtle shell my father had brought me from the Galapagos Islands told me it was almost noon. I had hardly slept at all. Not since my illness had I awakened to the day.

I tore at my shirt and buttoned it furiously. I felt like a stranger in an unknown city, going out into the sunlight that smelled like gasoline. All the familiar landmarks were only so in the dark. The light hurt my eyes. I squinted. Once or twice I kept them closed for a whole city block. I was suddenly afraid that I would not be able to find her house in the daytime. Despite the sunlight, there was a slight drizzle. It relaxed me a little. I didn't even mind the occasional patrol cars. I looked at my combat boots and was somehow unafraid. Suddenly, I was on her street.

Before me was the rusted wrought-iron gate left ajar. Strips of paint were peeling from the high open porch. The floorboards weren't level. Some were much higher than others. I hadn't noticed before. My little red umbrella was gone. I was so excited that I didn't even bother to look at her window as I left. I ran back to my room as fast as I could. I left my door wide open and began packing my things. There wasn't much to pack: some socks, a couple of shirts, one other pair of pants, government issue. An empty frame, a scrapbook of postcards my father had sent me. When I was done, I felt a sudden chill. I was afraid, afraid to leave my habitual room. I decided to wait until midnight. I could leave in the dark. No one would see me go.

I waited. She would be playing with the red umbrella. Still I waited. She would be nervous, but she would be glad she took it. It would give her courage to go outside. I waited. It would give me courage too.

When I got to her street, I noticed for the first time that there were small foreign cars and loud motorcycles passing me on both sides. I was walking in the middle of the street. It was not raining. One car screeched its brakes in front of me, stopped, then burst away faster than it had gone before it stopped. Another honked its horns as it passed me. I didn't care. The umbrella was gone.

The house was still there, but it was not the same house. The corners were pointed inwards. Then what I had taken for the corners before were only shadows. The roof was as flat as my table top. The curfew beacon shone dimly as it fanned the sky. I needed to adjust my eyes to the dark. The house was completely dark.

I ran through the wrought-iron gate. It creaked as it went. I was beside myself. I ran through the hall, up the long stairs and straight to the second door on my right. It was wide open.

I went in at a slant. I came to the closet on the right: wide open and empty. Only hangers still curled around the pole. I squeezed several until my hand hurt. I retreated and turned the light switch. The light did not come on. The smell of incense was thick as fog in the room.

I walked to my left. I bumped into the bed. It was flat and low. When I groped over its edge with my hand, I could see that there were no covers and no sheets. It had been stripped. Could this have been the woman's room, the woman at the window's room, my woman's room?

It was like walking in my sleep. I went to the window. It was closed. I could still see myself down the street, leaning on my umbrella, crippled ant peeking up. Perhaps I had seemed too insignificant to notice. I was filled with rage. I turned to the wall. There was no picture, only the bare nail and dozens of holes in the wall, perhaps bullet holes, holes which bored upward, as though from someone hammering from a seated position, as though from someone shooting from the street below. I hit the nail as hard as I could with my fist, then with my flat palm. It broke skin. In the corner was the chair: old, metallic, with its two big wheels.

When I left the house, I could not tell whether it was raining or not. I was only glad for the night. I walked straight back to my room with my half-empty suitcase banging at my side. I turned every corner at the corner without breaking stride. I thought that everything should always be painted in black and white, or better yet, in middle shades of gray. The world was ugly when it was colored.

I walked into my old room, locked the door behind me, and then I slammed the suitcase down on the bed. I lay down beside it and put my head near the handle. As I did so, I felt a slugging pain in my stomach.

Two little girls, aged ten and twelve by official guess, stop thirty yards at ten o'clock from us. The older one hurls her grenade to the right of me. From the ground, I look around. No one is moving, but I can hear the low moans of dying. Someone's severed arm has fallen across my leg. The two girls are laughing. I raise my gun and fire on the younger one. Both girls explode like confetti.

For a brief instant I dreamed that my father and I were picking mushrooms one day when he was on leave. I dreamed that I was a mushroom in the act of decaying, and that I was so hungry that I began eating myself.

I have never left Saigon.

Night Baseball

The ability to speak a foreign language is a gift from the gods. It is the only way left open to become another person. It is the only way left open to keep a lasting peace. War intervenes, and countries spread over each other in the missionary position, without even knowing how to say "excuse me" to the one on the bottom. I came to Japan unwillingly. As an intellectual in a time of war, enlisting for Japan was the only way left open to avoid conscription for Vietnam. I did not act like an intellectual in Japan. I became a mask in a mime play, whose reflections on the barest gestures were always hidden from my audience. I could have given more of myself, if the Japanese had only been able to speak English, think English, be American. I could have gotten more of them, if only I could have become Japanese. It is the only way left open to become another person. Commodore Peary must have entered Japan with only half a crucifix.

Where no common language is possible, rituals are the only avenue left open to the unwilling traveler. I lived out my sentence in Japan by losing myself in rituals, until the memory of Japan itself, until the memory itself, is no more than a ritual. I've lost all meaning in it by adhering to the clothing of it, the clothing which makes it visible, which covers up. My only consolation in all of this has been the knowledge that everything we do is temporary. I learned this from Yoko. I learned it just in time.

What impressed me most about the women I knew in Japan was their uniformity of expression, their collective giggles of embarrassment, their national ability to go from standing down to the floor without the hands or a crack in the knees, their group transformation in the evening's artificial light from yellow skin to almost beige, the color of cream gone sour. The sameness of the women to the Westerner who knows them only through films or photographs is similar to the sameness experienced by someone who's known them in the Inns under billowing sheets and rice pillows on tatami mats. The inability to tell an Asian woman's age by any Westerner is that woman's revenge on time told by bowing more than by clocks, on an island's isolation like an ingrown toenail, on big-boned soldiers too far away from home, too lonely and too gruff to understand how a woman's hair, black like all other hair around me, is sacred and hers alone to touch.

I never knew how old Yoko was and I never asked. It would have been imprudent to do so. Questions with her needed to be couched in the generic. If she cared to twist them to the personal, that was her prerogative. It seems to me that the Japanese. . . . I would offer. Sometimes she would answer. Sometimes she would simply giggle, the gurgling of a schoolgirl from the mouth with lines around the corners and hard as an almond.

I met her at the airport. I was on leave, going home for two weeks and coming back for two years. She was sitting there with a duffle bag, a tennis racket sticking out. The tennis racket was the entry to conversation for me, although I later learned that the chance to speak a little English would have been enough for her. She had this way of saying "I see" to everything I said, polite and in a monotone without feeling. It made me want to blindfold her when we talked. She was not the GI's woman, I could see that formality of her smile, the way she crossed her legs whenever she wasn't standing, as if the sitting on chairs was a custom to be kept foreign, unassimilated.

To see us in public, I could have been her cousin on a visit, except for the difference in skin tone. There was no hand-holding, no shared confidences in the eyes, almost no recognition of my personal intimacy with her, except in the faint, nearly imperceptible lowering of the chin. I expected this to change after we had gone to bed together. It did not change. The lowering of the chin was the only clue.

She took everything I said for the gospel truth, and, if she recognized that I was joking at her expense or tapping her for a sense of humor, she didn't show it. One day we were in the subway, and I noticed an old woman with a bandage wrapped around her mouth like a surgeon's mask. the sight is fairly common in Japan. It signifies a cold, a willingness on the part of the wearer to swallow one's germs and prolong the suffering rather than spread the infection to anyone else. I nudged Yoko and asked her if Japanese doctors always went to such extremes when they were off-duty. I expected the hint of a chuckle or at least the now-familiar "I see." "As you wish," she whispered.

In my more playful moods, usually after sex, I would call her "Loco Yoko." "What this mean," she would ask. "A train with the hiccoughs," I would always say. "I see." I'm sure she didn't. Her chin was too lowered to see anything but the nails on her big toes.

She accepted sex with me with the sameness of all Japanese before pleasure. Mechanically, clinically, with a precision unfettered by any rising in the pulse. She neither sought it out nor avoided it. The hidden tearing of the flesh, the muffled screams in pillow cases, the acting out of animal grabbing and pulling beneath the perfectly ironed sheets was something indulged in for the moment, with no prior anticipation and certainly no fond recollections that were ever verbalized afterwards. The silence after sex with Yoko made me feel inadequate, as though something were missing, as though I should be paying her something. She accepted sex the way the woman in the subway accepted her cold. Ever inward and not to spread around at any price. A difference in our cultures, no doubt: the simple "thanks" of a grateful man in English is "domo arregato gozaimashite" in Japanese. Two miles long and with the time to lower the chin or bow at the waist.

Activities were a problem at first. I was never invited to her home, that sector being reserved in Japan for family and close relatives. Nor could we go to evening spots like night clubs very much, for there the business men would come with their carte blanche expense accounts to smoke and drink and eye the foreigners' women. Yoko was sensitive about being seen with an American. She did not want it thought that she was my mistress. So we went wherever there were crowds, big crowds, mixed crowds, crowds that promised to be full of Americans.

We went to baseball games. The perfect metaphor for the love story of the American and Japanese. The transplanted game that the Japanese brought to their bosom and fashioned to their own idiosyncracies like a woman bears her pregnancy. I was amazed at Yoko, this bird-body of a woman with the almond eyes and the measured speech of a university professor. She was a true athlete herself and a connoisseur of other athletes. When we first played tennis together on an American military base, there were catcalls from envious privates' eyes that she ignored, so completely engrossed in the form of the game was she. I knew from the first point that she had studied the game thoroughly. This was no spontaneous encounter for Yoko. If she hadn't read thirty books on the subject and practiced in the mirror for months by herself, she didn't do it, whatever "it" was. I suspect that this included making love.

She lost most of the points, with perfect form and perfect politeness. She never stumbled and she never lost her temper. In my own spastic way, I would flail at the ball and usually win the point by sheer force behind the shots. Yoko would position herself, always position herself for the ball, even though the ball was hit in such a way that she would have to dive to get it. She never dove. She would lose point after point, but she never lost form. Form is synonymous with face for the Japanese, I soon discovered.

Everyone knows that sake is the national drink of Japan. But the Japanese embraced baseball the way they took to beer. When the first beer breweries were installed, they caused a crisis in the national behavior pattern. Beer was meant to swig, not to sip like sake. The Japanese began to drink beer out of sake cups, hardly enough for a good mouthful at a time, patient and insistent on their form. Drunkenness is something of a twentieth-century phenomenon in Japan. They began to swig the beer and the sake along with it. Middle-aged men suddenly let loose all their repressed lechery. Women in kimonos tied tightly to their chestnut breasts began to burp and stumble in public. The traditional haiku has no way of dealing with this modern corrosion in form.

They're slightly fanatic in the same way about baseball, the undisputed national pastime for men, women and children everywhere on the ingrown island. Crowded like the British in their bomb shelters during World War Two, the Japanese still build vast stadiums of grass and open grazing for the midget men with ball and glove. There's probably not twenty women in America who understand every rule of the game of baseball. The situation is reversed in Japan. Yoko knew the rules, the scores and the batting averages. It was all she could do to contain herself at the stadium. There was twitching in the lowering of the chin.

When I perceived this intensity in the Japanese about baseball, I resolved to be a student of the game, to understand this strangest of all nations and this queer bird-woman by the metaphor I could most easily extend to both sides of the Pacific: baseball.

There are two professional league in Japan: the Central League, comprised of six teams, headed by the Yomiuri Giants, the perennial winners; and the Pacific League, also having six teams, but different from the other league in that these teams play a double season, the winners of each split season squaring off in a playoff to determine which team meets the winner of the Central League in the October World Series. Contrary to American baseball, the Japanese teams bear the names of newspapers, railroads, big businesses, all except the Hiroshima team, which bears the city's name, the city where Yoko was born, the city where Yoko's mother was burned alive in the bombing. The Yomiuri Giants were the enemy, I discovered. It was unfortunate, because they usually beat the pants off the Hiroshima Toyo Carp. as the team was called.

We decided to go to a baseball game together one night in bed after hearing one of the games broadcast on the radio. I was trying to find mood music to ease the heavy silence after our sex. What I found were two announcers rattling away machine-gun accounts of the game, the words only slowing down to pronounce the inevitable borrowed terms:

"Rattatata unamono shomodozo. etc. . . . . homurunu ne?"

They couldn't have been further from objective reporting. The glee of children was in their voice when they pronounced "home run," the dead "e" on the end of "home" becoming a "u" just like the tacked-on ending for "run." I looked at Yoko. She was listening intently. A long flurry of words followed.

"What's he saying, Yoko?"
"He say the batter is good hitter."

I felt cheated by the translation. All those words for something so direct. It couldn't be that simple. It was, though, and I'm sure of it. The camouflage of many words for a straight statement is a way of lowering the chin. The Japaneses usually take American honesty and directness for harshness, vulgar speech. "Thanks" comes across as a grunt.

Baseball is a real happening in Japan. It's not the apathetic grinding out of games that the sport has become in America. The slowness between pitches is a welcomed chance to study the players for the Japanese. As fans go, they're quiet, somehow incongruous with the animated announcers' voices on the radio. I suspect their animation is a little contrived, a kind of compensation for those who can't get to the games in person where they would surely sit like stone in their seats. You can't tell the home crowd from the visiting crowd in Japan. They all stare with the same quiet intensity.

I discovered that each team can have (but is limited to) two foreigners (American). Ironically, most of these transplants from the States are blacks: ironically, because the Japanese have such a terrible prejudice against blacks. George Altman, formerly of the Chicago Cubs, was a big star in 1973. Yoko asked me about Willie McCovey one night. I found out later that several teams were trying to get him to come over, including the Yomiuri Giants, who really didn't need him, since they always ended up in first place anyway.

I learned something about time that night. The games never start on time, even when they're being televised. The Japanese have an obsession with the mechanics of time, but not with the practice of it. There are clocks in even the poorest farmers' huts off in the provinces. Everyone has a watch around the wrist. Clocks are everywhere in the stores and the subways. The correct time is announced every half hour on the radio. For all this attention to it, no one bothers to be on time. Yoko was surprised to find me angry at her coming late to our meetings. One was not supposed to notice one way or the other. Lateness is a modern notion in Japan. The government went so far as to establish a National Time Day in 1920. The day falls on June 10. Nobody bothers to observe it.

Yoko's brother had been a baseball player, a very promising one to hear her tell it. At the age of twenty-five, he'd had a disastrous season. His batting average dropped forty points, an incredible statistic in Japan, since almost every ball playable is recorded as a base hit. The most blatant errors in fielding are overlooked and recorded as base hits, since recording errors would involve shaming the players. No one loses face in this country, I decided. Yet her brother had.

"What happened?"
"It was the *yakudoshi.*"
"The *yaku*--what?"
"The *yakudoshi.* Man at year twenty-five and forty-two have very unlucky year."

Actually, it sounded like: "Man at yeal of tenty-fi an folty-too ha vely unrucky yeal." It always took time to translate and comprehend.

"You don't actually believe in that nonsense, Yoko?"
"As you wish . . ."

It's a hero's game played under the floodlights, applauded by millions. Strategy, as I knew it in the American game, was simplified and played on a more glorious plane in Japan. There was little distinction between starting pitching and relief pitching here. Both threw the ball. Their won-lost record, after all was said and done, was less important than the amount of home-run pitches served up. A pitcher could have a high earned run average and many losses, but if he was stingy with home runs, he was a good pitcher. Everything revolved around the grand swat. The homer hitters were paid ten times more than the singles hitters, even those who hit for twice the average. The Americans who played the game here were expected to produce home runs, not singles.

"Homurunu ne . . .?"

I remembered and finally understood the child's glee in the voice. Babe Ruth was the greatest player ever to play the game in Japan. He toured the island in 1934. He could have stayed and played for three times the amount he was getting in the States. Even Yoko knew his name, even though she couldn't tell me the current Vice President in America. Babu Lutu would have been his name. Even for three times the salary, I could never imagine the Babe staying in Japan and passing for a lute player.

The home run overshadows everything. They don't bunt here with a man on first and nobody out. They swing for the fences and next year's paycheck. The bunt is devious and a little beneath the national character. The sacrifice fly is denigrated too, unless it's close to the fences. The near-home run is more important than the run scored by it.

But I was most amused to find that the Japanese have no concept of base-stealing. Players their size in this country, like Maury Wills and Lou Brock, are earmarked for base-stealing, paid for it. They don't steal in Japan. That goes for baseball as well as for daily life. The woman need not lock her doors, and the pitcher need not check the runner. And where American players would lope around the base for a home run, savoring the moment's applause, the base runners in Japan tear around the bases, even though nobody's got the ball to throw them out.

Yoko seemed very pleased that we could go to baseball games together. It was an unexpected intimacy for us, one that needed little words. I couldn't keep myself from making jokes about the players, their seriousness, their miniature stature, exaggerated by our position in the stands.

"I see . . ."

She wouldn't move a muscle of those lines around the corners of her mouth. They either came from age or much laughter before the mirror in the privacy of her room. I kept hoping it was the latter, kept finding out it was the former. Yoko said she forgot how to laugh the day her mother burned to a crisp.

"Do you see . . .?"

I never knew how much she intended behind her clipped questions. I could have been a kindergarten child needing guidance or a war criminal awaiting sentence for all the expression in her eyes, blurred further by the inward tucking of the chin.

Baseball had been very popular in the Hiroshima of Yoko's youth. I asked her repeatedly what effect the bombing had had on the baseball team. She never elaborated. She would only say that the sport had been suspended during the war and then resumed at the end of the war. How could the Japanese return to the invader's sport, the sport that John McGraw and Charlie Comiskey had brought to the island, return to nine innings with the same fanaticism as before? Meanwhile, football had become more popular, the child of the foreign father. Yoko's home-town team was called the Hiroshima Bombers.

April was a busy month. There was Buddha's birthday. Yoko had to spend much of her time with her family for the birthday celebration. April was also the beginning of the academic year, and Yoko withdrew to her studies. Left alone, I began to wonder what I should do about her. I would be going home at Christmas. I had told Yoko nothing about my "early out," as it's called in the service. I had never even asked myself if I loved her or not, if I had any intentions of marrying her or not. I began to go to prostitutes around the base. I knew that if Yoko were to lose me it would be to the return home, not to another woman. I felt a kind of perverse excitement, the kind I used to feel burning anthills when I was a child. I went to the cheapest prostitutes, the older ones, the ugliest ones with squinting eyes, baggy shawls and barrel hips, the ones reduced to fellatio to make a living. When the others soldiers passed them at the gate to the base, they would flick their cigarettes at them and ask scornfully, "How's the lips, honey?" — I would stop and choose, stop and spend the night. I would go all the way with these sixty-year-old women, all the way without protection.

Yoko sensed a change in me. She was warmer, more open to me than ever before. She wanted to teach me the summer festivals, to observe them with me, to make love with me on festival days. But we had gone beyond the stage of foreigner and geisha, the sake and raw fish stage, the stage of animal sex and abrupt giggling without translations. The relationship had become familiar, comfortable, easy as a cigarette after supper.

June meant *Nyubai,* the rainy season in Japan. Yoko and I walked the streets of Tokyo. We walked through the Ginza where foreign tourists sported Nikons on each shoulder, and Yoko looked at me. We walked through Shinjuku where the glue sniffers gathered near the subway stops, and I looked at Yoko. This comfort was a kind of accusation, culture against culture. The more we knew of each other, the more we began to judge all Japanese and all Americans by each other. That awareness made us cautious. I stopped calling her "Loco Yoko."

Sometimes Yoko would skip a class or leave her friends to go with me. In the second week in June, we took an iris bath together in an Inn and drank iris wine until late into the night. I had tried to convince Yoko to go with me to one of the public baths. For old people, she said. For children, she said. Not for foreigners, she said.

The Hiroshima baseball team came to town for a three-game set. All three games were rained out. Yoko was very disappointed. She came to my bed depressed and withdrawn. When she had fallen asleep, I would sneak out to the gate and choose an aging, gap-toothed goddess. She would take me to her home, talking about her children as she stripped to layer upon layer of sagging beauty, her body like an escalator going down. She would fall on the bed, still talking about children, the television on in the other room.

On such nights, I knew I would never take Yoko back to America with me. Perhaps, when Japan finally mustered up the strength again to attack America a second time, Yoko would have an extra reason to wish the kamikaze pilots success. Each time that I resolved inside to go home alone, I also secretly wished to give Yoko a child before I left. At first, it was merely a fantasy but as the summer passed, the fantasy became purpose. My late-night excursions at the gate were a rehearsal for the moment to come with Yoko, a way of teaching me distance in pain, detachment from the unborn child.

July brought the *Tanabata* or Star Festival, the night when Altair and Vega meet in the Milky Way, the equinox of the consummated marriage among the constellations. We took a hot bath and lay naked in our Inn room, watching the stars until Yoko began to snore in the crook of my arm. I held the bird-woman in her song of sleep, and the feeling was warm and secure but not sexual, the feeling of stroking any animal that cuddles.

The second week of July brought *Bon*, the Lantern Festival, the week when all Japan lights up with rows of lanterns surrounding the Temples like candles lit in Catholic Churches, rows of lanterns around the boats in the harbors, rows of lanterns that move in the night, carried by children who dart like fireflies around their parents. The lantern festival is Japan's Buddhist All Souls Day, the week of ancestor worship, the week when Yoko most remembered her mother, burning like a candle in the wind, the high flame from her charred skin like a halo about her head. I learned that the memory of the dead was especially painful for Yoko this year, for 1973 was her *yakudoshi* year. If men must suffer at the ages of twenty-five and forty-two, then women must suffer their own year of curses and evil eyes at the ages of nineteen and thirty-three. The puzzle gathered its pieces. Yoko had been nineteen in 1959, the year that Alain Resnais made *Hiroshima mon amour* in Japan. She had turned thirty-three in 1973, her birthday having gone unnoticed between us. I calculated. she must have been four when her mother went up in flames. It seemed strange to me that this bird-woman was eleven years older than me, this bird-woman that I treated like a child. We had never talked about her family in any detail. I asked her if the memory of her mother was painful.

"Painful for mother, more for me. Mother lucky to die. I live. You see . . .? My whole life a *yakudoshi*."
"But, Yoko, you're young yet. You'll find a man, a nice man who'll marry you, take care of you. You'll have babies."

"I see . . ."

I knew she didn't. We lay naked in the bed, looking into each other's eyes. There was no lovemaking, no urge to move toward each other. There was only the heavy incense smoke of an ancestor coming between us, passing judgment on the daughter who slept with the murderer.

August was the hottest month. It passed without festivals, without the arguments we'd grown accustomed to, the arguments that usually ended with false translations or lack of the right words, ended with silence and snoring on my arm. The whole month was a night of sex, no one particular night standing out in my memory, but rather time after time melting one into another, my sweat appearing on her boy's body that never sweated of its own. One of those nights differed from the others in that Yoko took the initiative and went down on me the way the women at the gate did for the soldiers, the wide-open way the kamikaze pilots caromed off canyon walls, hollering obscenities to hallow their deaths.

Sex and baseball. August was the baseball games we faithfully attended, the ritual of Japaneses men swinging for the fences. I'm told by friends who were stationed in Spain that the Spanish children go around waving imaginary capes at invisible charging bulls. In the same way, Japaneses children in blue uniforms run through the temple yards, swinging for the fences.

"Homurunu . . . ne?"

The Hiroshima team was playing poorly. Yoko was depressed, as though there were a nationalism to be observed among the various teams. My interest in the foreign players on each team seemed petty to Yoko. The other teams got all the homers, the other pitchers were the stingiest, Hiroshima wallowed in last place in the Central League. And there we were, my *yakudoshi*-stricken Yoko and me, going to night baseball.

It's difficult to explain my feeling about night baseball. I have to resort to the analogy of the child getting to see his first Christmas lights, the child who sees the night lit up in neon miracles. The rules of the game seem suspended in frozen animation for the wonder of the lights. Yoko asked me about night baseball in the States. I had to look it up. The first night baseball went way back, arc lights hung on poles in 1880 for a semi-pro game. Larry MacPhail was the Edison of night baseball in modern times.

With President Roosevelt pressing a button in the White House, the lights first went on at night in Cincinnati's Crosley Field, thanks to MacPhail. Later, as general manager of the Yankees and Dodgers, MacPhail spread his mission to both leagues and both coasts. I'm sure MacPhail is enshrined somewhere in the minds of the Japanese for turning the ritual of man and wood into the lights, the lights brighter than Broadway, the lights that give the dream back to baseball. The ball looks faster under the lights. The men look smaller under the lights. Yoko's yellow skin looked bleached under the yellow glare of the lights. Japanese baseball rebecame the white man's game with this filter of yellow upon yellow becoming white.

The lights were bright enough to bring daytime to an entire city of fifty thousand people. One game for fifty thousand. I began to appreciate the seriousness with which Yoko followed the wallowing Hiroshima Toyo Carp. into the cellar of the Central League. Even under these lights ten times brighter than the light used by the average person for reading, the Hiroshima team remained in darkness, enigmatic in their ineptness, their lack of home runs, their failure to attract the foreign sluggers. I remembered the Lantern Festival and Yoko's mother, and I thought that both would burn more brightly, more meaningfully, under the lights of night baseball.

The atmosphere of a night game is more oriented to the stands, the celebrities who attend, the movie stars and politicians. Night baseball is big business; day baseball is baseball. I suggested to Yoko that a home run at night was worth two during the day. She smiled. She did not move her head. Her team was losing.

September brought the beginnings of Spring to Japan, the meaningful flower and fruit festivals everywhere. The full moon of September is said to be the most beautiful of all.

I watched the full moon rise and fall from the center field bleachers at the Tokyo stadium. Yoko stared intently at the batters' faces through binoculars. I stared at the moon, whose magenta light would have been enough to light up this game. Night baseball by the full moon: the thought seemed more poetic to me than it did to Yoko. I tried my best to distract her from the batters. I slipped my chilled hands under her sweater and around her breast. She jumped from her seat. She didn't even look at me. Her eyes never left the binoculars, but I knew that she was looking at me just the same. Her cheeks were red with embarrassment.

The third baseman for the Yomiuri Giants hit a towering home run into the center field stands some fifteen rows in front of us. Yoko began poking me to run after it. I refused, laughing. She began to beat me with both fists, her hair down over her face, her face crying into my coat. I didn't realize how much that one baseball meant to her.

She told me that night in bed that her brother had been playing baseball the night their father's sister died. The sister had been a substitute mother for them. The brother had brought disgrace upon himself and the family by missing her death. I wondered if this had happened during his year of the curse, but I didn't ask. Yoko was snoring in my arms. Her nose still drivelled from so much crying.

The season ended in October. There were no festivals, except the final baseball standings and the upcoming World Series. Those final statistics were important to me, because a year of my life with Yoko went into them.

Central League	Won	Lost	Ties	Games
Yomiuri Giants	66	60	4	
Hanshin Tigers	64	59	7	1/2
Chunichi Dragons	64	61	5	1 1/2
Yakult Atoms	62	65	3	4 1/2
Taiyo Whales	60	64	6	5
Hiroshima Toyo Carp.	60	67	3	6 1/2
Pacific League				
Nankai Hawks	68	58	4	(1-3)
Hankyu Braves	77	48	5	(3-1)
Lotte Orions	70	49	11	(2-2)
Taiheiyo Club Lions	59	64	7	(4-5)
Nittaku Home Flyers	55	69	6	(5-4)
Kintetsu Buffaloes	42	83	5	(6-6)

The season was over before I had realized that there was such a thing as a tie game in Japanese baseball. There were no extra innings to be found. The Yomiuri Giants had won the Central League again, and in October they beat the Nankai Hawks of the Pacific League for the World Series. The crazy Pacific League had gone through two seasons. The Nankai team had had to play the Hankyu team for the right to play the Giants. The poor Lotte Orions finished second in both seasons and didn't get to play anybody. I hadn't realized how close the teams were in the Central League. The Hiroshima team finished only six and one-half games out of the first. Still, they finished last.

It was small consolation for the city of darkness and for Yoko, but I suggested to Yoko that the Hiroshima team had only finished last once this season, while the poor Kintetsu Buffaloes in the Pacific League had finished last in both of the league's seasons.

"I see ..."

She spat on the ground. She obviously had not seen my point. All that was left were the statistics. In 1973, some eight million people attended Japanese baseball games. Yoko and I must have accounted for around fifty of that figure. The season was over for us but not for the teams. They awaited the arrival of the American team or teams. They would play well into November.

The festivals were nearly over too. In November there was the *Schichigosan* (7-5-3), which I found to be extension of the superstitions surrounding the evil eye years. In this festival girls aged three and seven and boys aged five dressed up in costumes and went to the temples. Much prayer for healthy lives and successful careers surrounded this miniature masquerade ball.

I never told Yoko about my departure, but somehow I think she sensed it. Or perhaps the end to the baseball season had somehow signalled to her the end to our affair. She began to distance herself from me again. Suddenly, her relatives had to be visited again. Suddenly, her studies became very crucial to her. And suddenly, one night rare for the lack of other nights around it, we made love in the cheap rented room without protection. That was the only night that I can remember Yoko not snoring between my arm and my chest.

In early December, with Christmas in the States next to my family and friends on my mind, the Japaneses celebrated *Susuharai*, the festival of soot sweeping. On a secular level, I took it to be similar to our rituals of spring housecleaning. On a spiritual level, it was the time when Japanese swept the sins from their souls, casting out all evil spirits before the New Year. Perhaps it was fitting that I should be going.

I never told her. I never wrote her, and she never wrote me, although she knew how to write to me. I guess the price for my cowardice came in the pangs of waiting, waiting for a letter to tell me ... to tell me ... anything at all. "I see" or "As you wish" or whatever. For every two foreigners lucky enough to make the Japanese baseball team each year, there must be several thousand like me who leave this island like an ingrown toenail, who cross the International Date Line and re-enter real time, who forget the squatting women with their bird bodies, their uniformity of expression, their collective giggles of embarrassment, their national ability to go from standing straight down to the floor without the use of their hands or the sound of a crack in their knees, who forget, finally and most difficult of all, their night after night of animal sex in the middle of the diamond under lights bright enough to burn fifty thousand people to a crisp.

The Interpreter

I left Kadena Air Base the day the Americans gave Okinawa back to the Japanese. It was the end of an era: the end of Iwo Jima, the end of the teahouse of the August moon, of twenty-five years of prefab houses, GI bars and steak-'n'-shake huts that had cluttered this anthill, sixty miles long and thirty miles wide that we called the Keystone of the Pacific. We were still going to keep our bases there and, of course, all the choice land, and the highways and super-markets would still remind one of suburbia in America. But now the Japanese ruled.

The riot police were out in full force that day. The Marines smoked ci-garettes behind jeeps that were parked sideways in the form of a barricade outside all the base gates. They all carried gas masks and M-16's. Next to them were the newly arrived self-defense forces from Japan, tall and skinny men in gray uniforms with pointed white hats and white shoulder straps that hung like suspenders down to their white belts and white holsters with the little red sun-ball on them.

The American Secretary of State and the Japanese Prime Minister signed document after document in Hawaii. Half an ocean away, the American Commander-in-Chief and the Commander of the Self-Defense Force shook symbolic hands in Naha. The Okinawan merchants continued to put their shoji screens and stolen combat boots, their gaudy Thai silk and colored glassware out on the sidewalks for the soldiers who would not come.

The day I left brought no Oriental faces to any of the bases: no maids to make the beds, no cooks to serve blunt steaks and french fries the texture of sauerkraut, no cabbies on the one-way streets. Officers' wives volunteered to do on this day what the Okinawans had done for twenty-five years. It was their duty.

I was debriefed before boarding my plane by the American customs offi-cers. They informed me that I was leaving Japan and going to Japan. Japanese customs officers daintily fingered my baggage with white batons that looked like billy clubs. I felt as though America had not won the second World War after all, only the truce between wars. I returned the scowl of the Japanese cor-poral who inspected my bags. The way he enunciated his few memorized lines of English, as though he had to make himself heard above the noise of the plane's engines by those already on board, made me furious. His politeness was arrogance. The way he fingered my clothing, as though he were a Buddhist priest who had mistakenly touched a woman, made me color with shame and rage. I began to sweat. I resolved to make him blush.

I began chattering wildly as he inspected my carry-on bag. Yup, that's tooth glue, my good man. You know, you wonder where the yellow went. That's after-shave. Go ahead and smell it. Like sake, isn't it? Take a nip. Get it? Of course you don't. Those are dirty clothes. Not enough bleach in the wash here. I apologize for the rips. You see, the Okies don't exactly pamper the clothes. They beat the dirt out against the barracks' garbage cans. Here I am going to your home and you're stuck here looking at my dirty laundry . . .

He didn't understand a word I said. I was surprised at my own anger. I had never given in to my prejudices so freely. I even began to feel sorry for him, even to like him, because I was showing him my teeth. The soldiers behind me began to giggle. The corporal giggled too, out of politeness, for he didn't understand a single word.

Eventually, he did lose face. I always chew gum when I take a plane, to keep the air pressure from building up inside my ears and head. As I spoke, I began to chew as children do, my mouth wide open. The saliva built up. I began to make my gum crack. Click-clack, click-clack. He stopped smiling. I blew a bubble. When it popped, his bowed head jumped. His look was incredulous. I stuck my tongue out, still smiling, to draw the gum back in my mouth. It was the ultimate insult. He shoved the bags toward me and looked away to the next man. I would be on the plane before the smile return to his lips.

I always sit next to the window on planes, perhaps out of habit, perhaps out of superstition, perhaps out of an inner need to help the pilot navigate. The only window seat left was next to a Japanese officer. I became so engrossed in my last looks at Okinawa that I didn't even hear the instructions of the stewardess. As she passed our seats on her way to the forward cabin, the Japanese officer stopped her and pointed. I had not fastened my seat belt. The stewardess just stared at me, hands on hips. The Japanese officer had made me lose face. He smiled sweetly at the stewardess, then looked humbly at me and said by explanation:

"It was my duty."

I stared out the window during the whole flight. I chewed my gum as loudly as I could, but it had already grown old and crusted in my mouth. I tried, but I couldn't make it crack.

***

Where the Japanese hide the traditional temples and gardens in Tokyo behind skyscrapers, neon signs and Olympic swimming pools, they flaunt the asymmetrical temples and the age-old gardens in Kyoto. From almost any street corner in the city, I could see at least two temples in any direction. I had heard that there were people who came to Kyoto on every vacation and still could not see all the temples. I had always thought it was a promotion device for tourists. Now I understood. In Kyoto, the temples were skyscrapers, a whole city whose rooftops stretched out to Buddha. The buses and taxis made as much noise as they could, but their sound was engulfed by the temples. Kyoto was a city of the past.

Two days before the tour ended, I met Hori-san. I had stayed with the tour for three days, and I had seen twenty-five temples. As hard as I tried, I could

68

not reconstruct more than two or three in my memory. I needed distance to remember.

I needed to feel my feet on the slippery, rain-drenched sidewalks. I needed to see the steam rise on the windows of restaurants no bigger than closets, to look at the colored plastic replicas of all the fish and noodle dishes for tourists, to hear the tapping of canes, the screeching of the trolleys, the clearing of throats and the spit that followed, the sound of the megaphones from the movie houses where the sound-track of the film playing was piped out into the street to induce pedestrians to come in. I needed to drown myself with noise, noise of the kind never heard at the temples. I smelled the exhaust fumes of buses, the clogged sewers, the smell of human sweat and sake breath. I needed to walk when I pleased, stop when I wanted, sit where I chose for as long as I cared. Most of all, I needed to break down the postcard memory I had of Japan and its too posed, too static beauty, which still hung over me like an off-color joke one can't forget.

I had stopped in a guitar store. Even here the wooden floor was covered with a tatami mat which made me feel as though I had intruded upon a private home. The guitars hung like skeletons, gathering dust on the wall. It was hard to tell which were the cheap guitars and which were the expensive ones. I felt ill at ease, fingering the guitars as though to show that I was interested. I used my fingers for language with the proprietor, who passively nodded his head and alternately raised or lowered his eyes. Even when his eyes were lowered, he still nodded his head. In the back of the store, the floor was raised. There the tatami mats were clean and new. Black-lacquer teacup and a red rice bowl sat atop a low round table in the middle of the enclosure. Even at work there was a small corner of the room which was home, a place for relatives or close friends who might drop by. A place of refuge from foreign tourists. A place to step out of the present and into the past.

It was only when Hori-san tapped me on the shoulder that I decided to buy a guitar. I hadn't heard him come in. He tapped my shoulder as one taps chopsticks on a table to get them straight and parallel between the thumb and fingers.

"Please to speak English for you, maybe once?"
"Oh, no thank you. I was just looking."

I answered reflexively, the stock answer I had always used in the States to keep the salespeoples' smiles out of my back pocket. I sensed that in Japan one didn't just look at merchandise. It would be too impolite, especially for a foreigner. Fingering the proprietor's instruments was a little like fingering his daughter's kimono in public. Even with dust, these guitars were objects of reverence. I had left the postcard Kyoto.

"You like guitar very many, sir?"
"Yes, very much. I'm afraid that I can't tell the difference between them and the American brands."
"Do you pray?"
"No."

I thought the question impertinent. My answer was blunt, a quarantine hurled at my questioner. I had forgotten that the Japanese often substituted "r" for "l" when they spoke English.

"All are good, if I may say, yes?"
"Yes, of course. I meant that I couldn't tell which ones were expensive and which ones were ch . . ., I mean, less expensive."
"You want expensive guitar, if I may?"
"Well, yes. Yes, I want a good one. Thank you anyway for your help."

I was shuffling my feet. He was probably innocent enough. He probably just wanted to practice his English, as so many Japanese do when they see Americans. But his words seemed to have fingers. They were crisp at the corners and staccato in speed, the feel of the the vibrating floor after a plane has gone by too quickly. I turned on him, as though to speak to the proprietor. I was immediately embarrassed. The proprietor had gone back to the little enclosure and was squatting on the tatami floor.

"Yes, I would be most honorable to be your help, soshite . . ."

He was motioning for the proprietor to rejoin us. There was no trace of any insult on his thin and bone-starched face. I would learn that in Japan I could commit the most unpardonable blunders in etiquette, and the Japanese would act as though nothing had happened. I could track mud on their clean tatami, I could eat with my fingers, I could leave soap suds in their baths, I could even strip in the middle of their streets, and they would walk by without looking. To acknowledge would be to accuse. To ignore is to deplore. The Japanese would speak to me when spoken to. Only those who wanted to practice their English would ever speak to me first.

We began the ritual walk up and down the long wall of guitars. I had to pretend to be thorough. I had to know the price of each guitar, even though I couldn't mentally convert the yen price to dollars fast enough for the ritual to make any sense. I gradually learned that those further to the back were more expensive than those near the front. Looking at the teacups, I decided that I should have been able to guess that much.

"Could you ask him if this one is expensive?"

It took five minutes to get an answer. Hori-san was smiling and directing the conversation. The proprietor, his eyes on the teacups, answered when spoken to, but never offered more. His answers were the cutting edge to Hori-san's buttered questions. Perhaps he was suspicious of any Japanese who spoke English.

"Takai desu."
"What?"
"He say it especially expensive. Totemo takai desu."
"Can you ask him if the wood is treated? I mean, will the wood crack when I go back to the United states?"

I was speaking English with a Japanese tempo. My words were machine-gun, evenly spaced. I had never changed my speech in Okinawa. If the Okinawans couldn't understand my vocabulary, if they couldn't keep up with my pace, then they lost my money.

"Wood good."

I still didn't trust him. Did he know the proprietor? Had they arranged this? I had spent too much time asking, looking, fingering the foreign wood. I had to buy. I realized that I didn't even know the exact price of the guitar I had just bought. I had only asked whether it was expensive or not. I paid the money. I didn't even want a guitar. I had only wanted something more than postcards, something more tangible than a guided tour.

Hori-san was waiting for me at the door. He was smiling. His gums were bleeding into the cracks between his teeth.

"Thank you for helping me, Mr. . . . ."
"Hori. Matsuhiro Hori. Please to call me Hori-san. And you?"
"Prine. Andrew Prine. Uh, Andy . . .?"
"Prine-san. I'm very pleasing to meet with your acquaintance."

He walked off with his hands in the baggy khaki pants, the cuffs rolled up so as not to catch the zoris when they came off the heel, his faded white shirt hanging over the back of his belt. I looked at the wrinkled card that he'd given me.

HORI MATSUHIRO. INTERPRETER. KYOTO.

The address was written underneath in Japanese. It was strange, this mix-ture of English and Japanese. It was as if he wanted only the Americans to know who he was and only the Japanese to know where he lived. I didn't trust him.

***

In a week's time I had come to be accepted as their son. I had eaten dinner with Hori-san and his family. I had flattered them with my laughter on which they smiled approvingly and asked: More sake? I had complimented them on their scroll paintings, all taken immediately and given to me. I had congratu-lated Hori-san's wife on her fine teacups, which were immediately wrapped up and given to me. When I complimented Erico, their thirteen-year-old daughter on her koto playing, she winced. At the end of the evening, I had to pretend to be drunk, so as to leave all their gifts behind. Hori-san saw me to the door, smiling through bleeding gums.

Hori-san took me to the family factory where the fine teacups were made. I was invited into one of those little enclosures to squat upon a tatami mat and sip the ritual tea. I was invited to the wedding of one of his cousins. She ac-cepted my presence with a bow, never once looking me in the eyes. She smiled weakly at Hori-san, as though he had transgressed and was, nevertheless, forgiven. He took me to visit his brother the painter, who did no paintings one August afternoon when we ate strawberries and watched the sun go down. His brother kept glancing at the blank canvas and at his younger brother, who knelt between us like a priest, the go-between with Japanese smiles for his brother and American smiles for me, both from bleeding gums. Everywhere he took me, he transgressed. And everywhere he went, he was forgiven.

He was never too busy to be with me. He had no work. Erico told me he had a bad heart and couldn't work. What she was really telling me was that it was bad for him to keep up with my tourist's steps all over Kyoto.

"Erico is new Japanese girl. She talk too many."

Hori-san shrugged off any suggestions that we rest between visits to all his relatives. He was apparently driven to show me Japanese customs and rituals, just as he was obsessed with speaking English. For such a man, the land of the rising sun was a desert. He spoke to me in hurried gasps and with some blushing, as though I was the first human being he'd seen in many years.

He seemed to know everyone in Kyoto. Merchants nodded knowingly when he passed by. Some taxi drivers refused my payment of the fare, nodding to Hori-san. And the cherry blossoms, in full bloom at that time, seemed a respectful backdrop for his bleeding gums.

***

Three weeks had passed, and I was AWOL. It was stupid. I had survived three combat missions to Vietnam and two years of boredom on Okinawa. My only remaining obligation to the U.S. military was to separate myself from it, by the books. I had severed ties in my own way. I checked out of the GI hotel and moved into the temple nearest Hori-san's house. He had asked the head monk. There had been no hesitation. I had only to remember to take off my shoes before entering to remain a citizen in good standing in this city of the past.

At the same time, I was becoming nostalgic for home. I wanted to talk about America. But Hori-san, who lived for the chance to practice his English, never asked me any questions about America. I forced the issue. Passing a hill of clustered temples and elevated gravestones, I said that it looked like the skyscrapers in New York.

"No elevators, Prine-san."

I looked at him. He saw that I had not understood. After momentarily closing his usually open mouth, to swallow a little of the blood, he explained.

"Americans crazy. Elevators. They have no touch with the land. They go up, down, not forward, backward. They go up, get dizzy, get crazy."

72

Instead, he plied me with questions about Okinawa. He was intensely proud of Japan's newest adoption. The television was filled with specials about Okinawa. I had no desire to talk about the squat people with rotten teeth; the officers' wives with their bouffante hairdo's, spiked heels and gaudy gift shops; the uniform and gray-green buildings, the close-cropped grass imported from Hawaii; the endless flow of B52's and the smell of fuel on my breath every morning; the year-round water shortages, the daily heartburn from overly-fried foods, the jack-knife highways with the 10 mph speed limits; the TV re-runs of the *Big Picture, Rat Patrol, Twelve O'Clock High* and *Hogan's Heroes.*

So I told him about the strawberries as big as baseballs, the fierce lions sculpted atop all Okinawan rooftops, the coral beneath the choppy waters and the screaming Okinawan theater, fashioned after the Japanese Kabuki.

There were TV interviews with a corporal who had just surfaced after twenty-five years hiding in the bushes of northern Okinawa where the roads ended and the gruff mountains began like a three-day-old beard. He told of making clothes from the stubble of stunted foliage. He told of eating bugs and wild berries that gave him diarrhea. He told of his few attempts to swim to Japan. The currents had been too rough. There were sharks. There were the American planes. He weighed sixty-five pounds. He had lived alone for twenty-five years. Hori-san translated his answers meticulously.

Most of all, the corporal spoke of the importance of holding out, of not surrendering, of surviving for the sake of Japan. A month ago, he would have been considered a fool, an anachronism, a candidate for the asylum. But now that Okinawa belonged once more to Japan, he was a national hero. He was given two new cars, a complete wardrobe and a season's pass to all the games of the Yomiuri Giants, Japan's best baseball team.

I watched and felt a strange affinity with this TV scarecrow. They had not caught me either.

***

I asked Hori-san about the war. He didn't answer. We toured the city. I asked him again. Finally, he told me that he had been a lieutenant who had done nothing spectacular. Erico told me differently. Hori-san had been wounded in Okinawa, a bullet close to his heart. Still, he managed to save four of his men, bringing them back safely through American patrols to the retreating Japanese lines. After the war, the last months of which he spent recuperating in a Tokyo hospital, he had distinguished himself in a different way. He had served as one of the leading interpreters for the American Occupation Forces. He interviewed the prisoners for them. He translated the cryptic comments of condemned generals, including his own, before the war tribunal. He accompanied MacArthur to the as yet unsubtitled movies. Erico told me this in a monotone, without the slightest tinge of pride in her voice. It was in her eyes that she expressed that faint blink of forgiveness.

Hori-san took me to the movies. We saw a "period" film about the samurai. By the end of the film, most of the samurai committed ritual suicide by sword, with much groaning and coughing of blood. I realized that in America we pride ourselves on our heroes' deaths. We ask only that they be swift and clean, with no complaints and certainly not a long drawn-out dying. I watched these samurai disembowel themselves and I thought of Hori-san's bleeding gums in the dark next to me. His voice bubbled as he leaned over to whisper.

"Like the kamikaze. Very beautiful, yes?"

And still they had not found me.

***

Hori-san has taken us to Lake Hakkone for the Lantern Festival. Everyone in Japan seems to be here, holding either a red baloon or a yellow and orange lantern. The children are all lined up against the railing of the ship, Erico and Mabu with them. Some of them let their lanterns go, and they bob like buoys before disappearing in the wake of the ship. The mountains extend on both sides of us. The boats go in soft circles around the harbor.

At night after walking up and down the harbor, parading our lit lanterns in single-file, we go to an outdoor hot-springs bath. Hori-san has blood stains caked around the edges of his mouth. He is tired from walking up and down the little streets. He has a chill. His wife stays with him, while Rico, Mabu and I go to the baths. The night air is windy, a slight frost is in the pine branches that whine their mournful songs, and I have goose bumps all over my flesh as I step naked into the steaming water that smells of sulphur.

Mabu comes running out behind me, jumping into the steaming water. Even though my teeth chatter, I enter slowly, one foot at a time. Then Erico comes walking very slowly from the womens' dressing quarters. She too is naked, her towel draped low at the shoulders, concealing her chest and abdomen. When she takes off her towel, I am amazed. At thirteen, she still has the face of a young child, but her body is close, very close to blooming. Her supple shoulders and legs have a luster to them from the nearby lanterns. Her little breasts are hard like sea shells. The brown nuts that are her nipples look like little hermit crab shells. When I look up, I see that she is looking at me. She blushes, smiles, lowers her eyes. There are goose bumps up and down her wispy body, but her face is warm and orange. She has not lowered her eyes from shame alone. They are lowered, but they are bulging with curiosity. She is looking at my towel, draped over my lap. In the middle my hardened penis sticks up like a sprinkler on a new-mown lawn.

I am overcome with desire for this pixie child. I want to cradle her in my arms. I want to bring her body to a boil, to give her body the first throbs of wailing and surrender. This is not safe or soft sex that I feel. The crunching in my stomach is that I have felt only in the air above Vietnam at the moment of bombing, the moment of release when the bombs light up the ground below like magic lanterns. I want to put a child in her belly, even against her will.

I am too excited to bathe. I ask Erico if she is cold, but she has already draped the towel around her body, and she refuses my willing arm by moving away. A matter of inches. Too far for my arm without moving my body. Not far enough to free me from this surge of phlegm in my throat.

Mabu glares at both of us. His little head is an accusation in the water. He calls us cowards. He leaves us running at full speed toward the bath-house. Without a word, Erico gets up slowly, gracefully, and walks away. And I am left alone, my towel damp, the steam rising before my eyes and the smell of sulphur in my brain.

Everyone is silent on the return trip to Kyoto. Hori-san will be bedridden with fatigue and irregular heart beats. I will be informed that an American soldier has been to the temple, asking for me. For the first time in three months, I will forget to remove my shoes when I enter the temple.

***

It has been two weeks since I last saw Hori-san and his family. Each day that I've gone to his house, his wife has told me that he is too weak to see me. She intimated that he might have to go to the hospital for tests. I am totally alone in this city of mythical temples.

Without Hori-san, without his guidance and his flawed English, I have become a foreigner again in Kyoto. Taxi drivers expect me to pay the fare and no longer nod to me. Plastic noodle and fish dishes stare out at me from restaurant window displays. I go in, sit down, wait for the waitress, go outside with her to point at the plastic dish I want. At night, there is no street life as there is in Tokyo. There are only the husks of temples, the deep silhouettes of Buddhist rooftops that cast their shadow over foreigners. The wind whines through the gravestones like the lonely rain falling sideways between the skyscrapers in New York. I buy the one English-language newspaper and spend my mornings reading every page and every column. Already the peace has been broken on Okinawa. A drunken marine pistol-whipped a Japanese policeman to death in a Naha bar. The question now is whether the marine will be tried by the American military courts or by the Japanese civil courts. One of the B52's from Kadena was shot down over North Vietnam. There is an editorial on the many Japanese writers and artists who have committed suicide in the past three years. A secret pact is said to have been signed by the Japanese, stating that they will assist mainland China in overthrowing Taiwan. I have all the news about everywhere else in the world in front of my face. And I know nothing about Kyoto. I desperately need an interpreter.

I have not gone back to the temple. I change hotels each day, walk different streets each day, point the different plastic bowls in different out-of-the-way restaurants each day. I have even begun to spend whole afternoons inside the temples, confident that no patrols will be on the guided tours. I have never experienced such freedom, such loneliness, such sexual longing. I dream of Erico each night.

I must try to see her one more time. Then I will take a bus to Osaka from where I can get on a boat to Canada and, eventually, home.

***

I didn't realize. I had walked by the guitar shop. And suddenly there was Hori-san putting his peanut-brittle hand on my shoulder.

"Prine-san! Thank to God. We thought you leave Kyoto without to say good-bye to Hori-san. I tell my wife no. I go to all hotels. I cannot understand why you not one many time visit, why you have leaved temple and . . . leaved expensive guitar there too, yes?"

His annoying habit of ending a statement of fact with a question was instantly familiar, welcomed. I was beside myself. I hugged the frail body, feeling all the creases in his too-big and wrinkled white shirt. For the first time since I had met him, I noticed no blood between his teeth. He said his heart was good, that Mabu had pitched a no-hitter for his school team, that Erico was about to give a koto concert at one of the temples. He noted that my hair had grown very long, and he scolded me. A good soldier must keep the little hair, he said.

We made an appointment to go visit one of his favorite temples the next morning. Then he ordered lunch for us at one of the few Korean restaurants in the city. It was I who had suggested it. He explained to me that few Japanese would come to such a restaurant. He added that many GI's would come and some "bad women." My stomach jumped.

"Hori-san, have any American soldiers come to your home, asking about me?"
"Prine-san, please to send as many friends, yes? We most welcome soldier friends of dearly Prine-san."

***

In the morning we went to Kinkaku-ji, the temple of the Golden Pavilion. From across the lake and through the spruce trees, the three-tiered temple with its shimmering golden roof looked like a storybook castle out of the Middle Ages. The temple was enclosed on all sides: by rippled hills behind, by the lake in front, by the spruce forests on either side. The green of the tree needles and the gold of the temple roof blended in the blue pool in which no wave moved. School children sat obedient and immobile in flat boats upon the lake. Frogs rivveted rhythmically and leaped from one lily pad to another. Entire Japanese families all crouched around the banks of the lake, while the father tried to capture a more breathtaking picture than the last with his Nikon. Monks walked by in orange robes, smiling on the silence. It was Hori-san who spoke at last in a whisper of bad breath, so incongruous with this perfect post-card setting.

"It is as beautiful from any distance. Some Japanese come every day to stand on a different place. To circle the Kinkaku-ji. To see it whole and different each times."

I nodded. I understood in every muscle of my body. This was the first place I had found since my childhood where I could pray without using words.

"I wanted Prine-san to see Kinkaku-ji. This is temple where our Erico play koto."

Then Hori-san told me the story of the Buddhist monk who burned the temple down some years back. He, too, had stood somewhere along the banks of this motionless lake and had found the perfect spot. I could picture the colors merging in the monk's mind, so that the cradled roof like an inverted casket was green and the singing needles of the spruce trees were golden in the afternoon sun. The monk had been transported by the beauty of kinkaku-ji, its perfect place in nature, his perfect place in it. Overwhelmed by such beauty, he had wanted no other moment to come after. So, he burned the temple down. Hori-san said that all the Japanese in Kyoto mourned the loss of the temple for months. Then they rebuilt the temple, slat by wooden slat, proving the poor monk wrong. They duplicated the perfect temple in the perfect setting for the perfect Buddha. Hori-san coughed and laughed at the same time.

"Prine-san, Erico like the Kinkaku-ji. I am like the monk."

***

Two days later, I met Hori-san in the same place. It was an hour before Erico's concert was to begin. I felt some sense of finality meeting Hori-san in a place where we had met before. His white shirt was ironed, his green tie looked plastic, artificial against the green spruce. He spoke fast, saliva bubbles erupting an off-color red out the corners of his mouth. I had asked him the question that had been on my mind since that first day in the guitar store.

Suddenly heavy hands were clamped upon my shoulders. I was turned around to see a Japanese policeman and two MP's in faded green uniforms, which seemed to me more plastic than Hori-san's tie. Hori-san seemed stone-struck and utterly pale. I was handcuffed and put in the back of a jeep between the Japanese policeman and one of the MP's. As we were about to drive off, I looked at him one last time. With a voice more quiet and more obedient than the school children we had seen in the boats, he said:

"It was my duty."

-Johannesburg Diary-

The Tower of Babel: The End
of the Old Testament, the
Beginning of the Middle Ages.

March 15. It is not a very propitious day for a journey. Dictators and whole civilizations with them have fallen on this day. Erostrate conceived of the destruction of the Holy Temple on this day. God must have rested on this day. Caesar was warned on this day. I have waited a long time for this trip.

I look out the window. The peephole, porthole, glasshole, asshole of the world. Just three gin-n-tonics brought that on. I'm not really looking out the hole. I'm writing down what I saw there. Can't keep my eyes straight. It's too damn early to be taking a plane. Something as momentous as this ought to be reserved for midnight. I look out the window. The smells of Bangkok's gritty open sewers, gaudy peppered restaurants, the neon signs of the massage parlors, the garlic-gracious women are all blotted out. The high-thatched rooves of the squatters' huts look flat and rusted now. Tops of temples glitter in the sunshine, their steeples pointing up at me. Within them Buddha reclines in quartz contentment, having traded the pleasure of the flesh several thousand years ago for the mocking smile and overweight belly that the hungry children and the withered old men admire so much. Joe is down there somewhere with his whore. I wonder what the hell she thought while Joe and I played a little blackjack and sipped our colored straws of gin-n-tonic in the airport. Probably nothing at all. If you got the money, honey, I got the time. Wait'll they hit the water pipe tonight, that old-time religion of the people, at the Hotel 99 where there are no walls or ceiling, only mirrors through which the pimps can watch the customers. Wait'll Joe's full of that opiate awareness, that sexual abandon, if he hasn't gone too far, that soft violence of the mindless. Wait'll he's rubbing his hands and twitching his fingers, ready for foreplay. Then the whore will be thinking. Hurry up, honey, the meter's running. What do I care? I just look out the window, breathe on it a little, play a little tic-tac, cat games, strung up like the gut on a tennis racket. Meow, meow, old Poozmerow. My old man's in that racket! Ha! All I can see are the tops of trees. Steep ascent. Hard to write when the plane is rising. I just looked out the window one last time. To see if I missed anything. Clouds as dense as the tops of trees. Fluffy, scruffy clouds that run and open up like wheelbarrows. December snow, a world of pillows. Now I lay me wish I could. Why the metaphors? I'm writing a diary to myself. Joe is down there with the whore. I no longer have an audience. Suddenly I feel very anxious to get the whole trip over with. Like Baudelaire, hurry up before the second glance comes to spoil everything. I don't need to look out anymore. I think I'll turn in. Sleep, deep sleep, close the curtain to the peepholes. Puffy clouds like pillows, handkerchiefs hovering over the snotgreen sea. Rejoice.

Ten minutes later. Took a cat-nap. Never even wrote down the reason for this diary. I am going to Australia. My mother wrote me - Son, you have the chance of a lifetime there in Bangkok, a good government job, exciting travel right there in Thailand, exotic food, why do you want to go off to Australia, a place after all where they speak English just like in America? Are you home-sick, son? - How can I tell a Colonel's widow fighting off the Middle Ages with bourbon straights in Florida's Eldorado settlement that I'm just plain bored with Bangkok? That it's like Cleveland to me now? Better not write at all. Too busy to write, Mother, what with taking the temple tour this morning and get-ting ripped off by a ten-year-old Thai girl I held in my lap. Too busy to write, playing poker with Joe. No challenge whatsoever because I always win. Would quit playing with him, except that I know he likes me and we have a good old time reminiscing on the good old times that never seemed so very good at the time. Singing the songs of our own destruction, singing always louder than the last time to drown out the words, - And my heart keeps telling me / datada / you're not a kid at thirty-three / dabbadabbadoo / you play around, you lose your wife / scoobiedoobie three / you play too long you lose your life. Better to write a diary.

I am going down under, as they say. Bangkok-Sydney with stops anywhere I want them. Stop, I say. Hurry up and stop. Penang, Bali, Christ Church. His church is full of aborigines, whooping and hollering, trading their rosary beads for a little firewater, just a little of that old black magic, lord. Wonder if Joe knows the whore's lord. Wonder what it does to him to see her bite into the succulent shell of a roach, decapitate it and suck the licorice stuffings out of it? Does she pray to Buddha with her breath of weasel piss? God! Stop, I say. I'm going to Australia to forget all that. One month is a long vacation. Maybe there's a carefree, live-and-let live job down there with some wealthy Australian widow. Winks most when widow spiders wince, lord.

Australia. I mumble the name of the place like a litany and I lose all sense of timing and direction. Everything must be upside down there. Buddha would be Humpty Dumpty there. Imagine all those white women with their round eyes and specious crotches all turned upside down for me. A veritable peep-hole, that. Who really knows how far away Australia is? They've never been in-vaded. In fact, they beg people to come. Like going off to Wonderland. Voluptuous blondes in peasant dresses, their fertile brittle breasts sticking up like camel humps. And yours truly with the eyes of a giraffe. Kangaroos and koala bears. Boomerangs and sharks off the coast. The Great Barrier Reef where coral is still a color. More than a vacation, that.

There are soldiers on the plane with me. Wondering what kind of beer they'll get down there and how much the Aussie women are going to ask for it. They've heard old Aesop's fables that love's for free in Australia. All the soldiers go there. Even if it's not free, the women will be white. The soldiers still sport their baggy green fatigues with the rolled-up sleeves, tatooed muscles, cereal-bowl haircuts, hair-trigger nerves.

They talk about women. Not a one is the least bit worried about the history of Australia, the native mores and customs. After all, it's not like going to Japan. More like invading the Old West of America, eh buckaroos? Not bad, Thomas. Come to mention it, these boys look like cowboys about to ravage the last fron-tier. I would like to talk to them, because I am lonely. But I don't want to see them again, once we get to Sydney. I'm not a part of the rodeo. So I won't talk.

Still I would like to get them into a little five-card stud, relieve the wad in their back pockets a little. But then I don't want to risk any sore losers. They're saving their money for something else.

Fifteen minutes later. I have a damned headache. From writing so much. Never realized how easy it is to think, yet how difficult it is to write down the thoughts exactly as they come out. I begin to hate the thoughts when I write them down, because they're not true. As long as I just think them, I'm not lying to anyone. Then again it takes too damned much time. I have a thought, but it takes me two thoughts to get it down: one for what it was and one for how to say it. I may not be able to keep up the diary. It won't be the first time.

The soldier next to me thinks that I am writing a woman. I can tell, because he's taken out paper of his own. Wonder if it's from the Hotel 99. Paper like the mirrors on the walls, lord. He had been staring at my paper. But I angled it so that he'd have to read everything upside down at a slant. Like Australia. If he wants to go to all that trouble, then who am I . . .? Now he is the one who writes. - My dear and darling Shirley-girlie-I am safe and on my way with some of the guys--Wish you could be going with me--there's a civilian next to me writing to his wife, I guess, so I thought I'd write a couple lines to you--I want to tell you a secret--It's that I---------he looks up at me. He would like to court-martial me if he could. I don't care about his fucking secret. I know what he's like. I know he's left-handed, squeezing his pencil like a football player. I know from his fatty cheeks he's going to have a heart attack some day. And I know he doesn't have the first cue as to what foreplay is with Shirley-girlie. He'd think it was for eighteen holes, not just one. Reminds me of Potter, my boss, ex-Army all the way, who told me to remember the old South Texas story about the two bulls when I got to Australia: -These two bulls, see, an old one and a young'un are standing at the top of a hill looking down on a pasture-full of luscious cows. The young'un says in a rush a slavver---Hey pops, why don't we hurry on down there and fuck us one of them cows? To which the wise old bull says--Whoa up, pardner. Why don't we take our time getting on down there and fuck all of them? Get my message, Cousin?--says Potter. Roger dodger. The soldier next to me is one of the young bulls. Thought I was writing my wife. Who might that be, Thomas? I just know I'm gonna spread my genes all over the lost continent, and yet I have an ache in me that says a wife would make this more than a vacation. Always the best man, never the groom. Groom and doom from womb to tomb. I've never had a honeymoon. Unless I count that little sortie to Tiajuana way back when. Even then I got more than I bargained for, eh Doc?

Thirty minutes later. I must have fallen asleep, dreaming of Nazi doctors in the camps, performing their experiments. How about it, Dad, you never told us about that one. I wouldn't fall asleep if I were writing to a woman. It doesn't matter. Soon the real thing. Caveat emptor but cherchez la femme. This soldier is probably packed with bills as far as a deck of cards to be doled out to the fair-hair sex. I'm sure he's kept this much a secret from old Shirley-girlie. But then maybe Shirley's got some sugar stashed on the side too. In any event he'll be sending her a post card of a cathedral, certainly nothing more secular than that. Wish you were here, lord. Was a great party after you left. I'll tell you all about it when I get there. Thomas, are you jealous of the Private's privates? If I had a woman, it wouldn't matter. But this wet pants sticking to the seat kind of waiting. Waiting for the wide-eyed lovelies with their quaint nasal voices, cups of tea with two lumps, their stroll me out in the parasol, their schoolmarm eyes and Roman orgy laughter. I know they will take my money. It doesn't matter. When I leave, I will have had more of them than they of me. I always get more than I bargain for. Keep the faith, Thomas. Put up with a little wet pants waiting.

March 17. Interruption. I got off in Penang, thinking I would sample the surf for a day or two, search out a topless Penangese or two in danger of drowning, saving her in the proverbial niche of time, of course. But I had one of those terrible sober lucid epiphany memories of Fraulein Alice from the past. Why should I remember her in Penang? It was like a bomb scare at Times Square on New Year's Eve, the kind of panic Mother's got in Miami about life gone by, the kind of memory in the gut, not in the head. Everywhere I looked out on the beach, I saw Alice. Felt like I was the one who was drowning, decapitated, since I was recollecting from the gut. I choked on several gin-n-tonics. Couldn't even swallow properly. I tried to write it all down in order to squelch it, but I couldn't even do that. Today I'm back on the plane for Australia, feeling a little more like the wise old bull. I have all the time in the world.

I just reread what I've written so far. There don't seem to be enough extended passages, enough historical insights, enough truths. Just the same old cold reportage, same old existential blues, same old verbal epilepsy that might be more interesting if I were Raskolnikov. I believe in his moral elite, but there are no more conquering Napoleans in the twentieth century. I'm more like the one who ended up with Raskolnikov's sister. Wonder if Joe thinks of Sonia when he fucks his whore. Jesus, is there no end to my perversion? I'm going to sleep this leg of the trip. Maybe I'll have more to say after Bali.

March 18. Bali was not high, as they say in the song. It was like trying to play Bach on the accordeon. The guidebook said the women were supposed to go around topless, dancing for the tourists. I saw them, but they weren't topless and they weren't dancing. They were sticking around just long enough to pose for a picture, pick up the fee, then hurry back to the chief. The hotel situation was a monopoly of one. At thirty dollars a night for an empty bed, I felt it empty. Now if the beds had come with company, that would be different. As it was, I found company enough camping out on the beach. Two giggling girls who'd dropped out of Smith to come smoke grass in Bali. We took a little naked midnight swim, and I played a little tic-tac on the clitoris of the one called Shane, which only whetted my appetite, but again it was like drowning. The other one fell asleep as soon as she had dried off on the beach, while Shane began seeing visions of the end of the world in the zodiac. For all practical purposes, she was incommunicado for the rest of the night. Out of the ages endlessly rocking. I pretended I was asleep like the first girl, leaving Shane to babble on to the universe. With my back to them, I masturbated in the sand, realizing that sex comes always as it must, not as it might. In the morning I kicked a little sand in the hair of the still lifeless bodies. What did they care? Their buttocks smiled back at me in mock triumph. They had bared themselves to me, taunted me, and still they had come through the long night unscathed. Drugs were a way of preserving virginity. I thought of Joe and the opiate whore in their bedroom of mirrors. I stopped at the Bali Hilton on my way to the airport and bought a post card depicting the Louis Quatorze lobby of the hotel. I signed my name to it and sent it to Mother in Eldorado, realizing that I too had spent the night in the

Middle Ages. I took the morning plane to Sydney, still thinking of Alice, my queen of castles on the Rhine, the specter of sex appeal.

It was Alice through post cards who first showed me what I nor anyone else would ever see again - Germany before the war, Germany ante-bellum, wiped out as Sparta obliterated Athens, as Rome decimated Carthage, in spite of the moral superiority of the victim's intellect. At the time I could not see the post cards for what they really were. I had read my father's letters to Mother, telling her that"the boy" should never forget what we were doing in Germany. How could I reconcile his descriptions of the bombing with her pictures of the cobblestone streets of Heidelberg, the fairy boats floating down the Rhine to the sound of the waltz and the smell of fresh bread? It was like the world of monsters in science fiction invading the world of Alice in wonderland. But the paradox existed only for me. The little Colonel, Louie (for Lieutenant, to his friends) Colonel had gone off with all his medals to the Fatherland to recapture I know not what. Mother received a new medal and a letter from the State Department as mementoes of his journey. His last letter was a deliriously happy one, telling us that he had found himself, that he was where the world really needed him. I have never understood what he meant by that, since I have never been there. Paradoxically, it seems to me that the old man went over there and sacrificed himself, so that Alice could come to America and take his place in my life. And so Daddy died with his boots on, Mother went to Eldorado with her baggage full of Jim Beam, and Alice came to America to study nuclear physics. It was all so very clear to all of them, except me, the history major with an unfinished dissertation on World War Two novels. Perhaps I am going to Australia to find out why the little Colonel flew the coop in the first place, why Mother would never let me talk to her of Alice, why Alice would never let me talk to her at all of the past, the past I so badly needed before I could commit myself to her, the past she so badly needed to forget in the future world of nuclear physics. Perhaps I am going to Australia to find out. Australia has never been invaded.

March 19. I am now in my hotel room at the Queen Victoria, care of Sydney, Australia. The plane trip was singularly uneventful. I goaded an Air Force Captain into a friendly game of gin rummy at a dollar a point. I was on the verge of forcing him to sign IOU's when the landing gear hit runway, and all our cards went flying. It's probably better that way. I would hate to think of meeting the Captain in every lonely alley and dimly-lit backstreet of Sydney. Sydney is full of colorless people, like any other city, socially alive, like any other city, depressing in the shop-and street-sameness of any other city.

I'm being very cautious about my stay here thus far. I asked the man at the desk if the hotel supplied a masseuse or companion. Apparently, this is not that kind of hotel. It goes without saying that I am probably paying too much as a consequence. I will look for another hotel in the morning. Tonight I have sent post cards to Mother and Joe. Neither will answer, for I have left no forwarding address.

March 21. It's been two days since I last wrote. In that time I have accosted around twenty women, some nineteen unsuccessfully. I cannot say whether the fault lay with them or with me. With several I no sooner introduced myself than I was invited home with them. One was the wife of a Unitarian minister who had gone to Perth. Another was a go-go dancer from Brisbane on holiday in Sydney. Another turned out to be an American school teacher from Des Moines. I refused most of them, because they showed no resistance. In Bangkok I would have given a month's salary for a night with any one of them, but here I feel like a glutton before I've eaten. One explained to me that Aussie men are "frightfully stingy" with their women, and that even the most respectable Australian woman would gladly give herself for a chance to go out in style. I backed away from a couple of them, because there was no conversation possible beyond the introductions. No conversation was what I had in Bangkok. A couple of them giggled and blushed at the discovery of an honest-to-goodness Yank. I felt like an archeological throwback to Neanderthal. With one or two others, my name was immediately changed from Tom to John, and I knew that I had strayed into GI traffic. Others I eagerly sought, because they ran away from me. I followed feathered hats, dancing mini-skirts, high boots and sweet perfumes through department stores and public parks. Somehow I was never able to catch them. I don't know whether the fault lay with them or with me.

When I had carried my feet as far as they would go, I slipped into the nearest bar and ordered a gin-n-tonic. As luck would have it, my table was directly in front of the piano where Claire, an overweight but sincere torch singer was just finishing up a melodramatic medley of Frank Sinatra hits. I had the waitress bring her a tonic, and she nodded "cherrio" to me as she left the bar. The next night, which was last night, I returned to the bar and began composing a message in the form of a song request. I wrote on the serving napkin: - Imagine yourself in one of the following situations and choose a song accordingly: (1) you are in the shower on a rainy night and your very first lover, whom you haven't seen in years, steps into the shower with you; (2) you have just made love with a man who didn't think love was possible, and he's crying on your cheek out of gratitude; (3) you have just composed a very beautiful song, and every other singer in the world is trying to imitate your way of singing this song; (4) or you have just felt my hands upon your heaving breasts, and you realize that the song you are about to sing will either draw me closer or drive me away. Again she nodded to me, this time without my having sent a gin-n-tonic. I always get more than I bargain for. Her song was a medley with which she closed her show for the night: Smoke Gets in Your Eyes / Over the Rainbow / I'm Forever Blowing Bubbles. On the first she winked knowingly from under blue eye shadow. On the second her voice cracked on the high notes. And on the third she hummed a lot when she wasn't projecting her wet lips in the shape of bubbles like a pregnant blow-fish. I couldn't tell whether she had responded to one of my alternatives or to all of them. I only knew that she always sang in medlies. She shut the piano and came to my table.

I finally fucked her about ten this morning. First she had to show me her scrapbook of clippings. All I can remember is one of her in a Chinese nightclub in Singapore. Then she had to tell me all about herself: Claire, husband left her with two kids who are grown up now, whole life is her music, even though she knows most buy her drinks for her body, not for her songs. She told me about how difficult it was sometimes to be a woman and a singer at the same time. Never knew who to trust and all that. Said she knew she could trust me from the start. Then she told me all about myself. I had that shy, intelligent look she admired in her men. I hadn't pawed her as soon as we got to her room. But most of all, I was a man who knew how to listen. I listened from midnight until ten o'clock when suddenly she whipped off her dress with an exaggerated stage flourish, as a vampire might whip back her cape to get at her victims. I couldn't believe it had finally happened. I was slow in getting undressed, and even slower in getting it up. I don't remember much about the fuck or about her body. I'm probably suppressing the whole memory. I have finger-nail scratches all over my back. The missionary position was never this violent, not even during the Crusades.

I promised her that I would be back with more song requests tonight. What else could I do? Obviously I'm not going back there. It's not just that I won't be able to sleep on my back for a week. No, it's more something she said between midnight and ten o'clock. I can't remember in what context she said it, but she did say it. -I hate the niggers.- My memory won't let me forget that much. She's not like the first who has told me that in Australia. All the women here seem to have a fetish about "hating the niggers," as if it gives them some sexual satisfaction to be able to proclaim it openly, even vehemently. I have no feelings one way or the other about them, but I do know that after she said that, her breath smelled like crushed cigar ash and her tongue tasted like melted butter. What could I do? As soon as I announce to them that I am American, they bring up the subject. I suppose if I were black, they would probably bring up the whites. Either way they completely distort America's true historical reality. They fail to admit our common European heritage, the British influence as strong in America as it is here. They love America more than anything else for having "liberated" the world in two world wars. The Germans are secretly admired, but publicly denounced as vehemently as are the "niggers". The Nazis taught the Aussies how to hate the Jews. I don't know who taught them how to hate the blacks. What can I do? If only I had a wife.

Alice, ich du. I have not been able to get you out of my mind. I have spent the whole day thinking about you. Why? Australia has never been invaded.

March 23. I have spent two days inside my hotel room without going out, without writing since I wrote the last paragraph. And still I cannot get you out of me. You with your way of punctuating everything I say with "Ja." -You're so good to me, Alice. -Ja.- You understand me more than American women do. -Ja.- You are such a part of me. -Ja.- As if you understood everything with all your voluptuous kraut smugness. Sauerkraut smugness, lord. I read what I have written, and I think it is a lie. I should never describe a place before I see it. I approach new countries as I approach new women. I always come away feeling like a fool, having spoken too soon, having thought too late, having never written. I have decided to address my diary to you, Alice. It will force me to be less introspective. I am tired of my own complaints.

Already I have taken a new interest in the diary. It's as if the diary has become what Australia should have been. Of course I'll have to lie to you, Alice, since I'm no longer talking to myself. But I will try this time, I promise you, to be as honest as I can. And when I do lie, the lies will be beautiful, not the sordid lies of self-pity that I've been telling.

Ten days later. Easter Sunday. Alice, I have already broken my promise to you. Not that I lied to you, but that I wasn't as honest with you as I could have been. Once I had decided to address this diary to you, I couldn't very well erase you. But I met a woman not ten minutes after I finished the last paragraph. I have spent the last ten days with this woman and her father, and since I became involved with the woman, I didn't know how to tell you. Perhaps it's because we were so entangled that I didn't have the time to tell you. Perhaps it's because I felt like the little Colonel flying the coop on you, immediately after the prodigal return, immediately after coming to roost again after all these years. Whatever the reason, I have left the woman and her father, and now I am on the plane to New Zealand.

I think I was secretly hoping that I would never use my round-trip ticket back. Perhaps, like my father, I was secretly looking for someone like you to give my return ticket to. No, what I've just said sounds too contrived. It's nothing but a sentimental lie. I want so badly to be honest with you. That is why I want to tell you now about the Vugteveens: Nell and her father. I have the funny feeling that you already know what I am about to say.

The woman and her father were having breakfast in the hotel restaurant. As it was late and the other tables had already been prepared for lunch, the waiter asked that I join the woman and her father. I hesitated, expecting them to be offended by our forced company. I hadn't shaved for days. Yet they seemed only too happy to speak with someone who spoke English without an Aussie accent. As if they wanted someone to interrupt their previous conversation. I learned that they were Dutch and that they were not just tourists in Australia. They had been separated from each other for thirty years. When I asked the reason, they became quite silent. I quickly suggested that we might do a little sight-seeing before lunch. They both seemed very relieved.

Alice, I'm not sure that I can accurately describe Nell, at least not her physical description, and still justify to you the importance that I am about to give to her in this diary. She does not look at all like you, except for the complexion of her skin and the whiteness of her teeth. She is not tall like you, nor is she thin and angular like you. She does not move silently as you do when you walk. She carries herself, as if the effort were the same as that of supporting her old father. She is a small woman, rather plain, except for a mole in the cleft of her chin. She has a small breasts and wide hips. She looks to be asleep most of the time because of her lazy eyes, but she laughs a lot, and her laughter is infectious. I have seen it work miracles on the old man's ratty skin. She is obviously better educated and better dressed than he is. She is very meticulous about what little make-up she puts on.

The old man, on the other hand, is very sloppily dressed. I have seen her scold him more than once for burping unexpectedly or for spitting on the streets. He apologizes like a little child, as if he weren't conscious of his actions. He is entirely humorless and seems to depend upon Nell to lift the frown from his face with her laughter. Yet, for all that, he is a very arrogant man, proud of his daughter and defensive about her. But despite the fact that he sometimes needs to lean on her for physical support, it is she who gains strength from the leaning, as if she were sapping the old man of all his remaining life's blood. I describe this to you as if it is just happening in the present, because the memory is still so vivid in me.

When the old man first realized that Nell was talking to me more than to him, that Nell was taking more than a passing interest in me, he began to scowl openly in my direction. He began to interrupt our conversations with complaints of whatever malady - arthritis, head cold, runny nose - he deemed appropriate to the situation. Ironically, it was his jealousy that drove us together. As I said before, Nell is a plain woman, and I did not think of her sexually until he began to interrupt. I must also confess that her age bothered me slightly. I learned from her that the old man was seventy, although he looked eighty. And after we had slept together, Nell told me that she was forty, although she looked thirty. They seemed to be aging in different directions.

As I said before, it was the old man who drove us together. After I entered the picture, he suddenly decided that he was tired of Sydney and suggested to Nell that they go to Brisbane. The suggestion was made to Nell and not to me. And so on what was supposed to be our last night together, I tiptoed past the old man's room and into Nell's. She was waiting for me in a blue nightgown, huddled on the bed, as if it were freezing outside.

Alice, you would probably laugh at my uncanny knack for putting myself into impossible situations. Not only was the light still on in the old man's room and the walls thread-bare, but Nell herself made the situation worse by being a forty-year-old virgin. To alleviate my fears about the old man surprising us, she told me that he always slept with the lights on. Even she was not convinced by that explanation. How could she be, when she didn't really know the old man's sleeping habits, having been separated from him since she was ten? Nor could she alleviate my obvious reluctance to enter what had never been entered for forty years. We looked at each other and said nothing the whole night long. I was impotent for the first time in my life.

It is not surprising, then, that in the morning Nell insisted that I go with them to Brisbane. I felt as though we had reversed the roles of Sultan and Scheherezade. She was waiting for me to come to her, and no amount of scowling from the old man would change her mind. She was awfully strong-willed. Yet she was the patient one, the one who knew how to listen. If it took a thousand-and-one nights, she was determined to give herself to me on the one following. I felt like I was drowning again.

We tried again that night in Brisbane. We really tried this time, and I was still limp. We could hear the old man coughing in the next room. I wondered if he could hear Nell crying quietly on my cheek. I began to feel like a statue in front of her, naked for no apparent reason. Yet what we did with each other was more priceless than a hard-on explosion without aftermath. We spoke with our fingers upon each other's body, as the blind do, recognizing each other, still afraid that the old man would hear us, afraid that whatever one of us might say to the other would only hurt the other more.

How can I explain these nights to you, Alice, hard as I try? I have had your body so easily and so many times, and yet it was so elusive that it defied me. I never did possess it. The very minute we turned away from sex to sleep, you rebecame a virgin, as if I had never touched you. So how can I explain the completeness of those nights with Nell, complete because they were incomplete and always demanded another?

Two nights ago, three things happened to change everything. First, I told Nell that I loved her. I broke the silence of our fingers. I'm not sure now whether it wasn't somehow compensation for my impotence. Yet at the time I was sure that it was the first time I had ever said it and really meant it. Does that make sense? Because it was so easy with you, it was always hard, it was always a lie. Because it was so pathetic, so futile with her, it was easy to say and still easier to mean it. I didn't have to say anything, so what I said must have been the truth. I realized that sex of itself is a mashing and tearing, a destructive consumption like drunkenness or cannibalism, and that tenderness, not sex, was really the prelude to mating, the prelude to staying alive the thousand-and-one nights.

The second thing that happened follows from the first. No sooner had I confessed my love to her than I realized there wasn't any need of such a confession. My organ pipes were humming. I gladly began to puncture the stiff folds like rococo curtains of her body. I began to feel the rhythm that polar bodies have on each other. In a minute I had found what I had never found before with women: sex without hunger.

The third thing that happened follows from the second. Nell bit her lips to keep from screaming. Her eyes were so wide and frightened, not their usual lazy shape, opening as her whole body was opening, her clitoris swimming everywhere, the thought of a pistachio nut opening. But her eyes told me all the pain she felt. Sex for her was like labor pains for other women. I was stretching her skin irrevocably. And although we were mute, we couldn't keep the bed from rolling on the floor each time we moved. Nor could we keep the creaking box spring quiet. It was inevitable. The old man burst upon us without knocking, and I came in fright. He just stood there livid, his ratty wrinkled face rigid as in death. He jerked his fingers abruptly, motioning for me to leave the room, but he never took his eyes off the naked body of Nell, her legs now leaking me out on the sheets. I left without a word in our defense. Whatever I could have said would only have been a lie.

How do you apologize to a seventy-year-old man just recently reunited with his daughter after thirty years? I am sorry for sneaking behind your shriveled back and stealing your daughter's forty-year secret, corroding the walls of her forty-year fortress? How does she apologize to the father after giving herself to the first stranger they come across? I'm sorry, daddy, but I prefer Tom to you, you old wheezing geezer? And how do I apologize to a woman to whom I've just confessed my love, at the same time making it impossible for that love to continue? In one minute I had succeeded in isolating her forever from me, for her father came between us, and in isolating her forever from her father, for I came between them.

Nell and I had breakfast alone in the morning. The old man refused to come down. He was packing his bags, and they were going off to Perth, this time explicitly without me. Nell seemed curiously calm during the whole breakfast. She looked to be asleep or drugged. She didn't laugh. She said she owed me one more thing before we parted, and that was the explanation for her separation from her father and the reason for this reunion. Her father had been a soldier with the International Brigade in the Spanish Civil War. He had gone of his own free will, a question of principle at the time. But after his first skirmish, his first sight of the wounded and the dead, his first taste of real hunger and filth, the smell of burning flesh, the endless hours of burials and boredom before the next battle, he had deserted. He could not go home, so he wandered from country to country - from Italy to Yugoslavia, from Yugoslavia to Greece, from Greece to Afghanistan, from Afghanistan to India, from India to Thailand, from Thailand to Indonesia, and from Indonesia to Australia, where he took on an assumed name and an insignificant teaching job. He wasn't even there with his family when the Germans invaded Holland. He simply waited out the years, too ashamed to go back, too proud to stay put in silence. His pain must have been very great. One day he had had a stroke, and the fear of death decided the issue. After his recovery, he wrote to his wife and daughter. The wife had already died, but the daughter still lived in Amsterdam. He arranged for her to come to Australia, if she so chose, because he feared that there might still be those in Amsterdam who had also fought in Spain. He placed his guilt of thirty years in the hands of his daughter. Thus had she come and so would she go with him now, her debt to her father far greater than her gift to me.

I told her of the canals in Bangkok. She said it must be like Amsterdam. She smiled then, and I think she pictured me on the Floating Market tour, floating by the high-thatched squatters' huts and the gold peeling off the spires of the temples in the noonday sun. I promised her that I would quit my job in another year or two and come to visit her in Amsterdam. By then her father might have mellowed, even died.

I realize now, Alice, that I am going to break my promise. I will never see Nell or her father again. In a sense it's somehow perfect, for I have received more from her than I had ever hoped for. Yet in another sense both the leaving of Nell and the breaking of a promise made to her somehow cheapen the experience a little, as if she were no more than a street slop after all; it somehow takes all the purpose out of my already aimless nomad's existence. The only purpose left in my life today is to complete this diary, which has come to mean so much to me, and to tell the truth to you, which I have done to the best of my knowledge. Which I have not done, for, having done it, I know I can never send it to you. Writing too comes as it must, not as it might.

****

Dear Joe:

I'm writing to say I'm sorry for breaking a promise to you, but I am not coming back to Bangkok. Right now I have neither the strength nor the time to send a formal letter of resignation to the agency. I hope I can impose upon you to see Potter and take care of it for me. In return I will cancel all your back blackjack debts!

About Australia and New Zealand: I left Australia in utter despair, coming as close as I have ever come to ending it all. The Aussies are a lively race, but they are narrow-minded, badly educated, extremely racist and insecure. In addition, I've never really felt what it must be like to live in a place with no real valid historical tradition before this. Australia has no past. They are a timeless, spaceless people, surviving in a void. They seem to be caught between an anxiety over what you think of the country and a desire to reduce the geographical isolation they feel from the rest of the world. All around are statues and monuments to the Boer War, Queen Victoria and the Empire. And what is evidently the central experience for Australia, the whole World War One Battle of Gallipoli, was, as you may know, a bad defeat marked by courage and death and bad generals. How many countries or continents have so little history that they identify with a defeat fought half-way around the world on foreign soil with Allied troops?

This real lack of history seems to affect their self-identity, much like a full-grown man saddled with a child's psyche. But perhaps I am painting a false picture for you, since many soldiers that I saw there said that they were having the time of their lives. Perhaps the fault is mine, not Australia's.

As for what really happened in Australia, I am sending you the diary that I kept. Please forgive me for any allusions I may have made to you and the whore. Also please disregard the fact that much of the diary is addressed to Alice. I think you know why I have not sent it to her.

I still haven't explained what has happened since I ended the diary. I arrived in New Zealand and immediately caught a severe head cold. That laid me up for a week or so. By then my travel time was up, and I fully intended to return to Bangkok, but I learned that I had contracted VD somewhere on my trip. Fatalist that I am, I decided to wait the blight out here and postpone my return indefinitely. Joe, the rub of the matter is that I don't really know which of the women, those I mentioned in the diary or a couple of pro's along the way that I didn't mention, gave it to me. Likewise, I don't really know how many of them got it in return from me.

The doctor who treated me was a Belgian named Felix in Portuguese Timor. He was working at the time for the UN. He happened to be organizing a trip into the bush of Timor, and I joined him for four days of roughing it through some of the most gorgeous country I've ever seen. Like going back to Stonehenge or Lascaux, back to where a man must depend solely upon himself. Me feeling like a b'wana on safari with all the dark natives carrying our packs. Can you picture those scenes from the old Tarzan movies, hundreds of blackies mobbing around the white man, dogging his every step? I can't really explain it all to you, Joe. It's not so much what I saw but what I felt on the trip. Felix felt the same. I realized that I had found what I had been looking for all that time in Australia. Whatever it is, it doesn't have a name. Otherwise, I would tell you. But I am deliriously happy. Felix has quit his job, and we are returning to the bush immediately and indefinitely.

Forgive me for deserting you, Joe. take good care of the diary, will you? It's the only thing that I've ever completed from start to finish.

Tom

****

November 7   Sydney, Australia

Dear Alice:

Please forgive me for calling you by your first name. But through my long friendship with Tom (Long for Tom, that is), I feel as though I know you very well. I am only sorry that I have never had the chance to meet you.

The enclosed diary and letter from Tom have weighed heavily on me, ever since I received them. The weight became even heavier each day that he did not come back. I have sent inquiries concerning his whereabouts and that of the doctor named Felix. No one seems to have heard of either of them. It has been three years now, and I do not believe that Tom will ever come back.

When I first started sending inquiries, I also started thinking about sending the diary and letter to you. I guess that you could say it has taken me three years to write this letter to you.

I fought against making this decision for as long as I could. You can understand that I wanted to honor his request in sending the diary to me, not to you. I also felt that he was staying away on purpose to test me, and that as soon as I gave the diary away, he would return from Portuguese Timor to curse my breach of trust and lack of loyalty. Yet neither of these considerations was stronger than my feeling that the diary did not belong to me. Tom once told me that he would never marry, and that some day before he died he would search for you and look at you one more time. You were the ideal woman in his eyes. I must confess that I tried awfully hard to convince him otherwise. I was not trying to insult you; I was just thinking of Tom's best interests.

As you can see by the address, I have left Bangkok since the date of the diary and have set up permanent residence here in Sydney. I will not take the time here to dispute what Tom said in the diary about Sydney. I can only say that I am very content here, except for the nagging possession of the diary. It belongs to you, Alice, and I am in effect returning it to you. If it causes you any pain, I ask you to forgive me, but again I am thinking rather of Tom.

Sincerely
Joseph Kunkel

****

Houston Space Center

January 23

Dear Miss Vugteveen:

It has taken me almost two years to find out your name and address in Amsterdam. Throughout my repeated contacts with the German Embassy there in Holland, I wondered whether or not I should not forget the whole thing. But I believe that the enclosed diary and letters rightfully belong to you, not me.

Perhaps I should explain myself. I am of course speaking of the diary in which I am addressed a good deal. But that Alice no longer exists and perhaps never existed, save in the mind of Thomas. I never realized how my memory remained with him through all these years. It is both flattering and distressing. I must admit that his memory is terribly distorted and overly idealized. I must also say that the comparisons made between me and you are certainly unfair ones. Thomas lost his father in the second war. He loved his father very much, and often he refused to accept his father's death, alluding to him or addressing him as if he were still alive. After his father's death, his mother became an alcoholic and was, of course, little help to Thomas. I fear that I became a substitute for the father who left and the mother who could no longer love him. I of course had my own personal psychological problems at the time, as you might well imagine.

But the truth of the matter is that I was the first woman Thomas had ever known so intimately. I don't in fact think that either of us was quite ready for what we shared together, but that is beside the point. You, however, were the last woman he ever loved, as far as anyone knows. To judge from the diary, I think that you were made to suffer much from this love, as much as Thomas obviously suffered. When I knew him, he was still very much a child. It appears that you knew him as a man. Consequently, I believe that the diary and letters were sent incorrectly to me. In sending them to you, I hope that they will increase your joy without adding any pain. I have no doubt that he must have loved you very very much.

Sincerely
Alice Gruenwald

****

91

May 15   Johannesburg, South Africa

To Whom It May Concern:

I am having my nurse inscribe this message for me with the purpose of adding the enclosed diary and letters to my last will and testament. They were received from the Gruenwald woman by way of Amsterdam. She had, of course, no way of knowing that I forced my daughter to come to South Africa with me instead of returning to Amesterdam. Nor could she have any way of knowing that my daughter died one year after the last date of the diary, after having given birth to my grandson.

I no longer harbor any resentment toward the man called Tom for my daughter's death, since I have been given a grandson in whom I see the mirror of myself. My grandson has given me great pleasure in these last years of my life. I wonder, if he knew the whole truth concerning his mother and father, whether he could give of himself so freely. Of course he is as yet too young to understand.

I would like for him to have this diary and these letters one day, when he is able to understand with maturity and perhaps some compassion. The picture of me in them is not very pleasing, but I do not deserve any better. There are many misunderstandings of the "old man" on the part of both my daughter and the American, but I shall not endeavor here to correct them. The boy will have to discover these truths for himself as he grows up. I have done too much harm already to those I love. I do not want to enlist the boy's sympathy any more than I have already done.

I hold myself responsible for the kind of woman that my daughter was. It is rather to enlist the boy's sympathy and understanding of his mother that I have chosen not to destroy this diary and these letters. I am getting too old to evade artfully the boy's persistent questions about his parents. Consequently, all will be explained to him when I die.

Our life here has been very isolated, although it has been comfortable. I do not sleep well at night any more, and I waste electricity needlessly with my sleeping with all the lights on. I cannot help that: I am afraid of the dark. I would have liked to die in complete and anonymous peace here in South Africa, whose climate and whose people remind me so much of my beloved Australia. But the country is infested with Negroes who threaten to destroy us all in a full-scale revolution. I do not fear so much for myself as I do for the boy. I do not want him to witness bloodshed if I can help it. It may be necessary for me to send the boy back to the Netherlands before I die. It would grieve me very much to die alone without him, but then I deserve no better.

                                                        Per Vugteveen

Recycling Dante

"Hello. You don't need to say a word. I know how you feel. I feel the same way. It's magnetic. It's electric. It's cannibalistic. My pulse has short-circuited, my brain is in flames, my flesh festers with expectancy. Permit me to be candid, my sweet. I broke the wishbone on my chicken tonight and I thought of your thighs. I sat down to pee this morning and I put Janus, my cat, on my lap. Janus could feel the tinkle below and he purred like a fire engine. I fondled his fur and I thought of your underarms. I smell French onion soup and I think of your aristocratic breath. Ah, language! How inept it is to capture my passion. I simply must be blunt. The thought of you excites me so much I get sick. I get diarrhea. I can't keep my milk down. I can't wait to see you. I'm wild with fever. I want us to fuck until we both throw up."

"Arnold!"
"Oh, mother, why does it have to be you? Can't you leave me alone? Can't you see I'm expecting someone else to call?"
"Frankly, Arnold, I'm appalled at your . . ."
"Your three minutes are up, mother. I'm going to hang up now."
"Arnold, don't you d . . ."
". . . click . . ."

His name was Arnie Kandinsky, and he lived in his own unique little world. He was a librarian at the New York City Public Library. He hated books, but he loved reading. He hated people, but he loved filing cards in the catalogues. He got his revenge on the books by mutilating the covers or by stealing them or by telling people that the books were on closed reserve when they really weren't. When someone would ask him to put a search on a book, Arnie would leave the desk and disappear for a coffee break until the person had disappeared. He refused to put a "hold" on a book, inventing outlandish stories about how desperately essential the book was to the research of its then-present borrower. In addition, Arnie was a tyrant on overdue fines. So he got his revenge on people too. I should know. I worked at the library with him. My name is Claire Lumiere.

Arnie never was a very important person in anyone's book, except his own. And maybe mine. His father died when Arnie was still a very little boy. His life apparently went inward after that. His body refused to grow any more. His mind remained at that same age of instant fantasy, total impulse and complete amorality that make children so charming. I've never had any children, myself.

Since Arnie never really reached the age of reason, he couldn't be held accountable for what he did. He must have loved his father very much, although he would never ever talk about him. It was as if he sprang from a virgin birth.

And that's why he got his father figures from Dante and the detective novels or adventure novels. He read the *Inferno* over and over, but he would never read the same pulp novel twice. His tastes in women came from the readings. If Arnie had known Elizabeth Taylor's phone number, I'm sure that he would have called her. But Arnie really didn't love the Elizabeth Taylor types he chased. At least, I don't think he did. I think he was really waiting, patiently and passively waiting, for someone like Dante's Beatrice to come bathe his morning soul with her body sunshine. It's a wonder to me why Arnie couldn't figure out for himself why the Elizabeth Taylor types would always run away from him and why the Beatrice types would never come to him. But with Arnie, each failure of reality meant a victory for fantasy.

He loved basketball, probably because it was the sport which stressed a person's height more than any other sport. Arnie knew all the scoring averages of every New York Knicks' player. Sometimes he walked around the library dribbling an imaginary ball or jumping up to get an invisible rebound, then pivoting with outstretched elbows to begin what he called the "fast break." Maybe that's why I cared for him so much. Arnie made all the breaks he ever got, because nobody else ever thought he was tall enough or important enough. If you were asked to remember twenty faces you had seen in the street on a particular day, Arnie's face would be the nineteenth. Mine would be the twentieth.

"Hello. Is this Susan Bodenheimer?"
"Yes. Who is this?"
"My name is Dan Vergil, Susan. I'm sure you remember me. You've probably been wondering when I'd call. I'm sorry if I've kept you waiting, but I've been frightfully busy. But I felt a throbbing in my muscle today and I knew that it was you sending me messages that you wanted to be seduced. And so I . . ."
"Wait. Hold on just a minute, buddy. Who the hell are you? I don't know any Don Virgin or whatever your name is. Where did we meet?"
"My sweet, there's really no need to be coy like this. Time flies while the passions ripen on the proverbial vine and the skin of the grape rots in the sun if you don't pluck it and all that . . ."
"Look, I'm going to call the police if you don't tell me who you are."
"There's no need for these silly threats of violence to stir our passions. I assure you that my blood boils already. I was the one who picked up your purse in the subway yesterday."
"You mean you're the creep who bumped into me and made me drop my purse, don't you? I remember you now, you little shrimp."
"Size is rather relative in the dark, wouldn't you say?"
"What the hell are you trying to insinuate, anyway?"
"I'm only giving free sway to our inner voices, Susan. You must realize that it's futile to resist the calling of two bodies who yearn to be one."
"God. You're an obscene little runt! I don't even know you. Now I know why you had to look at my driver's license before you'd give me my purse. I'm going to call the police."
"But, Susan . . ."
". . . click . . ."

Arnie was a victim of the technological revolution. He was just a mole of a man, but the fact remains that his species of dreamer and schemer could only have been spawned in the twentieth century. I said before that Arnie spent his every waking moment plotting ways to meet women. For quite awhile, I never knew about his direct approach. But the telephone was always his indirect approach. He would call women whose bodies were frozen in his memory after only a passing glimpse. He had learned the words of the casual male conqueror from the adventure novels. It didn't dawn on him that he spoke in cliche or that he offended his listener. he was completely oblivious to the effect he had on women.

"Hello. Is this Renata Murchison?"
"Yes. Who is this?"
"This is Murray Hill. We met yesterday."
"Excuse me, but your name doesn't mean anything to me. Could you tell me where we met?"
"On the elevator in the Switzer Building."
"I still can't picture you, Mr. Hill."
"You asked me to push four for you. I did."
"But what does that have to do with . . ."
"Then you got out and went into Dr. Samuelson's office."
"How did you know that?"
"I got out after you and followed you in. I got your name from the receptionist. I said I was your brother and that I wanted you to know I couldn't wait for you but that I would call later."
"So that was it. I wondered what that message meant. I don't even have a brother. Look, Mr. Hill, I don't know what your problem is and I don't really care. So why don't we just hang up now, okay?"
"But we've only just begun. Our relationship is still in its infant stage."
"I'm a married woman, Mr. Hill. Can't you please leave me alone? Why are you men all so bold, so insistent, so damned snotty?"
"Please don't cry, Renata. I only want to make you happy."
"Then leave me alone, please. I really don't feel well, and I . . ."
"Renata, are you pregnant?"
". . . click . . ."

Arnie never got far enough in his conversations for anyone to trace the calls. The police would have had to be set up with a wire-tap in the homes of every woman in New York City to catch him. He never gave his real name, but I don't think it was because he was afraid of getting caught by the police. Arnie was too naive for that. I think it was because his fantasy life was so strong that any name would be better than Arnold Kandinsky, New York nobody, moleman. I began to take more open notice of him, and I wanted him to take notice of me.

"Arnie, why do you like Dante so much? What is there in the *Inferno* that satisfies you so much?"
"It's really difficult to explain, Claire."
"You mean you'd rather not tell me, is that it?"
"I didn't say that . . ."
"You can tell me, Arnie. You can trust me."
"Well, maybe, I guess I could try. You see, everything is so controlled in the book: so perfectly planned, so mapped out, you know? I mean, there's three of everything. Dante must have been taken, you know, possessed when he wrote it, because it's so perfect. And yet in all that order, there's the unexpected, the totally unexpected. There's a surprise to every circle. And you know something,

Claire? You read these unbelievable things, and you have to believe them, because you just know that Dante believed them. It all boils down to that: was Dante telling the truth or was it just a bunch of lies? Well, I believe him. His form is so controlled that he couldn't have lied. You know, I've had nightmares like Dante's visions in the *Inferno.* The sad thing is, they're just nightmares. They're not real visions. Do you see?"

"I don't think so."

"Well, I think they're real when I have them, that is, I think I think that. But in reality I can't think at all when I dream. They just come to me, like I was some transmitter or something. I really don't think at all. I just feel them. And I know afterwards that they weren't real and that's why they vanish. That's why they don't stay with me. Because I can't think during the feelings. It's always one and then the other. So I know they weren't real, because I don't have the control to keep them real. Dante did. He could think at the same time he felt."

"Is there anything about the characters that you like? I mean, the Dante within the book, do you identify with him? Or with Vergil?"

"Vergil's so great, Claire. I have to laugh every time I read it. I mean, here's this pagan poet. He had to be great, and I guess Dante wanted to show that he was in some way Vergil's successor. But here he is, stuck in the fields outside of the circles, guiding poor Dante through the circles. And he's so proud of himself. I mean, he scolds Dante for his pride, but then there he is just as proud as a peacock himself. My father's name was Virgil."

"I see. And what about Dante?"

"Well, I can't quite figure out what makes him so good. Maybe because his name's the same as the author's. But he's so blind, you know, for a main character. I mean, he has to be told absolutely everything. But then I think I like him for that. He's the only main character I've ever found who wasn't very smart, who didn't have all the answers, who didn't know what to do every step of the way. It helps the suspense, you know? And then he's special. It's not really explained, and that's good. I like to guess why he's so special each time I read the book. But God and Vergil and everyone paves the way for him."

"Who do you mean by 'everyone'?"

"Beatrice and all the women saints. They're really something special.They're never there, and yet they're always there. It's like you could love them like Dante did and never have to see them. Excuse me, Claire, I'll just be a minute. Yes sir, may I help you?"

"Yes, I couldn't help overhearing. Were you talking about Dante's *Inferno?*"

"Yes. What of it?"

"I need the book for a class I'm taking. I looked in the card catalogue, and I saw at least nine cards for the book. But when I went to the shelves I couldn't find a single copy. Are they all checked out?"

"No, they're not all checked out. They've been removed from the stacks for inventory."

"Well, I really need the book right now. You see, we're having a test in a couple weeks, and well . . . could you tell me how long the inventory will take?"

"I couldn't really say. At least three weeks. You might try Benson's Bookstore down the street.'

'Thanks. Thank you very much. You've been a real big help, mister."

"Don't mention it."

"Arnie, why did you tell him such a lie? You could see he didn't believe you."

"Some people can't read Dante right. You can see it in their eyes. I could tell right away that he wouldn't understand the book anyway."

"Where are the books, Arnie?"

"They're in the drawer over there. I put them back every night when we close and take them out every morning when we open. You won't tell anyone, will you?'

"No, Arnie, I won't tell anyone."

"Excuse me, Claire. There's the phone. Hello . . . yes . . . no. I said no and I meant no. I thought I told you not to call me here. Yes, some other time maybe . . . no, I don't want your food. I'm going to hang up now . . . look, I told you, Florence, I'm going to hang up . . click . . ."

"Claire, please don't look at me like that."

"Like what, Arnie?"

"That look you have. It wasn't anybody really. You think I was rude, don't you?"

"Not really. No more than you were to the man who wanted Dante."

"That was different. Besides, I guess I'll have to tell you. That wasn't anybody on the phone. I mean it wasn't anyone important, you know? I mean, Florence is my mother's name. I call her that when she makes me mad. It makes her mad too. Then I can hang up like I did."

"I see."

"Claire?"

"Yes, Arnie?"

"I enjoyed telling you about Dante. I could see by your eyes that you can understand. I never asked you what you like to read."

"Oh, that's okay. I don't read much anymore. I don't have time, really."

"What do you do with your time, I mean, when you're away from here?"

"Oh, lots of things and not much of anything. I play with machines. Television sets and radios and tape recorders, things like that. I take them apart to see how they work, and then I put them back together again."

"I didn't know you did these things."

"Yes, well, that's what I was trained for. I have a degree in electrical engineering."

"Oh . . . you must be very good at it. The next time my telephone breaks down, I'll know who to call."

"You do that, Arnie. I'll explain to you how telephones really work sometime. Say, Arnie, I don't mean to pry into your private life, but I was wondering what you were doing this weekend. You see, the ballet's in town. My roommate got tickets, but now she's not going to go. I was wondering if you'd like to come with me?"

"Thanks, Claire. That's very nice of you to ask. But the Knicks are in town, and I have dates for both the Friday and Saturday night games."

"Some other time, then, Arnie.'

"Sure. Some other time."

I knew the Knicks were in town, and that Arnie would be their prisoner all weekend. Watching a basketball game must be something like working in a library, because of that same feeling of being trapped with no way to get out and the feeling that your space is getting smaller all the time. I knew Arnie had lied about the dates, but I couldn't say so. Besides, it wasn't really a lie on his part, when I think about it. I knew that he intended to have dates and that for him intention was the same thing as fact. I knew that he would be calling all weekend.

"Hello. Is this Patricia Schumacher?"

"Yes. Who is this?"

"That's not important, my succulent maid. What's important is that we've finally connected. Our eyes have made contact in the world of blindmen, and I do somersaults over you. I ate chili today and I thought of you. The palpitation in my pulse was the same. Imagine my fingers by candlelight, flickering and fluttering like a butterfly, undoing your bra, unravelling the perfumed secrets of your body like a ball of string. Imagine . . ."

"Hold it. Who are you? Did you just escape from somewhere? Do you need help of some kind? I know, you're going to kill yourself and you thought you'd call a complete stranger. Listen, I can get a number of a priest or something . . .?"

"Patricia! I need only you. Think of it. Soft lights. Italian music. A fireplace. Our arms entwined, drinking each other's wine. Closing our eyes to make a wish. Hurling our glasses into the fireplace. Smouldering in each other's breath."

"Look, just where exactly did we meet, mister?"

"Our paths were star-crossed, my sweet. We were fated to meet. I was shopping for the chili in aisle three at the grocery store. You were getting eggs in aisle eight. I saw you in the store mirror. I saw you putting extra large eggs in the container for small eggs. I don't blame you, with prices climbing like they are. But in the mirror like that. Like a vision. You were there and yet you weren't really there. I thought about it as I felt it. Beautiful. I turned it around in my stomach. I waited by the candy bars for you to go through the check-out line. I went behind you. Boy, was I glad you paid by check. When the checker took my money, I peeked at your name on the check. It was fate, I tell you."

"God, why me? Why do you freaks think you can just call a woman and pester her like this? I hope you weren't calling to see if I was all alone or something. I really hope not, because if you dare come here, I'll have several people waiting to beat you up."

"But that wasn't it at all. Please, Patricia, I'm really not that way. I just thought if we could talk, you know, just talk . . . I wasn't asking you to do anything, really. If we found that we could talk together, then maybe next week or even next month if you weren't too busy, well, maybe we could take a walk or something . . ."

"You know where you can walk, you clod. Don't bother to call again, because I'll have the number changed tomorrow."

"Please, Pa . . ."

". . . click . . ."

Arnie must have had a miserable weekend. The Knicks lost both their games. Arnie must have begun choosing his women at random. He must have closed his eyes, opening the phone book to wherever it opened and letting his fingers guide him to his choice. Knowing Arnie, I imagine it must have pleased him a great deal. It was like letting fate do his calling for him. He didn't even have to think about it. He was in complete control, and yet the thing was completely out of his hands. No more store mirrors. No more eye contact. Arnie 's fingers walked blindly, guided by a higher impulse.

"Hello. Is this Miss Ophelia Wampler?"

"No it ain't. Just a minute. Hey, Phele, the phone . . ."

"Yeah . . .?"

"Yes, hello. Is this Miss Ophelia Wampler?"

"It's Mrs., honey."

"Oh. I'm sorry."

"Ain't no need. It's my fault."

"Yes, well, you don't know me, but I feel like I know you. Do you know what I mean?"

"Crazy . . ."

"It's like . . . it's like when you read a book and you feel like you know the people in the book. And then when you see people outside of the book, they're not really that much different from those inside. Now do you see?"

"Man, you sure do talk funny. You from outtatown?"

"Sometimes I think I'm from a book, Ophelia.'

"Shit. Say, you on something?"

"I don't understand."

"I mean, you going up or coming down?"

"I still don't understand, my dear. Maybe I haven't explained myself very well. Shall I try again?"

"Why not? I got time."

"As I was saying, it's like a book. Your name's Ophelia, right? Right. Well, I picked your name by chance in the book, you know? But then I knew it wasn't really chance, if that makes any sense. You see, your name's Ophelia, and I've read all about you somewhere, you know?"

"What is this shit? Who's been keeping book on me?"

"I don't understand. It's a good book. Filled with beautiful poetry. *Hamlet?*"

"Don't know him. He an outtatown dude too?"

"I guess it doesn't matter. What matters is that we talk. We communicate. We're strangers, and yet we're talking together. I could be calling from two-thousand miles away or from twenty years ago in your past, and it doesn't matter, because this telephone has linked us. We're talking."

"Jive. Real jive."

"Ophelia, I was wondering if you were busy tonight. I'm a little lonely. Maybe we could go for a coke somewhere . . .?"

"Yes and no."

"What do you mean?"

"Honey, it's like this. I ain't exactly busy. But I ain't going for no coke with you neither. Know why?"

"I'm sorry. I don't."

"Like I said. I ain't exactly busy. But you don't sound like the right color to me. You dig?"

"Are you . . ."

". . . click . . ."

I cried for Arnie Kandinsky that night. I knew that he couldn't hear me. But I also knew that my crying would change his life. He had touched me. He was there and not really there. He was right about Dante, I thought as I felt.

"Good morning, Arnie. How was your weekend?"

"I'm too busy to talk about it right now."

"It must have been a good one. It's not like you to come in town hours late for work."

"Please, Claire . . ."

"I'm sorry. I didn't mean to pry. When I saw you weren't here, I went ahead and took all the copies of the *Inferno* off the shelves for you.'

"You didn't need to bother. It really doesn't matter anymore. Dante should have had better sense. He should have known that it would come down to this . . . this library, these people, these walls. He should have burned it when he finished.'

"Arnie, if I can do . . "

"Nothing. Nothing to be done, thanks. I need to be alone for awhile. I wonder if you could take care of the desk for me?"

"Sure, Arnie. Go ahead. Oh, Arnie?"

"Yes?"

"Your mother called."

Sometimes it takes the unexpected to bring two people together. Often, the unexpected comes from the most trivial of incidents, the most mundane of circumstances. I had almost given up on Arnie when I came to work one morning and found Arnie already there.

"Arnie, how come you're here already? Did you sleep here last night?"

"I had some work to catch up on."

He was nervous about something. Then I noticed that he had all the newspapers behind the desk with him. How could it be, I wondered, that Arnie would hoard the common newspaper in the same way that he used to hoard Dante? Something in me already knew. I stooped over his shoulder to see what he was reading. Arnie's hand went down on the paper immediately. Next to the hand I could see the headline: MAYOR VOWS CRACKDOWN ON ILLEGAL WIRETAPS IN CITY.

"Please, Claire . . ."

"There's the phone, Arnie. You'd better answer it."

As he walked to the phone, I could see the headline that his hand had covered: SUBWAY BANDIT CLAIMS THIRTEENTH VICTIM; POLICE BAFFLED. I suddenly felt as though I had overslept. I put my hands in my pockets to make sure the holes were still there. Suppressing a yawn, I ran my fingers back and forth across my lips. They were chapped.

"Who was it?"

"A bitch."

"Arnie!"

"It was only Florence."

It is not surprising when the New York City Police are baffled. It's part of their training. They seem to consider the media in the same way that they view the criminal at large: with a kind of swooping dragnet suspicion. They may be one lead away from apprehending the criminal, and yet they will still tell the newspapers that they are baffled.

I began to look at Arnie anew. It had taken me six months to wade through the camouflage. Without the element of surprise, it might have taken six years. A good detective doesn't mind. Patience will win out over pressure every time. I decided to test Arnie by confronting him directly.

"Say, Arnie, have you read about this mysterious subway kissing bandit?"
"No."
"You haven't, really?"
"If it's not on the sports page, I don't read it."
"Well, in a way, I guess it rivals anything on the sports page."
"What does it say?"
"It seems there've been, let's see now, yes, there's been fifteen, counting the one yesterday."
"Fifteen?"
"Yes, fifteen women who've been 'assaulted' on the subway by this mysterious man. The police say it's assault, but none of the women use that word. This man, they say he's about five-five, about your height, Arnie. He sneaks up and kisses these women right smack on the mouth. Apparently, he only 'strikes' when the cars are stopped at a station. After kissing them, he runs out of the car and out of the station. Most of the women were so shocked that they weren't able to give the police an accurate description of him."
"What else does it say?"
"You're curious, Arnie?"
"I'm only interested because you seem to be interested, Claire."
"That's sweet of you to say. Well, apparently the police are going to plant some plain-clothes detectives in the cars. And they're going to plant several young policewomen too. They hope that the criminal will make a mistake and try one of them."
"Do you think he's a criminal, Claire?"
"I think the whole thing is rather romantic. I wonder what I'd do if he came up to me."
"Oh, you don't have to worry about that, Claire."
"You mean I'm not pretty enough?"
"No, it's not that. I mean . . . working here in the library and all . . ."
"I won't be working here all my life."

Arnie continued to read the newspapers, charge overdue fines and deny patrons the books they wanted. Nothing seemed to animate him anymore, nothing except the continuing conquests of the subway kissing bandit. He thought my interest in the case a little perverse. I tried to get him to talk about the psychology of such a person. Was he an orphan? Was he maladjusted? Did he hate women? Why the subway? I suggested at one point that the kissing bandit was a little more colorful and slightly less dangerous than most psychotics, but that he was, nevertheless, a rapist at heart. Arnie wouldn't speak to me for three days. The victim count had reached twenty-five.

"Arnie, I had an idea the other day. The police are still baffled with this subway kissing bandit. Maybe they don't think it's important enough to bother with. But it seems to me that it's the perfect case for a couple of amateur detectives, you know? I mean, after work, you and I could ride the subway, roam through the cars, be on the lookout for him . . ."

"I never ride the subway."

"How do you get to work and back?"

"I walk or I hitch."

"Arnie, nobody hitches in New York. Well, anyway, everything's tailor-made. It's just like you said about Beatrice in Dante. There but not really there. I mean, a woman is suddenly kissed. The man disappears, and she's left wondering whether she was ever kissed or not. It's a game of disguises, false appearances, illusions, magic. The subway has always been so bare, so cruel, so impersonal. Statues riding on their pedestals, dangling on their poles, hardening on their hind ends. Now it's like a masquerade ball. I love disguises. Arnie? It would be so much fun."

"I never ride the subway."

We were like two beta fish staring at each other, waiting for some invisible knuckle to tap the glass of our aquarium, a signal for the fight to the death. Arnie trusted me, but he trusted my distance more. He lied. I knew that he had lied. He had never hitched in his life. The only thing Arnie Kandinsky had ever curled his thumb around was a telephone. The victim count had reached twenty-nine.

I decided to follow Arnie whenever he went out. He counted on not being followed, on remaining anonymous, on meeting his victims without their ever meeting him. He counted on my having to stay behind in the library. But what are cheap thrillers when compared with a real-life adventure? I decided to close the library after him every time he left. Let the overdue fines pile up. How could Dante ever compete with a headline? Purgatory was out in the streets.

I saw Arnie get his thirtieth. It happened in the noon-hour rush at Grand Central. There were some fifteen people rushing out the door between Arnie and me, but I alone knew what to look for. Fifteen baffled witnesses could not answer to what they had seen. His victim was a young secretary-type, obviously not born in the city. She still had a clean and wholesome look, the kind of face that would be perfect as the young housewife in a bread commercial. She was one of the million naive minnows from somewhere like Kalamazoo, Michigan, or Great Bend, Kansas. She had swum upstream to see the lights on Broadway and had gotten stuck higher up, probably on the forty-second floor of some nearby office building, stuck with typing letters to herself. I would love to read such a woman's diary.

Arnie gently but firmly swung her around from behind. He pulled her shoulders down and kissed her full on the lips. Kissed, then recoiled. Like a piliated woodpecker pecks, Arnie kissed his thirtieth. I was a little afraid that he would conk her on the forehead with his head and that she would suffer a concussion from his kiss. She only dropped her packages. She went limp and dropped her noon-hour shopping.

While others stooped to pick them up, from irritation at the traffic jam she had created more than from any genuine sympathy for her, she and I watched Arnie bore his way through the crowd and into the safety of the overpopulated streets. I knocked two widows down trying to get out myself. I stopped on the platform long enough to brush against the victim.

She was putting on lipstick. A sudden impulse took hold of me. I reached around and touched her breast. I tried to make it look as if I were just trying to get around her. How could she suspect me after what had happened? I could see my hand like some fleeting poltergeist from the underworld, there but not really there, flicker briefly in her compact mirror. Her image of herself would never be the same. My hand would always be in that mirror, I thought as I felt.

I had to take a taxi to beat Arnie back to the library. I felt alive and wonderful. I too was a fugitive from justice. After all, I had touched her breast. That was more than Arnie had dared to do. My cheeks were flushed, and there was no sun to be seen in New York. Does embarrassment stem from guilt or from courage that was never there before? Does blushing have anything to do with a temporary hormonal imbalance? I would have to avoid Arnie for the rest of the day. I had had an orgasm.

"Claire, There's a copy of the *Inferno* missing."
"What do you mean?"
"Just what I said. It's missing. I haven't checked them for some time now. But this morning I checked. There were only eight copies. There should be nine. I checked the files. It's not checked out to anyone. I looked through all the stacks. It's not misplaced. It's missing. It's gone. Disappeared. It's . . . it's stolen!"
"Catch your breath, Arnie. I'm sure it'll turn up. Who would want to steal it?"
"Claire!"
"You know what I mean."
"I'm just afraid that someone will think it was me. I don't want to be accused of something I didn't do."
"I'll vouch for you if anybody asks."
"Thanks, Claire. You're always so kind to me. I hope sometime I can return the favor."
"I'll let you know."

I took my vacation a few days before Easter. The subway kissing bandit was no longer a phantom in New York's collective unconscious. A composite drawing, based on the descriptions of thirty-two victims, had appeared in all the papers. It wasn't a very good likeness of Arnie. The lines on the face were too rigid, the look in the eyes too intense, the smile on the little lips too diabolical. Arnie's features were much more bleached, much more subtle than that.

There was danger now. The danger was not so much in Arnie's chances of apprehension but in the possibility, no, probability of multiplication. As long as the newspaper accounts were verbal, there was no danger. Most people haven't the imagination to see through words. But the drawing was the first visual clue. Arnie's would-be imitators would now begin to daydream more openly. All the mole-men in New York would see the picture. It would strike the right chord of guilt or courage in them. They would think of becoming the subway kissing bandit. Meanwhile, the police were still officially baffled.

I went to stay with my sister during the week's vacation. The change of residence was like a change of personality for me. I walked by the library and I smiled, because I knew a wallflower woman named Claire who worked there. I took the subway and I smiled, because I knew a little make-believe man named Arnie took the same subway. New York became as tiny and fragile and intimate as a bedroom closet. I showed my teeth to everyone who had the imagination to see me pass by. My machines were all unplugged back in my apartment.

It was Good Friday night when I left the egg-skillet gray of the New York sky and went down in the subway. It came as no surprise to me that Arnie got in the same car I did. He looked like a different man. He hadn't shaved for several days. There was the wild half-way look of a man without sleep in his eyes. He looked to be on welfare. He was no longer the well-kept slide-rule checker I knew from the library. His pants were unzipped. He moved his hands anxiously inside his pockets. The white of his underpants moved with them.

I saw Arnie go for his thirty-third victim near the stop for Time Square.

She was a tall thin girl. She looked like a detective with her sunglasses on in the false evening light of the subway. The collar of her overcoat was turned up, as if she were hiding from someone. Her tousled hair was wheat-field yellow, the color of egg yolks when they first come out of their shell. She was holding a little piece of paper in her hand. She wasn't one of Arnie's typical victims.

More mysterious than beautiful, more well-dressed than well-built, more Beatrice than Elizabeth Taylor, she sat hunched forward near the door, expectant like a question mark. The male voice with the muffled tone like that of a film shown too many times or like that of a man with mashed potatoes in his mouth began to say "Time." And before he had said "Square", Arnie was moving toward the coat-hanger woman with the lightbulb hair.

The cars were coming to their electrified stop. The doors were opening. The woman was getting up, snapping backwards like a wishbone, her body now a beanstalk for Jack the Ripper to climb. Arnie waited until she turned. From behind he reached up with both hands and grabbed the sawed-off branches of her shoulders. Then it happened. Her elbows shot back and into his stomach. Arnie's whole body snapped. He doubled over on the floor, his arms receding, shrinking, shooting back into his body like the tentacles of an octopus who survives through camouflage. He began to retch. As others walked around him, I could see from the platform that Arnie held a piece of paper in his hand.

"Hello. Is this Murrayhill 33933?"
"Yes. who would you like to speak with?"
"I don't know exactly. A tall woman with golden hair?"
"Golden hair? Oh, yes, you must mean my sister. Just a minute, I'll get her. Her name is Tris."
"Hello. This is Tris."
"Yes, well, you don't know me. I didn't know if I should call or not. I'm not in the habit of making calls like this, you see?"

"I'm sorry. Who is this?"

"Like I said, you don't know me, Tris. My name is . . . Arnie. Arnie Kandinsky."

"Hello, Arnie. I'm afraid I'm still confused."

"You were in the subway last night. It was near Time Square. You dropped a piece of paper. I was outside on the platform waiting to get on. I picked up the paper. This phone number was on it."

"I see. So. It was very kind of you to call like that."

"Tris, could I ask why you had your own phone number written on that paper?"

"Oh that. I have a terrible memory for numbers. You see, I'm staying with my sister this weekend. I'm not from the city, and I had her number written down in case I got lost somewhere."

"How long will you be here?"

"Just this weekend, I'm afraid. There's so much to see, and I'm afraid that I haven't really seen a thing."

"I hope you won't think I'm being too forward. But I have some time this weekend, and if I could show you around . . .?"

"That's sweet, Arnie. I don't know. I don't really know you . . ."

"I know. If you'd rather not . . ."

"Wait. There's a masquerade ball tonight. I'm invited. I hadn't planned to go, because everyone there will most likely be with someone else. Yes. It would be fun if we could go together. You seem nice enough."

"Thank you, Tris. I hope I won't disappoint you. What time shall I come for you? Where do I go? What shall I wear?"

"Too many questions. Let's see. I'll meet you at eight at the Time Square stop."

"How will I know you if you're wearing a disguise?"

"That's a problem. I haven't really decided who I'll come as. I tell you what, I'll find you. What will you be wearing?"

"I haven't got any costumes. Wait. I know. At my mother's house. There's a clown's mask my father used to wear and some funny clothes too. I can go get them."

"So I'll be looking for a clown. Not a sad one, I hope. Say, you won't feel too funny waiting in your costume like that? I mean, other people will probably give you some pretty strange looks."

"I'm used to it. I'll see you at eight."

Time Square on Easter Eve is amazingly different from Time Square on any other night. At Easter time, New York becomes a ghost town. Everyone stays at home, and Time Square becomes an empty and pallid yellow reflection of some crater on the moon. And because there is this moon at Easter, the ocean seems to swell off Long Island and threaten to deluge the world's biggest city. The skyscrapers look so vulnerable, like sand castles waiting for the waves. Like petrified trees, and the taller they are, the more breakable they look when there are no people around. I imagine New York as the toy construction of a ten-year-old boy's rector set. The subway hollows out like a gaping wound. It becomes a mysterious warp in time, a safe passage back to the womb.

"Claire. Is that you, Claire?"

"Arnie?"

"Yes, it's me. Just a minute. Let me take this mask off."

"But why on earth? Why are you dressed up like that?"

"I'm meeting someone. We're going to a masquerade ball."

"I read someplace that the Knicks were in town. I would have thought you'd be going to their games."

"Yes, well, I haven't really kept up with them lately."

"I see. Well, it's certainly a change to see you like this."

"And what are you doing downtown on a night like this? I figured you'd be on the beaches in the Bahamas somewhere."

"It would be nice. But I don't like to take trips by myself."

"But what are you doing downtown? The stores are all closed, aren't they?"

"You know, I see myself superimposed on the clothes and the china and the mannequins. It's like magic. Like a bad photograph that somehow turns out to be a miracle. I merge with everything I see."

"I haven't ever felt that. Have you been walking long?"

"Not really. I'm going to walk until midnight, though."

"Claire! Aren't you afraid to walk at night like this? I mean, all alone. It's dangerous."

"Do you really think so? I have the impression that the few people who are out don't even notice me."

"Even so . . ."

"I don't think there's any problem. You could walk with me and protect me if you'd like, Arnie."

"I'd like to, Claire, but I'm waiting for someone. I couldn't just leave."

"At midnight I'm going over to the cathedral and listen to the choir at midnight mass."

"Yes, well, as you can see, I'm not really dressed for church."

"I don't think anyone would even notice. Please come with me, Arnie. There's so much we could talk about. We could be each other's guide through the big city. We could have so much fun."

"I'd like that, but I really couldn't . . ."

"Please, Arnie. I feel so cozy next to you. We can talk. We can communicate. I've wanted to ask you for a long time to take a walk with me."

"Claire, you're a good kid. And I feel like I can trust you. So I'll tell you. I've met this woman. She's wonderful. So exciting and mysterious. So worldly-wise and yet so spiritual, like a dream that has a body. She's coming here to meet me."

"It sounds romantic."

"It is. It's funny, but I don't even know what she'll look like when she comes. She'll be in disguise."

"It's getting cold, Arnie. Would you put your arm around me?"

"Oh, Claire. I really couldn't. What would she think if she saw us?"

"Arnie . . ."

"Claire, you're a very nice person. I like you, but it's just that. She should be here any minute, and . . . would you be terribly angry, Claire, if I just sat here by myself and waited for her? I'm a little nervous. You understand?"

"Sure, Arnie, sure. I'll be leaving you alone now. Besides, I have a lot of walking to do before midnight."

"Thanks, Claire. You're a real pal. Be careful and don't let that subway kissing bandit get you."

"I won't."

"I'll see you again Monday morning?"

"Sure."

I left Arnie Kandinsky, the carnival clown, sitting alone on the platform at the Time Square stop. I left time frozen with him, as a widow comes out of mourning. I left him sitting there with the most visible mask he had ever shown the world, sitting there poking his fingers through the eye holes of his mask, as if he were dialing one last telephone number, sitting there in the underground, while the neon signs like magic tribal campfires danced incestuously in the empty streets above his head, danced like doves on fire above his head. Arnie was one of the chosen ones, and he would never know it. I left him sitting there, waiting nervously for his thirty-third victim to arrive in disguise. She had come willingly, there and not really there, and she would never come again.

I had lost and I had won. I understood Dante without thinking, without feeling, intuitively. No effort at all was the only valid effort possible. I rode the subway to the end of the line. The cars stayed empty where they stopped for a full twenty minutes. I had this awesome sense of power, knowing that New York subway time would never be the same again.

I put on Tris to seduce the conductor, knowing that Claire could never have done it by herself. He believed in the face of the impostor. He believed in her body with all its false connections, all its misplaced parts, all its wired strings. And he believed in her insanity, as all men must. He pawed her hair with mechanical fingers. He pounced quickly on her little mouth, as if he were guzzling a beer. Pounced as rabbits sit back on their haunches, then pounce. It thrilled him when he pulled up her sweater and saw that she was not wearing a bra. It didn't matter that her breasts were small and unused to the light. He grabbed them anyway, as children grab the handle bars of a new bicycle, as adults who return from abroad scurry to devour their first ice cream cone. There were pimples on her breast from the cold. It pained him that time was passing, while he stood still, and so he hurried himself, shaking her like a doll. She could hear the rattle of coins in the change purse under the belt he wouldn't take off, as he continued to poke her senselessly in this pantomime of dressed sex. And when he had finished, he was ashamed.

I was ecstatic. The rag doll had come to life. I had merged with Tris. Thirty-two more to go.

"At Time Square you will see a little man dressed in a clown's costume. He will be sitting on the platform. You will go out and give him this."
"But, lady, it's against the rules."
"The rules! You will do as I say, won't you?"
"Yes, mam."

The message that read "Vergil couldn't make it. You'll have to go to hell alone tonight." Would be delivered in disguise. Tris and I got off at the end of the line. I realized that I had not lied to Arnie. This really was going to be my last night in New York City. I realized that I had not lost Arnie to Tris but to Florence. I had won Tris to myself. We were twelve years old again, a tomboy and a woman, making love to New York's empty streets.

At midnight, I went as Tris to the masquerade ball. The cathedral was crowded. While everyone else watched the senile, sexless man on the altar, I watched the twenty-two choir boys up in the loft. They must have been twelve years old too. Their voices were the voices of angels, girl angels. And men call it falsetto. I knew that one year from now most of them would have lost those voices, would feel ashamed at the memory of having been girls when they were twelve. In my mind, I seduced them all, every little hairless penis. I gave them permission to keep their voices. The offertory came with the bells. The old man at the altar turned around slowly, the cue for the collection. The signal for all those who were not of the faith to depart before the magic began.

I could hear the coins rattle. They were far more real than communion wafers, those thin slivers of forgiveness to be swallowed whole without touching the teeth. I knew in an instant what my offering would be. I got up and waited for the ushers at the back of the church. When they got there, I put the *Inferno* into their Easter basket. I wondered if the Vatican could afford the fine. I smiled at the ushers and told them that it was a message for the old man in clown's costume, sitting up there on the altar.

I took my tap off Arnie's phone before leaving the city. I didn't need it anymore. It was Easter Sunday. The sun was shining on all the manhole covers in the city.

The Kleptomaniac

4:15 p.m. Visiting hours over, even for policemen. Girl named Candy, last person to see the suspect. Missing persons always suspect. Check again with suspect's mother. Why avoided subject of girl in preliminary questioning? Girl obviously suffering from malnutrition. Compounded by drug dose. Brought on by suspect's disappearance? Or perhaps one of causes of suspect's disappearance? Check suspect's apartment for more drugs. Lab men may have overlooked. Poor girl hysterical. In state of shock. Doctor says she feels no pain. Ironic when she obviously feels so much pain. Check back with doctor. Girl no help. Mumbled something about a pair of shoes and a ticket. A ticket and a pair of shoes. Check suspect's apartment.

Inspector Crowder from the Bureau of Missing Persons finished writing in his notebook and stuffed it back into the inside chest pocket of his trenchcoat. The rain still had not let up, Crowder saw, as he ran out of Mercy General Hospital and into the parking lot to his double-parked Chevrolet. When he reached the car, he was drenched. His shoes squeaked. Water squirted up over the sides, as toothpaste slithers out of its tube. Crowder gritted his teeth, Bogart-fashion. He had not rolled up the windows. Damp pants always gave him headaches. The driver's seat guffawed like a frog's croak as he sat down. He slammed the door behind him. He had to open it again. Part of his trenchcoat had gotten caught in the door. He turned on the engine as one turns the doorknob of a locked door. He looked up. A little white piece of paper, waterlogged, whirled in a semi-circle, wrapped around the windshield wiper. A ticket. Double-parking in an emergency zone. It was embarrassing for one policeman to get a ticket from another. No wonder people disappeared.

A man had disappeared, as usual, without a trace. Crowder's job was to find first the trace, then the motive, then the scent, then the footsteps, then the whole man. The man's name was Kane. This time it was Kane. What difference did his name make, if that was all that was left of him? It was like an epitaph, letters on a tombstone. A missing person is a dead person to those who knew him, missed him, asked for an outsider, a complete stranger preferably, to step in and find him. Make him reappear like magic. Change the wine to blood again. A missing person is not like a dead person. The living always manage to forget the dead, sometimes before decomposition. But a missing person doesn't decompose, not even in the memory that tricks itself into thinking he does. The more he's missing, the more he's remembered, like an empty bottle in an alcoholic's mind. There's not just the forgetting, there's also the forgiveness to think about. The outraged survivors demand to know why he just disappeared, as if he's never been born. They need to know why before they forget. Not once, but a hundred-thousand times, they need to be told. Perhaps that's why there are divorce courts. Perhaps the missing person knows all of this when he magically displays his hide without seek. Too many people always wanting to know why. Too many questions. Missing is maybe the only way left to be alone. So simple not to make the call, not to write the note, to just vanish as drowning persons sink beneath the soundless waves. Then all the questions are transferred from him to those who remain behind.

A stop sign. Crowder went half-way through the intersection before he saw it. His mind was not on the common traffic signs that other people follow. Fortunately, he was a plainclothesman in an unmarked car. He thought of the ticket.

A ticket and a pair of shoes. Mumbling, hocus-pocus mumbo-jumbo, slobber sounds a baby makes. Was it just to throw him off the track? Was it language posing for the truth, refusing as ever to take the lie-detector test? Or did it mean the girl named Candy knew that Kane was leaving? Leaving her behind to shriek to the doctors. If so, the shoes would probably be gone and the ticket used up. It wasn't likely. A man who disappears doesn't confess before the act, unless he wants to be followed, unless he's begging to be found. Sometimes a missing person is as much an exhibitionist as the rapist and drunks, the kidnappers and indecent exposures. Crowder had once followed a labyrinth of clues, laid out neatly like new linen, only to find the suspect waiting for him when the clues disappeared. "Took you long enough," the suspect had said. Once he had followed a man, only to find that the man was following him. He had only to turn around to solve the case. Crowder suspected that Kane was different. He had vanished so quietly, as if he thought that no one would miss him anyway. If it hadn't been for the girl's screaming, his disappearance might still be a secret. Crowder could go no further. He had come to the end of a dead-end street.

He turned off the engine and walked up the driveway to the suspect's apartment. The Bureau Chief always changed the word "suspect" to "missing person" when Crowder filed his reports. Crowder couldn't help himself. He was a creature of habit. A missing man was always suspect, unless proven otherwise when he was found. A a child, Crowder had always believed in ghosts, spirits that occupied the same space but who were centuries apart in time, spirits whose voices called him out of the dead of sleep, laughter singing "Lazarus" in the middle of the night. Of course, no one else would believe that a thirty-five-year-old man in his right mind could still believe in such childhood nonsense. But Crowder was convinced that missing persons were poltergeists, making saucers break in the kitchen, making windows open and shut, making the hot water faucet drip in the bathroom. He pulled out the key to Kane's apartment. He thought he heard the door slam twice behind him.

The apartment had not visibly changed. Kane's brown corduroy coat with the patches on the sleeves was still draped over the chair near the unmade bed. Crowder had already tried it on for size, but the sleeves were too short. The faded print of Van Gogh's self-portrait still hung crookedly over the bed. The bare lightbulb still dangled on a cord from the ceiling. The drawer to the nightstand next to the bed was still half-opened. Inside was the same jar of Vaseline with the missing lid. The lab men had checked. It was definitely Vaseline. The same grape juice stains were there on the dirty beige carpet. The lab men had checked. It was definitely grape juice, spilled all over the room on the carpet by the girl named Candy, whose blue-denim sailor's blouse had also been stained with the grape juice. Not with wine nor with blood.

A hand-written poem still clung by scotch tape to one corner of the cracked mirror above the writing table opposite the bed. In the lower right-hand corner of the mirror were two pictures, curled perhaps in self-defense, shriveled up with age. One was of the man named Kane, taken when he was approximately seven years old. Holes had been poked through where the eyes should have been, and a moustache had been penciled in. The other picture was of the girl named Candy. She was stretched out completely naked on a bed, one hand holding a cigarette in her mouth, the index finger of the other hand pointing down to the mound of pubic hair, the thighs spread-eagled, gigantic compared to the far-away face, stretching out to the sides of the picture, stopping just beneath the knees, as if the girl were an amputee. Between the legs was an inscription: "Come home to me soon. Here I am." Obviously written when Kane was still in Vietnam. Had he brought it back with him? Or had she never sent it?

Crowder felt dizzy from the poor ventilation in the room. He quickly stared again at the poem. Word-riddles. He tore the poem from the cracked mirror and put it in his pocket. Perhaps there was some clue in the poem. Then he walked to the closet.

Whereas the room was barren, austere, void of any objects of interest, the closet was cluttered beyond recognition. It was like a boys' and mens' clothing store. The clothes were of all sizes, styles and colors: from white shirts and knickers to fit a boy of five to coats of cashmere, suede and leather to fit a man of twenty-five. There was even a high-school football uniform. It appeared that Kane had never discarded a single piece of clothing, from the time of his birth to the time of his disappearance. In the whole apartment, these clothes were the only visible betrayal of Kane's family wealth. Why had he chosen this apartment, these surroundings, this austere, impoverished pauper's existence? And why had he kept all these clothes? The lab men had gone through all the pockets and had come up with enough small change and bubble gum and ball point pens and decks of cards and rubber bands and safety pins and fossilized candy bars to fill a laundry basket, supplied by the landlord's wife. Crowder had to remove six inches worth of hanging clothes in order to get at the shoe pile on the floor of the closet. What amazed him was that there were almost as many pairs of shoes as there were pieces of clothing. There were shoes of all sizes, styles and colors: saddle bucks, wing-tips, loafers, slippers, sandals, climbing boots, combat boots, and tennis shoes, ranging from size six to size thirteen. There were also several pairs of ladies' high heels. Crowder could not imagine the young Candy wearing any of them. At the bottom of the pile, Crowder found an old shoe box. Inside there were two books: a book of nursery rhymes with a shoe horn stuck in the middle and a book of philosophy, Oriental by the cover, with a ticket stub stuck in the middle. A ticket and a pair of shoes.

7:30 p.m.: Returned the book of nursery rhymes and the book of philosophy to the Branch Library where they had been overdue for eight years. Spent one hour and twenty minutes explaining to the librarian that I was not the one who took the books. That I should not have to pay eight years of overdue fines. Wouldn't it be simpler just to buy new copies of the books? Not the point, I was told. Took my name and address for further reference. Went to Gordon's Archway Shoe Shop with ticket stub. Gordon Senior dead. Gordon Son as furious as the librarian. Ticket stub from 1946. Had to go home to get his books for 1946. Ticket stub for World War Two combat boots in name of Kane Senior. Never reclaimed. No knowledge of what happened to the boots. Further fury from Gordon Son, suspecting that I would demand repayment for the boots. I laid his mind to rest. Only Gordon Senior would know where boots were. Gordon Senior dead. Dead-end. Stopped at station, Traffic Division, already closed. Check name of patrolman on ticket. Call Mrs. Kane. Check tomorrow at Bureau of MP's to see who has literature background. Get Kane's poem interpreted.

Crowder noticed that only one of his headlights was working, as he drove to the house of Mrs. Emily Kane. He had called her to give his report. She had insisted that he give it in person. She did not like telephones. There had been no telephone in Kane's apartment, Crowder remembered. Like mother, like son? The picture was never that simple. The picture was, if anything, double- or triple-exposed.

There were no current photographs anywhere of the suspect. The descriptions of the tenants next door and those of the landlord differed so radically that a composite for an APB was impossible. The tenants remembered Kane as a gaunt, emaciated Christ-figure with long flowing hair. The land-lord remembered him as medium height, a little stocky, balding prematurely, shabbily but conservatively dressed. The only point on which they concurred was the brown corduroy coat. Neither the landlord nor the tenants have ever seen Kane wearing anything else. A composite picture was impossible. Mrs. Kane had not seen her son for four years. He had steadfastly refused to see her since his return from Vietnam. She had not even known his apartment address before the disappearance. On finding out, she still refused to go and see it. The only communication between them, since he also refused to write letters, had been phone calls, always made by him to her. She had never known where he was calling from. The only person who could give an accurate description of the suspect was the girl named Candy, bleached-blond boyish haircut, pretzel-stick body, aged eighteen, hysterically mumbling on Ward Six of Mercy General Hospital. A girl named Candy and a man named Kane, the names like some ludicrous fairy tale from the Brothers Grimm, were all Crowder had to go on. And a pair of combat boots that were never reclaimed and so disappeared.

"What is your first name, Mr. Crowder?"
"Art. It's Art, mam."
"Arthur then. My name is Emily, not 'mam.' I insist that we call each other by our first names. Tea?"
"Yes, please. One lump."

The curtains were all drawn in the sitting room. Three candles alone on top of the piano kept the house from extinction of total darkness. The color of the sofa, the kind of flowers in the vase, the texture of the table, all were uncertain in this room full of shadows. Emily Kane obviously disliked the light. Crowder could hear them moving about in the room. The Kane house was filled with ghosts. Crowder regretted not giving his report over the phone.

"Do you find me sexually attractive, Arthur?"

112

"I beg your pardon, mam?"

She had returned from the darkness to the table in front of him. She was wearing high-heels and a loosened robe over a filmy nightgown. She had asked the question as she bent forward to set the serving tray on the table.

"One lump, right?"
"Yes, thank you."

She retreated to a chair near the piano.

"I'm afraid that I haven't much to report."
"Why is that, Arthur?"
"I don't know exactly. I've been to see the girl at the hospital. I've been to the apartment twice today. I found a poem and an old shoe box with some overdue books with a shoe horn for a book marker and a ticket stub from a long time ago for a shoe store and I . . ."
"Arthur, I'm afraid I haven't followed you."
"Excuse me. It doesn't really matter. I've just been everywhere and have nothing to show for it."
"Poor man. But surely you'll detect something very soon. You seem to be a very conscientious detective. I'm sure you'll find my son."
"I thought so too, at first. But I'm not so sure anymore. I keep feeling like there's something missing, some vital piece of seemingly insignificant information that would help me find out where he's gone."
"What kind of information, Arthur? How's your tea?"
"Fine, thank you. What was I saying? Oh. Information to help me feel like I know the man I'm looking for. It always helps, you know. But I know nothing about him. I don't know his likes and dislikes, his temperament, his habits, his faults. I don't even know what he looks like. You haven't seen him for four years. And the landlord and tenants, well, it's as if they've seen two different men. The only link is the girl, and she's in no condition to talk. I don't even know what your son's first name is."
"He hated it. He always called himself by his last name."
"Yes, well, you see, uh Emily, there uh just aren't enough facts. I feel a little like it's uh like a game, you know, where I'm it, and I'm supposed to be kept uh in the dark as long as possible, almost like the information, the facts I really need to know, are uh being kept a secret on purpose."
"Arthur, you know if I can be of any help . . ."
"Yes, well I think you can. What I'd like to do is go back to the beginning. If you could just answer a few factual questions, maybe I can get some kind of feeling for your son. You see, I need to know him as well as you do. I need to be able to step into his shoes, to think like him, to feel like him, in order to know where I would disappear to if I were him."
"You do make it sound like a game, Arthur. But ask what you wish. In fact, three wishes."
"Thank you, Mrs. Kane."
"Emily!"
"Emily. Your husband was a newspaperman, is that correct?"
"What does he have to do with my son's disappearance?"
"I'm just wondering how your son felt about his father, that's all. You were divorced shortly before the war, is that correct?"

113

"That information has nothing to do with what's happening here. You have no right to refer to it here."

"Please, Emily."

"Are you married, Arthur?"

"Mam, we can't get anywhere if you don't let me ask the questions."

"You'd be further ahead in the game, Arthur, if you answered as many question as you asked."

"Yes, well, I was married."

"Dead?"

"No. Separated."

"You never got a divorce?"

"No."

"Do you know where she is now?"

"Well, no, I haven't really kept in touch."

"Then you know. You don't have to ask."

"What's that?"

"My husband. He left me. I was his wife once. But he just suddenly left me and the boy. Now I'm a different woman. That's all you need to know."

"Well, is there anything you can tell me about your son's childhood?"

"Arthur, did you ever want to become a father?"

"I beg your pardon."

"There are so many things I could tell you about our son. I can't remember them all."

"Is there anything about him that made him especially different from other boys?"

"All boys are different. Especially him. I always did my best. I put him through the best schools. He even studied one year in Switzerland. He liked to travel. He knew more than most of his teachers. He had a perfect memory. He never forgot anything."

"That could be very helpful, thank you. Now, did your son have many friends? I mean, did he like girls?"

"I don't believe he ever liked any of them, but there were always enough of them around, certain kinds of girls. He tired of them so quickly. Sometimes he made appointments with several for the same night."

"I thought you said he never forgot anything."

"He didn't. He did it on purpose. He was always trying to make them furious. He wanted them to break it off, so he wouldn't have to be the one to do it."

"And did they?"

"Never. They always forgave him. They were too afraid of him."

"And what about Candy?"

"You know as much about her as I do, Arthur. You've seen her. Does she excite you? A sex-starved teenager. She wanted my son's money, I'm sure of it."

"That doesn't seem likely. I mean, that shabby little apartment. . . ."

"Are you asking or answering, Arthur?"

I'm sorry. Let me ask you something personal. Why is it that your son refused to see you when he came back from Vietnam?"

"Ask the girl."

"I beg your pardon?"

"The girl in the hospital."

"Yes, well, I intend to as soon as she's able."

"Do you think I'm cruel?"

"No, I don't think so at all."

114

"You're frowning."

"Am I? It's just hard to write in the dark like this."

"The person who came back was not my son."

"What do you mean?"

"The voice was the same. It was my son's voice on the phone all those times. But I could never see his face. It was like listening to a tape recording of my son's voice. It was like he was one of those prisoners of war that they never release. They just send the voice home to make you feel bad. It was his voice. But it never said what it used to say. I asked him many things. I wanted to find out if he really knew these things or if he was just a ventriloquist who's stolen my son's voice. I wanted to catch him in a lie. I asked him many things. I wanted to know why he changed. It was another man. He didn't remember any of the things I asked. He just said that he'd forgotten."

"The war can be very traumatic, I imagine. Perhaps the reason for his disappearance stems from something that happened over there. I hope to be able to get in touch with someone who served with him over there."

"Well, you'd better hurry. I know my son. He loves me. He wouldn't just leave me. He'll be back soon. He may be back before you get through sorting through your facts."

"I certainly hope so."

"Can I get you some more tea?"

"No, thank you. I must be going."

"I'll expect you tomorrow evening at the same time. You needn't call beforehand."

"Yes, mam."

"Emily!"

"Emily."

11.30 p.m.: Cannot quite trust Emily Kane. Too evasive sometimes. Too helpful at others. Insists on first names. Lives in the dark. Seems very lonely. Eccentric. Very beautiful in dim candlelight. Lied to her about Elaine. Next check sent to Owens in San Francisco, ask for more frequent reports. And photographs. Why hasn't he sent photographs?

Crowder dreamt that night that the whole Vietnamese army, all ghosts laughing and singing "Lazarus", dug up the coffin of Gordon Senior and found the unclaimed boots on his skeleton and the skeleton of Elaine, with high-heels and see-through nightgown, next to his.

9:15 a.m: Lewis in the Bureau an English major in college. Read the suspect's poem. Said it had existential overtones, likened it to man named Kafka's characters named just plain K. Said there were hints of Freudian symbolism, Marxist dialectic, art for art's sake and Taoist philosophy. I mentioned the overdue philosophy book. Lewis said it was leading to a breakthrough, a personal confession at the end. But last lines baffling. "In and out the room they come and go waiting for godot." Lewis said lines not suspect's. Came from men named Eliot and Beckett. Suspect must have stolen them. Lewis said such stealing quite common in English. Something about all the great lines already written by Shakespeare. But lines from Eliot and Beckett give conflicting testimony. Lewis said poets all liars when given chance. Poetic license, called it. Said poets wrote confessional, confessed to crimes, but always refused to name the crimes. Confessions as suspect as those of tenants and landlord. Received official communication from Marine Corps at Bureau. Suspect was not drafted into service. Enlisted in Marine Corps. Requested duty in Vietnam. Dishonorable discharge for the reason of discipline and personal integrity. Suspect found to be incompatible with Corps standards. Contact Sgt. Paul Ryker for details.

"Sgt. Ryker, this is Inspector Crowder from the Bureau of Missing Persons, New York City, calling long distance about Lance Corporal Kane. You were his immediate superior when you were in Vietnam, is that correct?"

"Roger that, mister. But I didn't have nothing to do with him being a pervert. The Corps Court said so. He was acting under his own volition."

"What do you mean by that, Sgt.?"

"The little bastard stole everything he got his claws on. Barracks was always full of government props. We'd call him in on it. Shamefaced little pinko, he couldn't even remember taking half the stuff."

"Excuse me, Sgt., but do you mean to say he was a kleptomaniac?"

"He was sure a damned maniac all right. Had half his barracks convinced that nothing was private property."

"What exactly did he take?"

"Anything and every little thing, it didn't make no difference. he weren't particular. Fountain pens, wallets, books, typewriters, the whole nine yards. Hell, we figured he must a memorized the combinations to the whole platoon's mail boxes. Got everybody all down in the mouth and demoralized. They weren't getting any mail for months. Shooting fly to forget. We found all them letters stuffed in the bottom of his trunk. I seen some loonie troops in my time, but he took it all.'

"So he was dishonorably discharged?"

"That's a fact, mister. Lucky for him he didn't get worse. We had another kind of discharge for him at the barracks. If he's missing, it don't surprise me none. You just better check out everybody else's gear. He's probably got a stolen plane somewhere, bringing all the loot to Castro and them cubanos. There was something definitely communistic about that troop."

"What do you mean by that, Sgt.?"

"Simple. We never recovered any of the stuff that was really valuable. Papers and weapons and uniforms, class A items. He give them all to the gooks. Kept only the dinky stuff, you know, them fountain pens and letters and all."

"Is this kind of thing fairly common over there, Sgt.?"

"Just what do you mean to be insinuating by that, mister?"

"I don't know exactly. I'm just trying to find out if perhaps the war was too much for him. Perhaps the war drove him to do these things."

"No chance. The Corps gets men, not babies. Gets men who want to serve. Who know how to be real men. The Corps don't keep no sissies nor perverts. That's why he got the boot."

"Did he have any close friends while he was over there?"

"Had two. An Irisher and a Jew. Irish got himself killed. Flying higher than a kite when he got it. Jew's still missing in action. Little liver-belly, probably deserted, covered up his mess behind him so's it'd look like a missing. Probably with them Swedes by now. You probably find Kane right there with them."

"Thank you, Sgt., for all your help."

"Mister, is my name going to be in the paper?"

"No, Sgt., this is strictly confidential."

116

"I respect that. Well, good luck to you. You'd be better off, though, if he stayed missing."

"Good-bye, Sgt."

A pair of shoes and a ticket. The clothes of all sizes and styles and colors in the closet. Two books eight years overdue at the library. A laundry basket filled with meaningless objects, objects that no longer belonged to anyone, objects that said nothing about the man named Kane. Kane was a kleptomaniac.

Did the kleptomania cause the disappearance? Many men disappear who are not kleptomaniacs. Or are they? If he was a kleptomaniac, why would he just leave all those clothes in the closet, clothes he had so carefully carried with him all these years? Perhaps it meant that he really would be coming back. Perhaps his mother had been right. But why hadn't she told him that her son was a kleptomaniac? She seemed so evasive, answering questions so perfunctorily on the subject of her son. Yet she seemed so interested, so animated when asking questions about him. What did it mean? The son, who had refused to see her for four years, suddenly disappears. Perhaps the disappearance wasn't that sudden for Emily Kane. Perhaps she was merely going through the motions of having an investigation. Kleptomania: an obsessive impulse to steal, especially in the absence of economic necessity. Crowder sensed that there might be some sexual explanation behind this obsessive impulse, especially if that impulse fully bloomed in the Marine Corps in Vietnam where the company of women must have become extremely appealing, but also extremely expensive and difficult to obtain. The girl named Candy. How many young girls would send pictures of themselves naked to their boyfriends? Perhaps there were more than one might expect. Perhaps that was why Kane had memorized the mail-box combinations of everyone in his platoon. How many other pictures were there at the bottom of that trunk? After all, hadn't he paid Owens to get such pictures, revealing and incriminating pictures, of Elaine in San Francisco? Crowder called Dr. Beatty at the hospital.

10:45 p.m.: New diagnosis on girl. Insanity. Maybe temporary, maybe permanent. Causes psychological, not physical. Transferred to Ballantine Sanitarium. Why hasn't Owens answered letters? In future ask for pictures before making payment. Check suspect's apartment again. Must be some clue overlooked. Kleptomaniacs certainly leave clues?

Crowder parked his Chevrolet in front of the dead-end sign. As he walked up to the apartment building, he nodded to the stake-out man. Crowder motioned for him to move from the building. Although his facial features were covered by the wide-brimmed hat and the bowed head, it was still fairly obvious that he was a stake-out man, sent by the department in the event that the suspect might return to the apartment. Crowder found the suspect's keys in his left back pocket, behind his billfold. He opened the door. For the first time, he noticed that the same door serviced both the entrance to the hallway and the entrance to the closet. As one closed the door to the closet, one opened the door to the hallway. As one opened the door to the apartment, one closed the door to the closet. Perhaps Kane knew that he would have visitors one day. Why hadn't he noticed it before? The rest of the room had not changed at all. Crowder was hoping that somehow something would have changed in his absence. Were all the secrets other peoples' secrets, buried in the cluttered closet? Would the suspect notice that anything had changed if he suddenly came back? One expects a room to changed, especially during the night, when the living are dead to sleep, and the dead are living, looting, breaking things. Crowder walked over to the cracked mirror above the writing desk and looked at the nude photograph of the girl named Candy. There was something peculiar, tactile, palpable, something almost too brutally real about this photograph of an underfed siren with protruding ribs, this naked child who'd lost her mind. Something sudden, brash, urgent, hungry, reckless, transparent and arrogant about the photo's stark black and whiteness. The girl with the cigarette in her mouth seemed to be accusing Crowder, mocking him, are you my father, tantalizing him, you dirty old man, telling him with smoke-rings to tiptoe come closer, her thighs like scissors ready to close, keeping him at a distance. The photograph seemed to be telling him that a detective was just a fancy name for a voyeur, a common neighborhood peeping tom. At the same time, the girl was so totally naked and unto herself in the burlesque. She seemed to be saying with all her muscles that she was showing all there was to show, and why did he keep coming back, looking for more? Perhaps she was already insane when this picture was taken. Perhaps the suspect had vanished from sight, because he had finally found someone who was not afraid of him. Ultimately, the picture told Crowder nothing. Nothing at all. It was a lie, another bald-faced, evasive lie. The girl in the picture, with all her looks of scorn and unabashed sex, did not conform to the screaming girl who trembled and cuddled up in quilts at the hospital. Crowder was convinced that any photograph he might have had of the suspect would not have been of the suspect, but of another man, a strange shadowy nameless half-man, a humanoid, a man who stole when he didn't have to steal, a man who never forgot anything, except the things he had stolen, a man who left a nude photograph and a closet full of other peoples' suits and shoes and a young girl who had waited for him to come back from the war, a man who just disappeared when there was no longer any reason to disappear. Crowder was still intimidated by the photograph, as if he were looking at a decomposing corpse at the morgue, which, nevertheless, still kept her legs cocked and ready to explode inside the picture. He tore the picture from the cracked mirror. It curled even more in his hand away from the embrace of scotch tape and cracked glass. He put her in his pocket. As he walked out, he closed the door to the apartment, and, invisible to him, he opened the door to the closet. Mens' suits stared from coiled hangers at the reflection of themselves, where once the girl had been. As Crowder walked out into the street and the blinding rain, he could no longer see the stake-out man. It was better that way. An invisible man stood a much better chance of catching an invisible man.

2:55 p.m.: Went to Bureau. Chief called me in on carpet. Accused of too much wandering, not enough looking, of too inconsistent and too inconclusive reports, of not having my mind where it should be, as per circumstantial evidence the parking violation, which had finally filtered up through all the slow and proper pipes from Traffic Division to Bureau of MP's. Said there were others at the desks who read the reports, reviewed them, summarized them, filed them, lead their quiet lives of desperation heroism, who would be more than thrilled to exchange places with me in the street. Showed him my notebook of copious facts and inductive reasoning about the suspect. Chief responded that we were a Bureau of MP's, not a TV team writing a script for This Is Your Life. Reprimand still stood as official, given verbally this time, would be written and reviewed and summarized and filed next time. Said I was to contact Dr. Ian Sample at the Sanitarium for update on the girl.

Dr. Sample was a man with a lot of hair around the temples and little hair on the top of his head, with lips too thin and white to offset the excessively thick glasses, a man who stuttered when he spoke too quickly, a man who ran the eraser of his pencil over the skin between his nose and mouth when he listened, a man who seemed to know his profession better than his patients. He produced a log which contained all of the patient's utterances since admittance. Many had to do with killing and suicide. Others made mention of a pair of shoes and a ticket. Dr. Sample knew of the investigation, and he hoped that Crowder would clarify the situation by telling him whether the utterances concerned the girl alone or also Kane. Crowder could not answer him. He knew the patient only through his pocket. He had questions of his own.

Was kleptomania common in New York City? More common than doctors would care to admit. After all, more goods available, more people living there, more goods stolen, more suspects on the run. Did kleptomania carry with it a sense of guilt at having stolen? Not enough evidence. Personal opinion said no, since most kleptomaniacs suppressed the thefts by remarkably forgetting that they had ever happened. Could kleptomania, with its implications of indiscriminate stealing, stem from an extreme inferiority complex, from severe feeling of alienation and loneliness, like in all those modern poets, from a poor self-image or a total lack of one? None and all of the above, again personal opinion, again not enough evidence, because kleptomania usually compounded with other crimes: petty theft, armed robbery, forgery, fetishism, amnesia, indecent exposure, rape, schizophrenia, manic depression, and temporary or permanent insanity. Then kleptomania was linked with sexuality? Most certainly, but studies in sexuality even more embryonic than criminal studies. Often, criminal studies legally suppressed sexual studies. Kleptomania, however, found more in women than in men. Where and in what jobs were kleptomaniacs likely to appear? They could appear anywhere. But kleptomaniacs were likely to change jobs and locations frequently, for fear of exposure. Also likely to change names, take on assumed names or pretend to be persons they had known and who had affected them for some reason or another. Kleptomaniacs were often very adept at espionage. Suspect could be impersonating himself for that matter, or someone in the act of looking for himself, like a man who checks into a hotel, then goes out of the hotel to a public telephone booth and calls the hotel, irately asking to speak with himself. Kleptomaniacs allowed to increase and multiply because of an almost reckless indifference in human beings to personal property, the old cliche being true that we only miss the water when the well runs dry. Kleptomaniacs in less evidence in societies without personal or private property. Take the goods away from everyone and you starve out all the kleptos. All our laws and regulations produce polarizing opposition in those who must follow them. A no-trespassing sign is an invitation to trespass. Religion sometimes relieves the guilt without solving the problem. Forgive us our trespasses as we forgive those who have trespassed against us. Could kleptomania be the overriding cause of suspect's disappearance? Personal opinion that of course. But kleptomaniacs don't usually disappear without leaving traces, because of their uncanny knack of forgetting things. Then again, men disappear for other reasons too. No personal opinion, since field or specialty not kleptomania, as he well knew.

Dr. Sample, his professionalism piqued to the quick, feeling that Crowder had turned him into a patient instead of a doctor, abruptly called a halt to Crowder's questions, saying that he hoped he had been of some help in Crowder's investigation, implying that Crowder had been no help at all in his investigation. Crowder sensed the falsetto laconism of rivalry in Sample's voice, as if Sample's career would be ruined if Crowder were to find Kane before Sample found the antidote for Candy's insanity.

Dr. Sample dismissed Crowder with a soft, moist handshake. He said that insanity, if temporary, was like amnesia and could be cured by weakening the patient's resistance and inhibitions through drugs and by aiding the patient to go back to childhood and retrace his or her steps back to the present. The same methods had been applied successfully to the concentration victims from World War Two and to the Prisoners of War from the Korean conflict. He said he would keep Crowder informed of any new developments in his patient. Crowder thought twice about surrendering the nude photograph to Dr. Sample. He decided against it. The testimony of the doctor had been too evasive, too helpful, too suspect.

4:05 p.m.: Rain has not stopped since case began. Roads too slippery to drive. On return from Sanitarium, car skidded, brakes failed, ran into parked car. Knocked out remaining headlight. Damaged fender of parked vehicle. Impact knocked license plate loose. Accident unobserved. After reprimand, cannot possibly report accident. Took down license number of parked car. May be able to pay owner anonymously.

Crowder returned to the suspect's apartment. As he parked in the street in front of the dead-end sign, he noticed that the stake-out man ran from the front of the building toward the back. Undoubtedly, out of professional pride, he did not want to be told again to move away from the entrance. Crowder went into the building and opened the apartment. The picture of Kane as small boy stared freshly from the scarred mirror, unobstructed by the picture of a too-naked older woman. In Crowder's mind, it was as if the nude photo were merely a childhood obsession of Kane's, a prelude to wet dreams in the mind of the young boy, who now seemed to have regained his pre-pubescent state. The poked-out eyes and the penciled-in moustache, now stripped of their sexual symbolism, seemed less threatening to Crowder, more like the pure mindless pranks he played as a boy. The more he looked at the picture, the more fascinated he became. It deserved further study. He ripped it free of the mirror and started to put it into his pocket before he noticed that there was something attached to the back of the picture. It was a ticket. A lottery ticket, number 345917, or was that the license number of the parked car? Crowder pitied Dr. Sample, impatiently trying to cure his patient's sanity. Crowder looked at the picture again. The boy was barefoot. He was wearing a blue-denim sailor's blouse, much too big for a boy of his age.

For the first time since coming to the apartment, Crowder looked into the mirror itself, not at the objects of another, but at his own image. For the first time, the cracked mirror was in total deshabille. He felt like he was seeing himself from the inside of a dream. His eyes, from lack of sleep, were bloodshot and bulging. Above his mouth, the traces of a moustache were beginning to appear. A sense of brute force, raw energy, unleashed violence came over him. He bent forward and kissed the image in the mirror. The image stepped back and became smaller with him, but a circle of slowly disappearing fog remained on the glass like a bullet hole. He ran out of the room without locking the door.

7:17 p.m.: Got headlight fixed by friend who works in garage, thus removing any evidence linking me with parked car. Called Emily. Demanded to know why she had not mentioned son's kleptomania. She refused to talk on phone. Said very curtly she expected me in person, usual time. Called Lottery Office. Ticket had been one of winning tickets in lottery six months ago. Ticket entitles bearer to cash prize and free trip to Switzerland. Ticket never cashed in, fortunately for bearer, since plane had crashed somewhere over France, killing all aboard. Called Bureau. Asked Chief about stake-out man. Repeat of reprimand. No stake-out man had been assigned to apartment by our division or any other division. Letter there for me at Bureau, San Francisco post mark, return to sender, no forwarding address.

Return to sender. Crowder was driving back to the apartment. Owens and the stake-out man were merging in his mind. No forwarding address. Elaine had discovered Owens, Crowder was sure of it. Had she motioned him to be more discreet, to move surreptitiously away from her entrance, the first time she saw him? Return to sender. Sender alone was left to follow the suspect. The inconsistent and inconclusive reports from Owens all came back to Crowder, like reading other peoples' mail. No wonder Owens had never produced any photographs. He was either taking them for himself, or else he was in them with Elaine. Case closed. Crowder knew that he would never find Kane, because Kane never stepped into the nude photograph with Candy. Not enough evidence. Always missing. What really caused the phlegm to ferment in Crowder's throat was the knowledge that he had so carefully stalked his wife from the moment she left him until now. So quietly, so invisibly. He had kept in touch. He could persuade himself that she had never left him for other men, since he always knew where she was. But Owens had been unfaithful. Crowder choked on the sobs, mesmerized by the wave of the windshield wipers that never quite succeeded in doing away with the rain. Like a flushed toilet, the water kept trickling back. Crowder knew that with Owens' expertise Elaine would vanish without a trace.

He ran into the apartment building, his keys in his hand. The door to the apartment was open. Shoulder first, his body exploded cannon-fashion into the room. A man in a trenchcoat turned quickly around, his hands in the pockets of the corduroy coat. Before he could say anything, the man was at his stomach, biting and tearing and flailing his fists. Breath gagged out in gasps, like throwing up. Wrestling like lovers to the floor. Heavy breathing, deep raspy animal grunts and screaming, like the screaming of a woman. The man in the trenchcoat, pistons pumping up and down, riding his stomach like a rodeo bull, all of his weight, both hands on his face, gouging the eyes, bashing the head on the stained carpet, everything blurred, the fingers too close, like seeing through grates, the fingers so close, eyes crossing over, fingers not there, withdrawing to curl, to close up and harden, saying "I'll kill you, Kane," knuckles like bullets, biceps and blisters, propelled from a cannon, a penis a cannon, shoot to his face, ooze there like oil, eyes white and swimming, drowning in darkness, lids closed like sewers.

He woke up alone, the throbbing of footsteps out in the hall or inside his head. The pain in his eyes, the sadistic pleasure-filled pain of squinting, like popping the pus from a boil, made the room dance all dishevelled, a burlesque before him. Soon they would come. All would be known. He felt for his wallet. It was gone. But what were these keys, where the wallet should be? He stumbled over to the door. One of the keys worked. There was another. He ran to the stairs, half-falling down them, dizzy from the height, like coming down a ladder backwards, look ma no hands, defying all the laws of gravity. The key fit the outside door. He ran through the rain to his car in the street. His momentum made the gear shift go beyond all reverse to full forward. He ran into the dead-end sign. It bent, but it did not break. He backed away. He drove blindly. His eyes on the road were inside his head, watching a movie, his life going by, the camera running. He drove out of instinct. He knew where to go.

"Emily."
"Where have you been all this time? You knew I'd be waiting."
"I know that. I know . . . that . . ."
"Don't hold your head down like a spoiled child. Your face is a mess. You know you can't hide it. I can see in the dark."

The darkness flickered, a lightbulb gone crazy. Short-circuit darkness. The smell of the wax, burned at the stake. The candles in darkness. Winked when they flickered. Piano keys playing low left-hand notes. Dirges in darkness, fingers that flicker. Pound keys staccato. Fistful of fingers, knuckles of ivory, elephants dying, candlestick tusks, flicker but dying cannot forget, hammers all pounding, staccato wax smells, sewer lid shut on ebony coffin.

He woke from his nightmare of ghosts greeting him with handshakes of wax, singing laughter and "Lazarus," chorus of low whining women. He woke to the rustle of bedsheets, clinging loosely to him, like Mexican prayer shawls over the black body hair, perforated in the darkness like Queen Anne's lace, rustling in the wind of the breath of a woman too close, like breathing through grates. He woke to the smells of fresh sex, which so permeated the room that even the pillow smelled like wax. He woke to the soft, cushioned feel of a woman's breast against his side, blowing him out, sucking him in. The woman, her legs crossed in his, was rocking herself back and forth, humming the low chant of the possessed. When she moved, he could hear the thick syrupy chirping between her legs, like cicada songs. He pretended to be asleep, but he knew she could see in the dark the whites behind his closed eyes.

"You have finally come. I want you to go back and come again."

Her fingers were searching the tangle of legs like a spider excavates its web. And he knew why the other had left her. Because no amount of touching would ever quite quench her. Because not to touch her was torture to her, was shameful to him who could not keep on touching. Fully awake, he realized with a shudder where he was. He jumped out of bed and began dressing, ignoring her protests like muted flute sounds of wounded birds. He ran from the bed-

122

room to the sitting room where the night squashed the morning through closed curtains. He ran towards the door. Running, he tripped and fell headlong to the floor. His hands groped behind him, an ancient runner groping for the pass of the baton, the eternal flame. His fingers were clutching thick leather. He squinted, and pins from a brooch pierced his eyes. He was holding a pair of old boots, high-laced boots, boots with a dried cellar smell, like relics of saints in the catacombs, all that remained from an ancient war, a blood-feud fought for the rightful return of the whore named Helen, who had run off with another man. He realized that he'd forgotten his shoes. He got to his bare feet and ran to the door. He paused, his nose like roots of trees pushing in against the wood, his hand already turning the handle, hearing her echo move through the room, a poltergeist looting all in its path. He turned the handle one full circle and let in the sunlight. First his body, then his shadow, then his whole memory vanished from the floodlighted room.

Krishna's Flute II

It was like having early Christmas, Reed thought. He was going home for free. Lieutenant Thomas Morrow, missing in action for three years, had been given back and was going home. Reed was escorting him back to the States, because he had the good fortune to come from the same home town. There would be a parade waiting for them. Reed would share in their joy. He had not known Tom Morrow in the States. Vietnam is a melting pot.

The headline in the Stars and Stripes read: PRESIDENT HINTS PEACE CLOSE AT HAND. They were fighting in the DMZ, they were talking in Paris, they were hinting in Washington. And Reed was going home with a hero. He brought the paper cup of Coca Cola to Morrow's lips. The latter drank some, drooled some. Nobody in their home town knew what kind of hero was coming home to them. Morrow still suffered slightly from malaria. He had amnesia. He suffered recurrent dizzy spells. The Viet-Cong had cut off part of his tongue. The State Department was pleased, seeing this as proof that Morrow could not have defected, could not have broadcast propaganda speeches for the VC. He was going home a hero.

Reed had spent eleven months as a supply clerk in Saigon. He had never been captured. He had never been in the "field," he had never done anything but stock combat boots and K-rations. But he, too, was going home a hero. Back home, anyone who came back was a hero. The Army had assured Morrow's wife that all his limbs were intact. That was all they needed her to hear. The Mayor and town council had voted unanimously that the day of his arrival would be declared Tom Morrow Day. Officially. The American Legion would sponsor a dance that night.

Reed would see his mother again. His father had died in Korea. His brother had been killed in Vietnam. He was all she had left.

Reed read the newspaper cover to cover, sometimes outloud for Morrow's benefit, although he never blinked an eye, sometimes quietly to himself. Somehow the rush of printed words compensated for the lack of conversation between the two.

WORLD AIRWAYS ANNOUNCES THE IMMEDIATE LOADING AND DEPARTURE OF MAC CONTRACT FLIGHT WOT5Y. ALL THOSE HOLDING CONFIRMED RESERVATIONS ON THIS FLIGHT PLEASE ASSEMBLE AT GATE NUMBER ONE WITH BOARDING PASSES IN HAND.

"That's us, Tommy boy. World Airways is taking us back to the world."

Reed helped Morrow to his feet and guided him through the gate. Reed turned around and took a last glance at the green walls of the 8th Aerial Port of Ton Son Nhut Air Base. He would have to come back here in two weeks. He wasn't about to complain, though. He would come back with confetti in his hair, his mother's kiss on his cheek, roast beef and mashed potatoes in his belly. For two weeks he would wear real shoes and eat real food. He could come back to combat boots and K-rations after that.

On board the plane, Reed helped Morrow into seat number three and he took seat number four. The stewardess announced that they would stop in Hawaii and pick up more passengers, most of whom would be coming from Japan. Then they would stop in San Francisco. Doctors would look at Morrow one more time, and then they would be going home. Reed could not sit still in the present. He was filled with future expectancy.

Ten minutes into the air and beyond the bomb fog that hung over Vietnam, Reed couldn't stand it anymore. He itched with the thought of spending so many hours in the air with a mute. They would be crossing the International Date Lane, they would be skipping a day, and Reed wanted to share it with somebody. He had to talk to somebody. Morrow just sat there, staring out of the window. He might not turn his head once during the whole trip. Reed turned to the GI next to him in seat five.

"It's good to be going home, huh?"
"Huh? Yeah, I guess so."
"Name's Chris Reed. What's yours?"
"Livingstone. Elroy Livingstone."
"You getting out or just on leave?"
"Neither, exactly. I'm taking my friend home."
"Where's he?"
"In a box."
"Oh . . ."

They fell silent. Reed wanted to tell Livingstone about Morrow. He wanted to tell him that they were both escorting other people to the States. He felt strangely close to this man with enormous feet and a Southern accent. But he didn't know what to say. Anytime anyone mentioned death here, it was like that. You just had to keep still and keep on keeping still. Reed asked Morrow if he was comfortable. No answer. He knew he was talking to himself. Besides, he knew that Morrow wasn't comfortable. He couldn't be, with part of his tongue gone and no memory of where it went.

After the stewardess had served them drinks, Reed thought he could try again with Livingstone.

"Your buddy. What was his name?"
"Carter."
"Say. I think I just read about you guys. Wasn't there a big rescue . . .?"
"Yup. Look, I don't mean to be impolite, but I'd rather not talk about it right now."

"Sure, I can see that. I mean. I'm sorry . . ."

More silence. This time it was Livingstone who broke it.

"Your friend's awful quiet."
"Yeah. He can't talk much. Had his tongue cut by the gooks."
"Too bad."
"Tough all right, but he's lucky to be alive. He's going back for good now. Medals, citations, parades, he'll get 'em all. He's going back on top as far as I can see."

Livingstone uncrossed his long legs before he responded.

"There's worse things to lose than a lip."

Reed nodded. It was all they said to each other. Livingstone complained of a headache and slept until they landed. Reed read the newspaper again, the same words he had already read before takeoff. He smoked cigarette after cigarette, not noticing that Morrow sometimes coughed from the smoke. And in Morrow's mind there was only the reflection of what he saw out the window. White fluffy clouds danced freely in the mind without memories.

***

Elaine Morrow couldn't sit still. The news about Tom had come as a shock, even as an imposition. It had taken her most of the three years to convince herself that she would never see him again. He wasn't missing, he was dead. He would not come back. He did not come back. He is not coming back. She would never have his child.

She had kept his drawers clean, the shirts folded and the socks tucked in the proper places. She had kept their wedding picture over the fireplace. She had watched the news on TV avidly for the first year he was over there. He had promised her that he would do something big. His infrequent letters rarely coincided with the accounts of the war on TV. Tom's letters were filled with reminders of their past togetherness and the reasons for America's rightful involvement in Vietnam, with plans for their bigger house and two children to come, with predictions for Vietnam to become a peaceful place, a satellite country, a resort area much like Hawaii. He told her that one day they would vacation together on Vietnam's sandy beaches. Walter Cronkite's news accounts only showed the casualties.

When the letter came, telling her that Tom was missing in action, she did not believe it. At first, she thought it was some kind of trick, some secret mission, some Army error. Her brother Bob had been over there. He had spent two years teaching in Thailand, had even fallen in love with a masseuse in a Turkish bath named Varee on his last day there. He had fallen in love. Perhaps her Tom... She imagined the worst. Bob had returned. So, missing or not, Tom would return too. Bob thought so too. He had assured her that the Army's mania for statistics caused them to list him as missing in action. Why, a man could get lost going to the bathroom in Bangkok, he said. Tom probably took a wrong turn in the jungle. Or maybe he was being careful, making his way back to base slowly, a little at a time, safely. Or maybe he was a little bit wounded, and some Vietnamese were caring for him. They hadn't found a body. They hadn't listed him as dead. Or captured. The VC hadn't announced anything about a capture. She had nothing to worry about.

Gradually, she got used to living alone, really living alone. Her husband was, after all, a runaway husband, not so uncommon these days. She would manage. She had to find a job. There was the first year of looking, of spending weeks on interviews, explaining to male executives that she used to be able to type, that she was a quick learner. There were the weeks of boredom and anxiety at home, playing Beatles records and learning how to be a drunk. One whiskey sour after another, she stared at that picture over the fireplace, massaging her tired feet, wondering if she shouldn't be going back to school. Would she be too old? Too dumb after all this time? Would mere "boys" in the classroom want to ask her out? She was more comfortable with the beady-eyed executives who helped her a little too much with her coat, who spoke too much of working overtime, who shrugged her rusty typing off with a wave of the hand, a wedding ring on that hand, all the while peering over the desk at her legs.

By the second year, things had changed drastically. She worked as a cocktail waitress at the Holiday Inn, making around $80-$150 in tips a week. She learned to be meek, to be coy, to cater. Still, she didn't like being touched. No night went by without someone pinching her ass, bumping her breasts as she leaned over to clean the ashtray or just telling her outright that she was probably a fantastic lay. She spent her off-days recovering, avoiding people, drinking more whiskey sours at home. The picture over the fireplace had dust on it.

The Army was acting strangely. They continued to send her form letters that they were doing all they could to get her husband back, that she should continue to wait patiently and be courageous in this time of trouble. The letters assured her. She saved them all. On the other hand, the Army sent visitors to interview her. Had she received any communications from her husband, either directly or indirectly? Did her husband ever express doubts about the morality of what we were doing over there? Had he ever been depressed with her? Was he ever overly fatigued? Did he still believe in God? Eventually, the visitors came right to the point. Her husband was said to have written letters for the VC, denouncing American imperialism and proclaiming his conversion to the cause of the peoples of North Vietnam. He was accused of making TV appearances in Hanoi, apparently in good health, apparently of his own volition, listing the "war crimes" of the United States and its "pig president." The letters assured her, the visits unnerved her. What could she tell them? Tom had never confided anything to her, except his future plans for a bigger house, two kids and a vacation of the Vietnamese beaches. The visitors took the few letters Tom had ever sent her away with them. Handwriting analysis, they said. They would be returned to her, they said. They were never returned.

She conducted her own letter-writing campaign. She corresponded with other wives whose husbands were missing in action. Such letters alternately spoke of the strength of their cause and the horrors of their present existence. Some of the women wrote long laments to Elaine. They were on welfare. The children were starving. The parents were urging divorce. Elaine had even gone to Washington once with a group of these women, to march outside the White House. Pat Nixon offered them cookies in the Rose Garden. Richard Nixon came out and shook their hands. Nothing was ever done. Elaine wrote letters to Senators Church and McGovern. She wrote Jane Fonda and others who had been in North Vietnam. Of the few who answered, none had seen or heard of her husband.

The biggest problem with such a campaign was not the frustration nor the futility, but the guilt. She never knew whether she had done enough. It was becoming too difficult for her to do more. She had forgotten Tom's touch, even in her dreams. How could she continue to protest for she knew no longer what for a complete stranger? If she pressed too hard, would the Army stop trying? If she pressed too much, would they find out for her that Tom was dead? She could bear that far better than the thought of him being tortured, which was what the inquisitors intimated as the only possible reason for his betrayal of America. She could even live with the thought of Tom as a traitor, if that meant that he really was alive. But if he was alive, how would she deal with his coming back? At this point, she would have to get over layers upon laden layers of anger before she could really be with him. She felt so abandoned, so cheated, so fooled by this man and this country that she couldn't write any more letters. She even stopped writing to Bob. She was buying cocaine from the neighbor's son.

She began to live in her fantasies. Tom has been a make-up husband. He was never really there. And since he was made up, she could make up any number of husbands, boy friends, playmates. She bought some baby clothes. She could even make up children. She talked to them at night, she set extra places at her table sometimes, she left little notes around her apartment.

She began to listen more to the husky voices in the darkened bar of the Holiday Inn. There were incidents. She went up to one man's room, then beat him with her handbag when he tried to force her to bed. One customer, angered by her resistance, complained to the manager that she was a prostitute who had accepted money from him and then had not performed. The manager knew better. Long ago, he too had tried and failed. Other waitresses introduced her to their "cousins" or long-lost friends, all losers. She took a night course at the university in book-keeping, but the male students who asked her out were ten years younger than she was, and they all complained about the draft. She didn't want to hear about that. The few men who didn't paw her immediately, who let her talk, lost interest when they heard about the husband who was missing in action. They didn't want to hear about that.

One of the letters circulated among the MIA Wives group even suggested that those who had lovers should share them during this time of crisis.

Elaine was caught between her groin, her heart and her memories. She desperately needed to fuck, she desperately needed to fall in love, and the two were miles apart. Then there were the memories, even if they were make-believe. When Elaine realized that even her memories of Tom had accumulated dust, she removed the picture from the fireplace. She put it in his top drawer, with the socks.

She had too many problems and too many principles. In the beginning of the third year she announced to a make-believe memory of a make-believe Tom that it was her turn to do something big. She "suspended" her principles, which buried the problems in with the layers of anger. She had not lost her man, if she could find other men. She had not been abandoned, if she could leave these other men. Her nurtured fantasies helped her be outrageous. She seduced the manager and became the hostess. She greeted the men when they were still sober. She found them tables. Others waited on them. She cornered her accounting teacher after class one night and took him home with her. She got the highest grade in the class. She fucked the neighbor's son and got free cocaine for three months. Men were actually very easy to please. They usually wanted a single night for which they would repay for years. They wanted quick compliance, no questions, no problems, no strings in the no-tell motels. At this point, Elaine wanted the very same things. She make-believed with all of them, changing their voices, their faces and hands into those of movie stars. In the dark it was easy. Dustin Hoffman was her favorite.

She was suffering from amnesia.

***

When the plane landed in Honolulu, Reed exhaled with relief. The longest part of the trip was over. He was officially back in America again. The flight to San Francisco would be much shorter, and the flight home from San Francisco would be still shorter. Both remaining flights would be less than the one now behind him. He was happy that the plane had landed safely. He feared landings much more than taking off. His ears popped when the planes brakes' were applied. He was happy that Livingstone was gradually waking up. The smell of Livingstone's sweating feet was making him nauseous, and the rush of air from the open forward cabin door revived his stifled nostrils. He stared over Morrow's shoulder at the charcoal fires lit beneath the palm trees. He could almost hear the ocean waves.

The crew changed, the passengers from Japan and Hawaii came on board, the newspapers changed, but the plane remained the same. Reed stood up and looked around. In the seat directly behind him, he saw a man staring at him. The man was in uniform, a red umbrella between his legs, his right hand handcuffed to the soldier next to him who was sleeping, snoring loudly. Reed found himself raising his eyebrows and tilting his head as if to say: "What can I do?" No response from the man with the umbrella. Reed turned again to the front of the plane. An MP was leading a soldier, handcuffed right hand to right hand, down the aisle past him. The soldier was carrying a guitar case in his left hand, vertically, with difficulty. Reed was tired of looking at people. He sat down to read the new batch of newspapers the new stewardess had given him.

The headlines read: "Nixon Warns Peaceniks," "Race Riots in Johannesburg" and "Bowl Games About to Begin." Reed paced himself, read slowly, just in case Livingstone wasn't up to talking during the next flight. Instinctively, Reed realized that headlines are tomorrow's news, not the condensation of the columns that followed.

Reed read an article on war brides and "battle" babies. He had known plenty of seventeen-and eighteen-year-old GI's who married the first prostitute they slept with, just because it was the first woman they'd ever slept with. He knew that most of these women were ten years older than these GI's, and he suspected that these "boys" got a substitute mother as well as a wife in the bargain. It wasn't much of a bargain. The article estimated that fifty per cent of these marriages ended in divorce or separation before the GI's had even separated from the military and gone home. Of the fifty per cent that made it back to the States intact, another fifty per cent would fail, were already failing. Over seventy per cent of these war brides already had children from a previous marriage, long since dissolved because their Vietnamese husbands were conscripted for life, or from previous liaisons with other GI's.

Reed had just begun to know the circuit in Saigon, to be able to distinguish between the black man's whore and the white man's whore, to guess the age of the women by the wrinkles around the eyes and the number of hidden children somewhere by whether they spoke good English or "pigeon." Reed had found a steady woman in one of the bars on Tudo Street. He amused himself, thinking that the difference between an American woman in bed and the Vietnamese whore was the difference between highway driving and bumper cars at a carnival. The latter gave you a rougher ride, sometimes all the more interesting for that. He knew his woman had a husband somewhere who would never come back. And even if he did, he would never find the woman he had left behind. He felt guilty about this woman, not for the sex they had shared, for she was well paid for that in money or in gifts, but for his leaving her behind one day. Reed knew that eventually the cost of the war would catch up with America, that we would pull out in a flurry of honorable words and fast helicoptors, leaving the rouged women of Tudo Street to fend for themselves. In North Vietnam's scheme of things, they would be expendable. Their children would be spared, taken away from them and put on collective farms to refertilize the craters that used to be rice paddies. Reed had allowed himself the fantasy of bringing this woman home with him, but he knew his mother would not be able to live with that. Her people had killed his brother, her only other son. She would be too much of a reminder of that death. So he never told his mother and he went on lying to his lady. Ironically, the first name of both was May.

He was daydreaming, the folded edges of the newspaper still stretched like a napkin across his lap, when the plane took off and Morrow suddenly grabbed his hand. Reed was frightened by this abrupt first contact with the hometown hero.

"What is it, Tommie boy? Did you just remember something?"

Maybe there was something in the lift of the plane and the tilt of the body backwards, maybe there was something in the loss of ground visibility and the ears popping that frightened him. Or maybe something in Reed's newspaper reminded Morrow of his three years of forced non-existence. Did the ego go with all the memories? Reed tried to get Morrow to look at him, to tell him in the eyes. Those eyes had jumped out of their window-watching stupor. Red and bouncing like a spilled sack of mung beans, his eyes darted back and forth, up and down like those of a man possessed.

"What is it, Tom? I'm here with you."
"You want me to call the stew?"

It was Livingstone asking, staring at Morrow, wanting to help. His voice was warm and musical, his breath was bad and crusted with the thick film of one asleep.

"No, there isn't anything to be done. He gets a little stirred up once in awhile. Mostly, he just sits there kinda comitose. Poor bastard. He might have been better if they'd just killed him when they had him. But to make it, man, to go back to the world this way . . . A fucking vegetable. It's a shame. I don't think his ole lady knows the half of it."
"Yeah, shame. But he made his own bed, that's sure. We all got to make our own bed."
"Well, looks like he's okay now. Hey, you want part of this paper?"
"You got the sports?"
"Yeah. Right here."

It was always like that. Reed had never played sports, never watched sports, never talked sports in the States. But of twenty-five pages in the Stars and Stripes, over ten were always sports. The rest was either too depressing or too far away to care about. Only the sports crossed the ocean as an area of action, a clear field of escape and no controversy. Reed read every line score for every game, whether it was skiing in Grenoble, kick boxing in Thailand or sumo wrestling in Japan. The best thing of all was the time lag. Nothing was "live." Reed sometimes sat in the base bar on a Sunday night, watching last week's condensed Grambling football game. He didn't even know where Grambling was, but all the players were black and the action was fast, the scores high. It was first down and a long pass, cut, it was fourth down and kicking. They'd removed all the waiting, the time in the huddles, the plays on which no ground was gained. And the scores were 41-40 and 38-36. You didn't have to know the rules of football to appreciate that kind of action.

So, Reed had followed the sports with everyone else. Would Denny McLain win thirty-one games again? He didn't. Would the Dallas Cowboys ever win a Super Bowl? Would the Boston Celtics ever grow too old to dominate the NBA? And how about all the stick-checking and brawls in hockey? Who scored the most points, who earned the most money, who had the best chance of retiring from touchdowns to make movies? These were the questions that Reed and everyone else asked themselves in Vietnam where the only sport was dying.

Livingstone read the sports and Reed either reread them over his shoulder or slept with the dreams of his bed at home waiting for him, fresh sheets, clean pillows, new flowers in the vase and all. Next to him, Morrow's teeth still chattered quietly around his severed tongue. His body slept, but his eyes still searched for the white fluffy sheep he had counted.

It was all going faster for her now, like a movie being rewound. Elaine Morrow had been reborn in the third year of Tom's missing. She could laugh again, she could take pride in buying new dresses befitting her job as hostess at the Holiday Inn, she could notice the children playing in her neighborhood without wincing or feeling the sense of now-too-late, which is the opposite of deja vu. She still went nude about her apartment, but now it was out of choice, not stupor.

Suddenly, the letters from the Army stopped their charade of assuring her that all was being done. Suddenly, the visitors stopped coming to ask about Tom's patriotism and fidelity. Bob thought that something was "up," that some exchange was being arranged. Elaine really didn't care.

Just as suddenly, she had met Joseph Kunkel, an American who lived in Australia and who stayed at her Holiday Inn on the third stop of an extended business trip all over America. He had come into the bar, he had asked to be seated, but he had not drunk the one drink he was forced to order. He just sat there, rolling a pair of dice and staring at her. She let him sit there in his eyes for about two hours. She was nervous. She wanted to make him wait but not too much. Finally, she walked over to his table.

"Everything all right?"
"Yes. Thank you."

She had expected some kind of compliment on her dress., some kind of leading question about what there was to do in a town like this, some kind of overture behind the thank-you.

"You a gambler?"
"Used to be, I guess. Not anymore."
"Why's that?"
"More profit in business. Safe betting. Besides, I only gambled to get enough to make a start."
"But you still carry the dice?"
"Yes. Habit, I guess. It relaxes me. I like to keep my hands loose. When you travel as much as I do, you do a lot of thinking with your hands."

Elaine was excited. She rolled some images around in her mind involving Joseph Kunkel's hands doing more than throwing dice. To her surprise, he wasn't eager to play her tune. He seemed content to spend his stay alone in the gaudy golden sheets of the Holiday Inn. Elaine began to suspect that he was married. He was not. She thought he might be a little bit gay. He was not. After three nights of the same ritual one drink undrunk, dice crackling against the unused ashtray and small talk between customers, she went to bed with him. He was slow in bed, patient with himself, attentive to her needs. He laughed a lot and said his business was for hurrying up, but people were for stretching out, lingering, fingering like a connoisseur of antiques. He had learned that from taking opium in Thailand. Elaine told him Bob had spent two years in

Thailand. Despite her best intentions, she told him about Tom too. He listened but he asked no questions. He said that he had lost his closest friend in the Far East, a man named Tom who had disappeared one day in Portuguese Timor. She nodded, knowingly, although she had no idea what he meant.

For three more nights, she slept in his room at the Holiday Inn. They had sex when she came in at three a.m. and once again at eight before she left down the backstairs, avoiding both the maids and the manager. In the morning after the third night, he confessed that he was checking out that day, that his business had been over for three days now, that he had cancelled too many appointments in other cities already. Suddenly, she deflated like a rubber raft. The shock of his leaving translated as the realization that she had not invited him to sleep with her at her apartment. She longed to bring him breakfast in bed.

Would he write? Probably not. Would he come back? He said he would try. He said none of the usual words to soothe a lover left behind, and so the leaving was less awkward. And for a month after his leaving, Elaine felt more loss than she had ever felt for Tom. Another make-believe husband had abandoned her. What was not make-believe this time was the pregnancy she carried inside like a time bomb.

And then the news had come. Tom had been returned by the VC. His health was poor but his spirit was good. He was being examined. He would be coming home soon. The State Department was ecstatic. Tom had never been to North Vietnam. He had been imprisoned in a camp in the Mekong south of Saigon the entire three years. So he could not have been a traitor. They knew she would be happy to learn that. They wished her and her husband "continued success" and a "normal" life together.

But nothing was normal. Suddenly, Elaine was a celebrity. The newspapers wanted to interview her, the various clubs all wanted her for a guest speaker, the governor of the state invited her to a reception in her honor. Suddenly, it was too embarrassing to have this brave woman working as a hostess in the bar, so the Holiday Inn management put up a sign, saying, "Welcome Home, Tom, from Elaine and all of us at the Holiday Inn where the best surprise is no surprise," and they gave Elaine a paid vacation.

For the first time in three years, she didn't have to scrape for an acquaintance. Everybody knew her and loved her. She was a celebrity. Editorials in the newspaper praised her patience and steadfast courage. New visitors pounded on her door. One had been sent by Walter Cronkite and the national nighttime news, which she hadn't watched for two years. She was more surprised to find out that Walter was still alive than that Tom was alive, a hero and coming home.

Bob called.

"Lainey, don't expect too much. They don't let somebody go like that just because it's Christmas. He must have been pretty sick for them to let him go.

Try to get ready for that. I know it's been rough on you, but it's going to get a lot harder for awhile. Please tell me if there's anything I can do."

There was nothing he could do. She had already done it. She vacillated between wanting Tom to disappear and never come home and wanting him to get back very soon or the welcome-home parade would be too embarrassing. She was two months pregnant.

***

Reed was the first to see the Golden Gate Bridge beneath them, and he nudged Livingstone who was dozing. As the plane descended, the bridge rose up, got taller and dwarfed them. In the distance was McDonalds with its own golden arches. When they separated, it was Livingstone who broke the awkward silence.

"Maybe we'll be going back on the same plane."
"Maybe so. If we both go back . . ."

The two smiled at each other, sheepishly, the way lovers do.

"Have a good parade."

Reed walked Morrow through customs. Everything had been readied for them. Officers were curteous to them. They were celebrities. One of them even nudged Reed's shoulder and winked.

"Ridin' on the lion's ass a little, huh?"

Everything accelerated in the artificial light of borrowed glory in which Reed bathed. Check-in went fast, travel to the base headquarters to shake hands with the Commander went fast, the gun salute for Tom Morrow went fast. Morrow's physical took only an hour. They would stay the day in San Francisco. They would sleep that night at the nearby Holiday Inn instead of the usual military billet. They would fly out United Air Lines, heading home in the morning. The parade was waiting.

Reed was too exhausted to take advantage of his one free night in San Francisco. Besides, he wanted to be fresh in the morning. He bought all the newspapers he could find and curled up in the gaudy golden sheets. He leafed through them all like a bank cashier counting bills, stopping only to lick his fingers for the next headlines. They read: "Newspaper Heir Kane Surfaces in Sausalito," "New York Subway 'Kissing Bandit' Gets Thirty-Second Victim" and "President Hints Early Troop Withdrawal." Reed read them all at leisure. And for the first time in over a year the sports page was up-to-date. He had caught up with life in the real world. Back in Saigon, someone else was still stocking yesterday's combat boots for him. He laughed. If the world suddenly were to come to an end, Stars and Stripes would carry the story a day late. He walked barefoot out onto his balcony and watched the evening trolleys curl up and down the city's hills like caterpillars in search of butterflies.

The mayor called Elaine that night. Everything was ready. The high school band would be at the airport two hours early. A chauffeured car would pick her up at ten. She would sit with the Mayor in the Distinguished Visitors' Lounge at the airport while they waited. The Methodist Church had donated a $5000 scholarship in Tom Morrow's name for the most deserving high school senior. The American Legion President, who was also the high school principal, would decide who was most deserving.

He wanted Elaine to know that she and Tom would be given the keys to the city at the airport and that he and his wife would personally treat them to a dinner at the restaurant of their choice the following night.

There was only one setback in all this stampede of joy. May Reed had had a heart attack. She wasn't expected to live through the night.

***

In the morning, Reed was surprised to find that Morrow had already dressed and shaved himself. He was sitting on the next bed, his hands folded in his lap, his eyes puffed closed, as though he were meditating.

"Tomboy, you devil you. I think you know what's coming down, don't you?"

There was no answer, then or ever from Tom Morrow. Reed guided him out of the hotel, into the limousine and onto the plane. Unlike any other plane he had taken in over a year, this one promised to be different for Reed. He was too nervous to read any newspapers. He was too happy to be worried about taking off or landing. He would just sit there suspended in the air, taking it all in like a child sitting at the top of the circle of a ferris wheel.

Morrow took the window seat again. Reed took the middle seat. And next to him in the aisle seat was a young man, mid-twenties, with long hair, a madras shirt with the sleeves rolled up, even though it was mid-December, and a long sword perched between his legs.

"My name's Chris Reed. What's yours?"
"Cooper. Everybody calls me Coop."
"Pleased to meet you. Excuse me if I can't sit still much. See, we're going home, my buddy and me. God, it's so exciting."
"It's gonna get more exciting."
"What do you mean?"
"Oh, you know, you're never there till the bird's gone down on its feet instead of its back."

Reed didn't like the tone of his voice. He resented the very possibility that this plane might not automatically drop like a soft football on the fly to a fair catch on the ground below. Momentarily, Reed experienced what he could only call later the trauma of giving birth. Of course, eventually, everyone was born. But for a few queasy hours on wobbly knees, one had to go through the possibility of death as well. Months later, Reed would remember this moment more than any other that followed.

"That looks like a quite a sword you've got there."

"It's the last one. I used to have lots of swords. I used to swallow swords. I gave them all away. Except this one. It belonged to my grandfather. I haven't been able to let go of this one. You know how it is."

"I think I do. My mother gave me this one shirt when I went to Vietnam. It had belonged to my father. You could still smell his sweat on the sleeves. Couldn't wash it out. Well, I never wore that shirt all the time I've been over there. But I kept it all the same."

"You were in 'Nam?"

"Still am, I guess. I'll be going back in two weeks."

"I feel sorry for you."

"It's all right. I got a safe enough job. I'll make it."

"I didn't mean it that way. I feel sorry for all that waste time. All that counting time. Then one day you get back to the world, thinking you've arrived somewhere, and you're still counting. You live off your fingers. I mean, don't you ever want to just quit counting and do something really big?"

"What do you mean?"

"I mean really big. I mean that guys over there aren't really afraid of dying. It's not the dying that rips the guts apart. It's the God-awful fear in the bones of dying without having done anything bigger than the peep-sight of the enemy's gun."

Reed was feeling threatened again. He still had not understood. Coop was still speaking, but he was looking straight ahead.

"And ten years from now high school kids will go to college. They won't even know that this war went on. We'll all of us be dead, and they'll have proved to be the better counters. They won't even remember . . ."

The captain's voice interrupted on the speaker system, announcing the approach, the start of their descent. And Reed still had not understood. He looked out the window, expecting to see flags waving and bands playing. But there were only white fluffy clouds.

"I still don't understand . . ."

"I don't have time now to explain it any better. You'll just have to wait and see. Excuse me . . ."

He got up and put his sword down on his seat. The stewardess passed him on her way to the front and asked him to please sit down and fasten his seat belt. He remained standing anyway. Slowly, he began walking forward up the aisle, his hand in his pocket. And suddenly Morrow was up and hurdling over Reed's knees. It was all going by so fast now. As though watching a movie, Reed saw Morrow grab for Coop's shoulder. He saw Coop's hand come out of his pocket. Months later, he finally heard the shot.

***

The local and many of the national headlines read: "Vietnam Hero Dies. Thwarts Skyjack Attempt by Vietnam War Vet." Forever behind the times, the article beneath concluded with the statistic that this was the forty-second skyjacking attempt by a Vietnam War Veteran in the past decade. That evening Elaine got to see what had happened in the morning directly over her head. Her husband's last few seconds of life had been captured on the plane's video cameras. And there was Walter Cronkite, talking about Tom. Elaine didn't hear a word he said. She was dreaming of kangaroos.

Two weeks later, President Nixon announced on January 1 that he would do something really big in Asia, and the Sixties came shuddering to an end.